Antoine Bloyé

Antoine Bloyé

a novel by Paul Nizan

Introduction by Richard Elman
Translated by Edmund Stevens

Monthly Review Press
New York and London

Originally published in Paris, France
copyright © 1933 by Editions Bernard Grasset

Second Printing

Monthly Review Press
62 West 14th Street, New York, N.Y. 10011
21 Theobalds Road, London WC1X 8SL

Library of Congress Cataloging in Publication Data

Nizan, Paul.
    Antoine Bloyé.
    I. Title
PZ3.N658An [PQ2627.I95]   843'.9'12   72–92034
ISBN 0–85345–277–6

Introduction
by Richard Elman

Paul Nizan never reached middle age. He died in 1940, aged thirty-five, with the French army at Dunkirk. He wrote six complete books: the novels *Antoine Bloyé*, *La Conspiration*, and *Le Cheval de troie* (translated in England as *The Trojan Horse*); two polemics, *Les Chiens de garde* (American edition, *The Watchdogs*) and *Aden Arabie*; and *Chronique de Septembre*. He had been a philosophy student of the idealist academician Leon Brunschvig at the Ecole Normale, a writer for *L'Humanité* and *Le Soir*, a Communist who broke with the party over the Hitler-Stalin pact. According to his former schoolmate Jean-Paul Sartre, he enjoyed the company of women. Nizan's was a short though not an ordinary life and *Antoine Bloyé* is a major novel of such great intensity and compassion that its strength is still available to us. It is one of the few truly great Marxist novels I know of, a work that incorporates the imagination of Marx to treat of the alienation of ordinary men from their fellows and their work, yet does so without once becoming scolding, combative, or sneering. It's a thirties book that has not become time-locked.

This edition of *Antoine Bloyé* uses a translation that was published in the Soviet Union in 1935. Edmund Stevens, then Moscow correspondent for the *Christian Science Monitor*, found a way to make hard, clear, intelligent English out of Nizan's precise thoughtful French with its meditative echoes of Pascal. Published only a year before the Great Purges of Stalin, it must have had the force of novelty in party-hack Moscow literary circles. Nizan had been a Communist but, in literary matters, never a Sovietist. His literary inclinations were gravely modernist and French, and English publication of a novel such as this in the Soviet Union had to be something of an anomaly, explained perhaps by the fact that it was issued by the Co-operative Publishing Society of Foreign Workers in the U.S.S.R.

The translation came into my possession through my friend, the writer Tilly Olsen. Once in a letter I had mentioned that I was reading Nizan's *Aden, Arabie* with my freshman composition students. *Aden, Arabie* is a fine example of anti-bourgeois invective with, as well, a high sense of place; its theme is inauthenticity, and like nearly all of Nizan's polemical writings, it is full of burlesque and hyperbole aimed at the then-current philosophical stances of detachment. It originates in autobiography, in Nizan's own journey as an incipient colonialist to the Arabian peninsula, which is why I wanted my students to read it.

He was a better writer than I, says Sartre in his by now well-known essay in *Situations*. Earlier, he writes: "Young and full of rage, struck down by sudden death, Nizan can break ranks, speak to the young people about Youth. . . . They will recognize their own voice." What moved my students and me so much was Nizan's anger; it seemed to us to be almost visionary, leaping beyond the grave to speak to us today about our own anger with a greater force, we thought, than the rhetoric of most American youth-culture charlatans: "We knew one thing: men do not live as men should. But we still did not know the elements of which a real life is composed; all our thoughts were negative."

"To claim the right to a human act is to attack the forces responsible for all the misery in the world."

"No one will make me believe that growing up is the answer to everything."

Something in Nizan's voice and stance was like a Weatherman

communiqué, like one in particular that had moved me greatly. "Not to love is to die," the youthful revolutionists had declared. "This we refuse."

Tilly wrote back that *Aden, Arabie* was indeed very youthful writing: fierce, brilliant, rash, mixed up, unjust—to Nizan himself, and perhaps to the world. The power of this artist, she observed, had only once been expressed—in *Antoine Bloyé*, a book which she said had been important to her life. Tilly's gift of mind was shortly thereafter followed by Nizan's text.

The feelings aroused by my first encounter with Nizan's funereal moral fiction remain with me even now, like a hurt one cannot forget. Tilly spoke of *Bloyé* in the reverential way that one reserves for masterpieces, although, as with any true masterpiece of this century, its language and feelings are understated, and much of the force of Nizan's work derives from his ability to transform an ordinary life into a drama of suffering without redemption, of failure without pathos.

Antoine Bloyé's terrible death in life was to manage his existence so that, in fact, he had never lived. Sartre tells us Nizan was obsessed by his father. All his life the man had cheated himself. He had led a life that denied his own humanity, his feelings. But within this parable of the career of the railway functionary is the choice each of us confronts, almost daily: to remain vivid and in touch with one's experience, to grow, to be one with one's comrades, brothers, friends, and lovers; or to withdraw into oneself and bitterly await death, to suffer the slow, wasting passing of the timid, the intimidated, the encapsulated, the bourgeois whose life is wrapped "in cotton wool" (to use Nizan's phrase), those whose selves have been shrunken into the deals they have made with their own lives. It is this constant test of all humankind which Bloyé so plainly fails.

So much of recent literature sees how men falter and deny themselves their own lives, only to mock or sneer or to deform such men as expressionist grotesques. But Nizan is always straightforward with Bloyé, and compassionate. "Day after day, night after night," he writes, "Antoine lived this life. It permeated him with its ease, its thousand sources of indifference and forgetfulness. He let himself go, he no longer struggled. He was settled. He would say, 'Everything is settled. How calm you become as you grow old!' He told himself these things because he had need of such assurances, because he was not so sure, after all, that they were true. . . ."

Antoine Bloyé is a child of the working classes, a locomotive engineer who seeks to better himself by becoming petty bourgeois. He joins the bosses: he marries his boss's daughter. At moments throughout his life, he is seized by a certain dull anger and regret. For he has given up everything in his life that was vivid for certain smug assurances. As Nizan puts it: "All his work only served to hide his essential unemployment. . . . There were times when he would have liked to quit the life he was leading and become someone new, a foreign someone who would be more like his real self. . . ."

Time and again Nizan wants us to see Bloyé's defeat as our contemporary defeat. It is the sort of life, Nizan tells us, that one could sum up in two brief obituary paragraphs in one of the provincial papers; that is just what he refuses to do. He treats Bloyé's promise and vividness and yearnings empathically. He is able to make us accept, like breathing, the subtle social and political corruption of youthful spirit, that cruel banalization through marriage and getting on that our culture imposes on so many men as their rite of passage. He forces us to know this nobody—but never abstractly, as Camus might do, or with Sartre's contempt. Bloyé is an authentic man set loose on a course of death, who lives in a world of schedules and trains, of honest accomplishments, domesticities, and occasional celebrations. He seeks to improve himself. He becomes declassed. He becomes a traitor. He dies alone, with only a wife to look after him, their pretense at love and sharing long a waste. His education has been to be selfish. He has been encouraged only to be isolated, greedy, and resentful, a mere atom, or monad. His oppression is the cultural—finally political—oppression directed against so many males: because they have been told they must get on, they must choke themselves emotionally.

The anger of this book is never dressed up with facile ironies. Bloyé's chance was simply to be human, to be alive; he was never very great; most men are not. But we can be better than we know. Nizan's social anger is like the conservative Flaubert's distaste for provincial society in *Madame Bovary*, a book after which Nizan seems to have modeled some of his style, tone, temper. He is in despair that men like Bloyé were driven to choose the fantasy of safety, alienation from their fellows, that they effectively died so young, that they then went on to exist as empty-eyed, gray-haired children. Paradoxically, Nizan manages to make his prose alive to their numbing of feeling, of sex, of ebullience.

Paul Nizan did not enjoy his despair. From his own childhood, from the life of his father, he saw the ways men's hopes were maimed and crushed; he knew the mates men choose and the women they betray; he constructed out of the particulars of that betrayal this most eloquent dirge and fiction.

It is in describing how Bloyé's sexuality is maimed that Nizan is most acute. Bloyé has had the love of one woman but he chooses to marry someone very different, and they become wedded to a pretense, to role-playing. Nizan writes: "Antoine rarely thought of Anne as of a separate individual. Perhaps in reality she was not, but who would dare assert that another human being conceals nothing? He lived with her, five or six hours a day, that was all. Their married life was an exchange of phrases and services, where the only human undertaking was undoubtedly their nocturnal copulation." And how human was that? Nizan calls their love-making a "tawdry collusion." Anne wants children to reduce her boredom. With the birth and death of their first child, both their lives are, in effect, over. They have succumbed to the condition of death that is the ordinary person's adjustment to hopelessness.

Nizan writes: "He worked because sorrow and death are slothful and the whole of his wisdom consisted simply of obedience to work. He never suspected that within him were other inclinations to laziness, other temptations, besides death, opposed to work. He was a man who scarcely ever recalled the nightmares and dreams of triumph he experienced at night. His trains had to run just as ships must reach port—the trains leave, the men work, and the trains must run on time and the men must do their job. . . . You can't go wrong if you do your job well. . . . The simplest arguments of social life . . . crowd out the whole of man."

Paul Nizan wrote to find what a revolutionist could live by within a dying culture. He was a Communist, and then an antifascist. He perished in a war that confirmed his worst fears about the culture which he had grown up to share. To the New Left in France today, he is very much alive, as Régis Debray has noted.

Nizan hated his father for what he had done to himself. He refused to be a coward. He wrote a book that is as current as the slogans of the best of our young people. It is a Marxist book: not only, or simply, because it sometimes incorporates into its analysis the language of Marxist economics as diction and metaphor with which to dramatize Bloyé's betrayal; nor because its central event is workaday life, its action the precise way in which the illusion of well-being is manipulated to imprison most of us and, in turn, to make us exploit our wives, our so-called friends, our mistresses, our children; but also because, as in most of Marx's finest work, its instincts are poetic, its seeming prosiness is about a way of feeling that is materialist; and its expression is by psychological insight.

The Marx who wrote "the invitation to abandon illusions concerning a situation is an invitation to abandon a situation that has need of illusions" would surely have quickened to this novel's power to provoke and dramatize just such a state of uneasy consciousness in simple, forceful language. Marx studied history, knowing all along that the problem was to change it, and also supposing there were clues, in the repeated acts of men, to how this might be done.

Nizan abandoned philosophy to go among ordinary men. For men like Antoine Bloyé, he wrote, to be "philosophical meant to accept anything, to take life as it came"; in other words, to be ordinary. Nizan's father, he perceived to his shame, had been among the most ordinary of all men, and while he despised him for cutting himself off from his strengths to be so isolated, he understood how even his own birth had contributed to this state. While lamenting all this, Nizan steadfastly refused to fall victim to such ordinariness.

Part I

If communism is to put an end both to the "cares" of the bourgeois and the needs of the proletarian, it is self-evident that it cannot do this without putting an end to the cause of both, "labor."

Karl Marx and Frederick Engels
in *The German Ideology*

1

It was a street where almost no one passed, a street of detached houses in a city of the West; grass grew on the trodden earth of the sidewalks and in the roadway. Before Number 11 and Number 20 the ground was stained with the oil drippings from the street's two automobiles.

At Number 9 the knocker, wrought in the shape of a hand holding a sphere like an emperor's orb, was draped in black. At the foot of the three granite steps of the entrance was a black box with white filaments, adorned with a cross and white teardrops. There had been a death in the house.

The door stood half ajar, visitors could enter without knocking. The tinkle of bells and the echo of knockers in the depths of houses bother the sleep of the dead. Now and again, perhaps once an hour, a passer-by glanced up at the blue and white enameled house-number and turned in. He pushed back the black door with its knocker draped in black and its various brass fixtures: a peephole, an oval nameplate, and the slot of the letter box. On the nameplate was inscribed the name: Antoine Bloyé. The visitor took one or two steps on the white and red tiling, where a loose tile creaked underfoot like a warning note. An old woman in felt slippers appeared in the semi-darkness and took his cap or his umbrella. The visitor asked, "Can I see him?"

The woman answered, "Yes, you must go upstairs. . . . We

carried him up there. . . . He fell in his office. . . . We couldn't leave him there."

The visitor climbed the polished oak stairway. On the first floor landing an unaccustomed yellow light, as during an eclipse, shone through a half-open green door. He moved forward, painfully conscious of the irreverent squeaking of his shoes. At the end of the room stood the dead man's wide bed. The flickering flames of candles in crystal chandeliers that had not been used for years, that were only used when someone died, lighted up the sheets. A man and a woman whose features were hard to make out rose from the armchairs where they were reclining and came over to recognize near at hand the visitor from out of doors with the February cold on his cheeks. Every visitor said:

"I learned of the great misfortune that has befallen you. . . ."

Or else:

"Whoever would have expected it, seeing him so active and so fit? What a terrible thing! . . . Life hangs by a hair."

Or else:

"I'm sure you know how I share your sorrow."

The man, who was Pierre Bloyé the dead man's son, retreated toward the window without uttering a word, once he had shaken the proffered hand. The woman, who was Anne Bloyé the dead man's wife, resumed her sobbing which weariness had interrupted. Every word of friendship and of sympathy set her off afresh, as though reminding her that her husband was actually dead when she had already forgotten it. All the visitors would take the thin evergreen branch that stood soaking in a gilded bowl, and sprinkle two or three drops of holy water on the bed. The women went near the body, sprinkled it and crossed themselves with the assurance of beings who go through their motions with the instinctive unconscious certainty of an insect. The men made the sign of the cross, bowing awkwardly. The visitors then asked, "When is the funeral?"

"The day after tomorrow, tomorrow, this afternoon, at four

o'clock," Pierre Bloyé would answer successively as the hours passed by.

They would leave at last. Outside on the street, they would tread cautiously, hush their footsteps for several paces till they were out of the magic circle where the presence and the power of death held sway, until they again felt the right to rejoice in being alive. And all at once they would begin to breathe freely again and let their shoes squeak unrestrained.

In the city papers, in the *Populaire* and in the *Phare* appeared the notice:

MADAME JEAN-PIERRE BLOYÉ, widowed
MADAME ANTOINE BLOYÉ,
MONSIEUR PIERRE BLOYÉ,
sorrowfully convey the news of the cruel loss they have just
sustained through the death of
MONSIEUR ANTOINE BLOYÉ
Retired engineer on the Orléans Railways,
Official of Public Education
Their respective son, husband and father, deceased in his
sixty-third year:

The funeral service will take place Thursday the fifteenth of this month in the Church Saint-Similien, his parish. The mourners will meet at the house of the deceased, 9, Rue George Sand, at three o'clock.

This notice invites your presence.

In his room, Antoine Bloyé was stretched out at the peak of his sixty-three years. His countenance was half illumined by the candles on the bedside table, while at the other end of the room a kerosene lamp was burning; its light cast three shadows on the wall.

Pierre Bloyé studied this face. It was not sunken like the faces of the dead, emaciated by long days of struggle: his father had died from a clot, without fighting. He was one of those dead of whom people say: "Didn't he look handsome on his deathbed?"

His lower lip, drooping below a short white moustache yellowed by nicotine, lent him an unbearable expression of deceit, of arrogance and scorn. Pierre knew perfectly well that this was the natural effect of death on a toothless mouth, but he could not help seeing in it his father's last conscious expression. The expression of a living man, the last evidence he left of his last thought, of his last agony, the final meaning he had read into the abrupt ending of his life. Pierre drew his eyes away from this stone mask where they always were returned by an invincible attraction. His mother cried, sometimes with sobs that shook her body like paroxysms of laughter, sometimes with the stingy tears of exhaustion, a spent trickle of salt water in the corners of her burning lids.

Thus they watched the dead through three chill nights of February. Now and then the old servant woman, or a neighbor, or a cousin of Anne Bloyé's would relieve them of their watch. In the kitchen, coffee simmered over the gas jet. Pierre and his mother drank shivering and went to lie down for two hours, like sentinels who have stood their turn. They fell into a deep sleep, from which they would awake in alarm as though father had been merely ill and had called from his bed for the medicine or the chamber pot or to ask the time, and they felt guilty over having slept. They went back to the room where the neighbor, the old servant woman, or the relative had stood watch, wrapped to the waist in an old plaid blanket. How cold it was in the room! The window was half open: the chill of the night preserves corpses. They looked at Antoine, secretly astonished that still he had not moved, that he had not fallen into one of the accustomed postures of his sleep; before the immobility of death all men grow anxious and uneasy, like animals or children. But Antoine had made no effort to shift his position, he had not budged, he already possessed the rigid patience of the dead.

The last night the son remained alone. The neighbor, the servant woman, and the cousin were tired out. They were back in their beds, in their own homes that did not know the spell of death, the disorder it brings to the routine of everyday life. The neighbor left for his country house, the cousin had gone to sleep with his wife. Anne Bloyé, overcome by weariness and the intoxication of sorrow, slept in the neighboring room and tossed heavily in her sleep, making her mattress creak in the winter silence. Antoine's old gold watch went on ticking on the marble mantelpiece, clipping the night with uncanny precision. Thus do men's possessions, made of sterner stuff than their owners, continue to serve their purpose long after them. Their furniture outlives them; their clothes, their houses, and their thoughts do not accompany them. Sometimes Pierre, chilled by his motionless vigil, rose and paced the floor with long slow steps. Each time he turned, by the door, he saw his face loom up in the big mirror over the mantelpiece: in the dark this livid apparition rose like the figure of a drowned man returning from the depths, and Pierre snatched his eyes away from the still water beyond which begins the land of the dead. Several times he went to touch his father's naked forehead or the chilly bloodless hands of this once strong and hearty man. He touched the cold of this stone being whose warmth and laughter he had known. In the hours that followed Antoine's death, Anne had likewise touched her husband, saying at first: "He is still warm. . . ."

Then: "He begins to grow cold. . . ."—as though she wished to retard the progressive recession of life, its retreat step by step, or sought the evidence or warrant of an unuttered hope. When she discovered that the body was really stiff and cold, she burst into tears. At that instant only did she understand that Antoine was dead. She stopped talking to him, calling to him, shouting: "Antoine, Antoine, answer me!" She began speaking of him in the third person, only in the third person.

A man's death releases a well-ordered sequence of words and actions. This transformation of a living being into a silent object

that no longer asks questions or issues commands, that is no longer questioned, that no longer answers "I," this metamorphosis
from a human state to that of a mineral, mobilizes a host of people
who make decisions for him and each of their decisions brings
him closer to the cliffs of death. In the first two days the neighbors and friends, notified by the closed shutters, the announce-
ments in the papers, the servants' gossip at the baker's and
butcher's, came to offer their services and pay their conventional
respects to the dead. Two women from the Rue Monselet, whom
Anne had never spoken to in her life, had shrouded the corpse
with the help of a nun from the Sisters of Mercy. The good sister
said to Madame Bloyé, "Madame, all I ask of you is to put his
pants on. . . ."

What an outstanding show of modesty! Anne commented on it
later: "How prudish these nuns are! After all, a dead man is no
longer a man. . . ."

On the second day the undertaker's agent called. He wore
black rubbers, and carried a large patent-leather brief case like a
commercial traveler with his bag of samples. Madame Bloyé made
him sit down in the dining room. He trotted out his patterns, his
gadgets, and his phrases. Madame Bloyé did the talking and her
son kept silent. Death is a woman's business; sorrow does not prevent her retaining an uncanny presence of mind that enables her
to distinguish accurately between the appropriate and inappropriate and then and there to measure the scale of the funeral costs to
her means and her budget. Pierre smoked, leaning against the
Henri II sideboard and biting his fingernails, while he heard the
last rites being planned with a detail that left nothing to chance.
The electric center light was on in this ground-floor room, even
though it was ten in the morning, a wrought-iron center light
shaped like the crown of a Merovingian king.

Madame Bloyé said, "We could open the shutters. . . . You
would see better."

She made this proposal with her tongue in her cheek, worried lest the agent accept. But he knew the customs. From his practice in dealing with families he knew shutters are never opened in the house of a dead man. He refused. Anne Bloyé wept and bargained; sometimes she yielded to the salesman's persuasions. In the end he made her agree to a fourth-class burial with hangings on the door, coats of arms, etc. He could hardly hope for more from a bourgeois family anxious to reconcile the rightful honors due to the dead and the economy that modest means impose. He again made his calculations, saying apologetically, "Nothing must be overlooked. It's always embarrassing both for the customer and for ourselves to have to ask for an extra hundred francs."

They discussed the coffin. Anne liked beautiful coffins, coffins with furniture finish. She had learned to love fine wood, to distinguish cabinet work from vulgar carpentry. She had always wanted to have a padded coffin when she died. She loved to imagine herself settled in a comfortable and restful death. She wanted all her loved ones to be provided for in the same fashion. She wept at the thought that she was giving Antoine the coffin she had often made him promise her. Her husband was ten years older than she. She was shocked by the trick of fate that had made him the first to die.

The agent went on: "We were saying, then, a coffin of three layers; spruce, polished oak, and zinc, with six handles, a crucifix, screws, rings. How would you like the handles? We usually supply very large handles, all one piece."

"That will do very well," said Anne sighing, "but I wasn't planning on the crucifix. There was no crucifix when my mother died."

"In these parts it's always done," said the man, "for coffins of a certain price; the crucifix smartens up the coffin. . . . For an additional hundred francs we can give you a capadine, a lining with a lace border. It will make a very beautiful, substantial coffin, sim-

ple, without frills. It will include padding and a pillow, of course."
"If that is agreeable," said Anne. "He will lie very well in the
padding."
"Certainly," concluded the agent, "not bad at all. All told, it
amounts to 2,800 francs."
Thus Mme Bloyé felt she had done the right thing by her husband. This coffin, these ceremonials were exactly in keeping with
a solid, modest, bourgeois life. Solid, simple, without frills, such
was her whole existence. She was entirely satisfied with all that.
Moreover, these funeral decorations were a parting gift, they
were like a last token of love for Antoine. She would have liked to
overwhelm him, giving him at one fell swoop all the gifts and all
the tokens of affection that he deserved, that she had perhaps neglected to lavish on him. The coffin was a bit expensive perhaps,
but it was as it should be.
"We really owe him that," she said. "He was so good, so devoted."
As he was about to leave, the undertaker's agent, who knew his
job and was familiar with the springs of human sorrow, turned toward Mme Bloyé.
"In addition I have provided four men for the ceremony, four
candelabra, in fact everything that's needed. On the other hand,
there will be the opening of the tomb, the newspaper insertions,
the cemetery expenses, all the matters relating to the cemetery
administration. . . . I shall tell you about all that later. I might
add, Madame, that you may purchase wreaths from us. It is the
employees' concession."
At last he ran off, after making an appointment with Pierre
Bloyé at the church to arrange for the service. Pierre turned toward his mother. He detested her air of knowledge, her assurance, her politeness in relation to her dead husband. To forestall
her making some remark over the order for the coffin, he asked:
"Why is it one can't open the shutters in a house where there is a
dead person?"

His mother answered that she didn't know why, that it just wasn't done. That in the room of the dead man it was quite un-understandable. There the shutters were closed because light hastens decomposition. But there was no point in arguing over customs, there were even stranger ones. In some provinces they emptied all the pails and all the wash basins to prevent the soul from drowning in them. Pierre was still somewhat annoyed. He knew it was useless to argue, that it was impossible to convince his mother. He shrugged his shoulders. He sensed that these customs, these beliefs and observances distracted his mother from her sorrow, and he didn't want to depress her still further by giving offense to the wisdom that was the stuff of Madame Bloyé's thoughts. They were going to bury his father after a religious service. The idea of it irritated him. He kept saying to himself, "After all, it's a sort of insult to my father. He laughed at all this nonsense about the immortal soul."

Aloud he said: "It's ridiculous. He took no stock in this nonsense. It's like a violation of trust."

Madame Bloyé, who was seated, sprang up, roused from the torpor of the sorrow that paralyzed her like a poison. "How can you talk like that, Pierre? If your father were here he would accept everything, for my sake."

Pierre left the dining room without answering. He was thinking that his father had been sufficiently duped by this phrase in his lifetime.

Later, in front of the rectory of Saint-Similien he met the agent, who walked along beside him with the humble and servile bearing affected by the procurers of death, not unlike the procurers of a certain category of amorous relations. An old maid with chalky skin, her hair done up in a frowsy bun, ushered them into the presence of a big ruddy squint-eyed priest ensconced behind a desk dirty and stained like that of a police commissioner. He smiled familiarly, recognizing the undertaker's agent. He got up, took a step forward on the red tile floor, and shouted "Good morning" in a voice that bore traces of a peasant accent.

In a twinkling everything was accomplished; the service was made to fit the class of the funeral. The vicar closed his register with a bang and said, "It will come to exactly six hundred and eight francs monsieur, not half a centime more."

A smile spread from his countenance to his neck which bulged around the greasy collar of his frock. How witty he was, this savior of souls! He added, "Had your deceased seen a priest?"

Pierre answered that he had not, that sudden death snatches many a soul from the designs of the devout, from the extraction of the last confession and from the oil of extreme unction. The vicar stopped smiling. The smile fell from his face like a carnival mask and he assumed the mean, scornful look of a merchant for a customer who spurns his wares.

Pierre left.

The morning of the funeral the corpse was placed in the coffin. The undertaker's men set the coffin down in the parlor. It filled the room; it crowded back the armchairs—a huge piece of furniture, of a size unsuited to the dwarf's apartments that living men inhabit. Open, it disclosed its satin lining, its lace, like the paper lace that fancy cakes are wrapped in. The men had carried Antoine downstairs, wrapped in his shroud. They had had considerable trouble. The stair turned sharply and was slippery. The body was a dead weight. A pallbearer said, half aloud, "We could never have carried a coffin down this way."

Another murmured, "It was high time."

For the body was beginning to decompose. Once it was deposited in the coffin a pungent nauseating smell of decay began to permeate the dark parlor. It contained, like the after-scent of hyacinth, a strange reminder of the fair grounds in early spring. This smell was unknown to Pierre. He had not the bitter knowledge of men who have killed and who have lived among the dead. He had not been to the war. The only smell of death he had ever experienced was that of a dead rat he had once discovered in his childhood. As he drew near to embrace his father before they covered his face, as he leaned over the broad naked forehead and the thick ridge of his nose, the smell overwhelmed him. He recoiled, he fled as far as the doorway, where his mother stood, her eyes at last dried out by horror. The smell welled up like an insurmountable barrier between himself and his father. It denied him this last contact, as though it were the dead man's wish to repel the living far from him. Pierre Bloyé came to know death at that instant, and he shed tears of mingled despair and revulsion. The undertaker's men poured a pinkish disinfectant on the shroud and started soldering the zinc lid. Their soldering irons were heating on the hearth on a charcoal brazier, and they worked with the easy motions of good workers. The ends of the white line of solder met. The last likeness of Antoine Bloyé, his body's mold under the sheet, disappeared. Pierre Bloyé offered the men a glass of rum. They clinked their glasses.

In the afternoon people arrived. Together with their black clothes, they wore a mournful look, drooping slightly, with the conscious slouch that imitates the mask of sorrow. After shaking hands with Madame Bloyé and her son on the way in, they gathered in the dining room and on the veranda. They flung hostile furtive glances at the closed coffin under its black pall, its wreaths and silver fringe. They did not venture to talk, they coughed, shielding their mouths with their gloved hands; they made each other gestures of recognition. They were thinking of their business affairs, their lives and their appointments; they thought of the influenza that was rampant in the city. Some of them even imagined their own death, others vaguely recalled Antoine Bloyé. All took stock of the details of the tapestries, and the painted plates hanging on the walls. Two women supported Madame Bloyé, who was sobbing, invisible under her heavy veil. Pierre Bloyé walked back and forth unceasingly from the coffin to the door.

He awaited the hearse as impatiently as someone about to leave
for a vacation waits for a taxi. He returned to the coffin as though
this limbless, faceless box of metal and wood, with its black pall
for a skin, cold and forbidding, was his father's body: he wanted
to embrace it, to pat it gently with the flat of his hand, as one pats
a man's shoulder in token of friendliness or to comfort him, to remind him of one's presence. Again he painfully imagined the succession of terrifying metamorphoses that was beginning to unfold
beneath this shell of metal and wood, beneath the ceremonial rai-
ment that Antoine had been clad in. Amid a breathless silence
charged with the impatience of the guests who strained every ear,
the hearse drove up, drawn at a trot by black horses, their shoes
clattering on the cobblestones at the end of the street. The car-
riers sitting on the rear end let their feet swing like children who
run a long way to climb on a truck for the pleasure of watching
the road rush by between their knees.

The funeral train fell in and left in disorder like a company of
soldiers after a halt. Behind house windows, hands pushed back
the curtains, disembodied hands that fluttered like birds. Thus
was the body of Antoine Bloyé taken from his residence. Pierre
Bloyé walked alone behind the coffin, which was covered with
the inert vegetation of the wreaths and the purple ribbons of the
inscriptions. He saw the men along the sidewalks doff their hats,
and the women cross themselves. The idiots looked as though
they thought they were doing a favor and expected gratitude. By
turns the affected voices of the choristers and priests quavered,
subsided, died down and swelled forth like the crops of pigeons.
Blown away by a strong wind in the endless streets and squares,
where once battles had been fought, in Saint-Similien the voices
massed beneath the black streamers that festooned the pillars of
the choir. They copiously poured forth their Latin with the long
notes taught in the seminaries. Now they shouted, then they
bleated: *De profundis clamavi ad te, dooomine . . . dooomine, ex-
audi vocem meeeaaam. . . . Dona eis requieeem sempiternam; dona*

eis, dooomine. From time to time the legs of a prayer-stool clat-
tered. The beadle would lower his stick. The crowd stood up and
sat down, with frequent coughing. The priests in their black
capes performed before the altar like dancers in a weird derisive
ballet. They ranged themselves in the stalls. Then they rose and
bowed before the tabernacle. They swung the censer, returned to
their stalls, and resumed their singing. The performance was in-
terminable, it dragged on and on, like the end of a bad dream. Yet
it finished suddenly. Everything speeded up; the priests came
down the nave. At the end of the church they revolved about the
catafalque like black sorcerers around a magic stone. The censer
swayed on its old chains; from the aspargillum a meager spray fell
on the wooden case and on the cloth.

The procession reassembled. On the steps of Saint-Similien a
choir boy dragged one of the choristers along at a run; the chorister, who was blind, stumbled behind the impatient youngster.
The chorister lifted to the clouds his ashen face, with its huge
twitching mouth of a semi-paralytic, with its black brows and
hairy cheeks.

From the summit of the steps could be seen the low-lying city,
its black slate roofs sloping to the towers of the cathedral of Saint-
Pierre and the invisible river. Through the sky raced cloud
streaks of shredded lead. A steady rain began to fall and veiled the
whole city. Through this film floated the smells of the nearby
slaughterhouses and the gasworks. Before the church the mourners stamped their feet while the horses pawed the ground. The
bearers slid the coffin into place and reattached the wreaths.
Ahead of the horses the clergy grew restless beneath their umbrellas. The undertaker's agent poked at the ground with his
black cane and muttered between his teeth: "Let's hurry, let's
hurry. We'll never get through before dark."

The Cimetière de Miséricorde was like a large city. As the
procession passed through the big gateway, a bell clanged, like the

bells that ring at the heads of harbor breakwaters on foggy days. The main avenue was well paved. It crossed the section of the wealthy dead, builders of fortunes, businesses, and tombs. In the depths of these mausoleums of polished granite and tufa, through the glass of wrought-iron doors, you could glimpse small family altars adorned with embroidered altar cloths, blue bowls, enameled portraits, and painted statues of Christ and the Virgin, Sacred Hearts, and doves. Many sepulchers let in the daylight through stained-glass windows like the studios of rich painters in the Péreire district. Some were built in Roman style and some in Gothic. Some were crowned with polygon domes, with glazed domes scaly as ceramic lizards. Others, done in the style of 1900, were adorned with lilies, iris, human hair carved in stone. You could not enter these vaults without first wiping your shoes off on the metal doormats. The skeletons of bankers, shipowners, generals, women of fashion reposed in the depths of these monuments. Their scrolls were inscribed with names of nobles and those hyphenated names of the bourgeois nobility that mark the great alliances of commoners. At the end of the avenue there was a sand heap where the poor children of the Miséricorde district had built gardens, canals, fortresses, and harbors and they singsonged tunes of Paris in the rainy dusk.

The procession reached the central plaza; in the middle a gray cement dome, pierced by openings covered with sheet iron, like the mouths of sewers, rose slightly above the wet sand that crunched beneath the wheels of the hearse. It was the roof of the common ditch where they threw those bodies whose concessions had expired, bodies that were only entitled to five years of solitude. Roundabout were heaps of decayed decorations, wreaths, palms, unstrung beads.

The horses turned right, entering a new section devoid of chapels, altars, and bell towers. It was a simple unpretentious district built over with substantial graves, large tombstones of polished gray and black granite, like huge books with plain solid bindings. Tall marble and granite crosses with gilt lettering towered above the graves—clover-shaped crosses, Latin crosses, double crosses, crosses of every shape. Some graves were neglected, but most of them bespoke regard for the dead. They were adorned with fresh flowers, with living plants and porcelain wreaths, some of them festooned with pansies and everlastings, others smooth as automobile tires. They were encircled by aisles of sand raked, rolled, and tarred. Though it was already late, a woman in mourning went back and forth behind the graves with a zinc pot and a green garden watering can. This was the burial ground of bourgeois comfort, of people who lived lives troubled neither by great riches nor care for the morrow, the burial ground of merchants, engineers, professors, obscure close-fisted men, cruel men, on whom, before the era of catastrophe, the security of the state rested. Here the concessions were generally for thirty years; some were in perpetuity. Among these tombs was the Bloyé vault.

The bearers lowered the coffin with ropes. Night was falling. They had a hard time making out the juttings on the walls and the coffin bumped with hollow thuds in the boundless silence, broken only by the distant barking of a dog, the bell of a trolley car from the far-off city of men. A gravedigger in the shadow of the vault called out: "Easy there. Hold it! Hold it!"

His voice issued as from a well. He climbed out covered with dirt. The onlookers then filed past and sprinkled the invisible coffin with holy water. Bits of gravel fell and bounced on the wood with a noise like large drops of water. Madame Bloyé walked away, staggering under the weight of her sorrow. For an instant Pierre Bloyé clutched the iron post of the railing as though to communicate for the last time with his father through this antenna. Then a man climbed on a neighboring tomb and read a brief address in honor of Antoine Bloyé. He hesitated often because of the deepening darkness, holding the paper close to his eyes.

"Antoine Bloyé began his career as engine mechanic in the employ of the Orléans Company. He climbed every rung. He became main stationmaster, assistant engineer. In 1920 he was appointed engineer at the main division, a post he held until only a few months ago. Wherever he passed, our comrade Bloyé left the imprint of his character, his strength, will power, and clear intelligence. Endowed with unusual energy and remarkable initiative, he possessed to the greatest degree the spirit of achievement. His integrity, his loyalty, the friendliness of his relations, the genuine sympathy that flowed from his personality made him a manager loved and respected by all. May his family's sorrow, with which we all sympathize, be lightened by the expression of our heartfelt condolence. My dear Bloyé, after a beautiful life of devotion to work and duty, you have died without suffering. Your comrades, through my voice, bid you a last farewell."

These words renewed Anne Bloyé's sorrow, but with it mingled the beginnings of a proud consolation. Pierre Bloyé was asking himself difficult questions.

"How pleased that big, pompous imbecile is with the sound of his own voice. There is the outer shell of my father's life. It's like a police report. After all, I know nothing of his life. What sort of a man was my father, anyway?"

Everyone filed past the wife and son, who thanked the man who had spoken. There were Antoine Bloyé's former locomotive engineers in their Sunday clothes, with black string gloves and knitted scarfs, retired railway employees who shook the son's hand with an air of complicity. Then the mourners dispersed among the graves, all scuttled off under the shiny domes of their umbrellas like speedy snails. Night had fallen. The caretaker's lantern glimmered all alone. When everyone had left, he closed the gates and went home.

Antoine's corpse, at last at rest, at last alone, continued its metamorphoses.

Anne tried to think of him. She comforted herself with the

thought that he was in the company of other dead, of his mother-in-law, of his father-in-law, of his daughter who died long ago. She fancied a sort of endless conversation among the inmates of the family vault, a sort of intimate enclosed life with its warmth and joys. The last arrivals brought the news of the world. They added to the common treasure their portion of recent memories, of new stories, and the older ones learned these riches by heart. Anne also tried to believe that in this grave the dead were not corrupted. Her veneration, her memories, must relate to incorruptible figures. One day she had asked the caretaker how the bodies were preserved at the Cimetière de Miséricorde.

"There's an underground spring," the caretaker had told her. "The coffins are in the water. This completely preserves people. We've dug up some that have lain there for years and years. They've scarcely changed at all. You'd think they'd been buried yesterday."

She thought hazily that after she died and came to fill the latest place in the vault, bringing the latest stock of images to the still and frozen voyage, she would recognize her husband and could say, "Good heavens, Antoine! You're scarcely changed at all."

Back on Rue George Sand, Mme Bloyé opened the windows and took off her hat. The wife, the son, and some relatives from another town ate and then went to bed. In the attic was a trunk full of papers, notebooks, and reports that Antoine had accumulated in the course of his life. In the closet his clothes began to lose the wrinkles his movements had given them. His watch stopped short, like a heart. The lamps were extinguished. Through the open windows the last smells of death, of the candles and the flowers drifted off.

Thus does a life evaporate, thus does a man leave his fellows. . . .

2

In 1864 a child is born. He reaches the light of day like all men, in the midst of shrieks and blood and water with great maternal suffering. He emits his first cry with closed eyes. The birth occurs at Pont-Château, a town in the department of Loire-Inférieure, at the foot of the last hills of the upland on the borders of the Brière country. It is Sunday morning, in those hours when the noises and echoes of men's work are still, those hours of respite when their voices and their movements are suspended. And when the bells of the village church have ceased their ringing, the wind from the Brière brings the chimes of Saint-Joachim, of Saint-André-des-Eaux, of La Chapelle-des-Marais, of Montoire. It is an extensive region under a broad curved sky, remote from the world, a land gnawed by the waters and salt of the sea. Through the Brière, between the reeds and cattails, the flatboats go down the canals and the canals go down to the Loire.

It is March, one of those damp windy days of the Breton coastland. It is drizzling and the tracks glisten like mercury along the railway embankment that dominates the house where Antoine Bloyé has just been born. A mist, borne from the sea with the incoming tide, creeps up the valley of the Brivet, overgrown with rushes, water plants, and arrowhead.

The child is registered the same day under the name Antoine Marie Joseph Bloyé. On the way to the town hall acquaintances stop the father and congratulate him on the birth of a son; to them a son seems far more important than a daughter. Afterward the father goes for a drink with his two witnesses at the wine shop across the way from the station.

Jean-Pierre Bloyé wears the uniform of a railway employee. He is a porter in the Orléans line station. A poor man, he realizes that he is anchored to a certain lot in the world, a lot ordained for the rest of his life, a lot which he surveys as a tethered goat measures the circumference of its rope, a lot which, like every lot in life, was willed by chance, by riches, by the rulers. "By God," his wife would say. God is the same as chance or governments, all of them that crush. He realizes his destiny promises little for him in the way of honors, possessions, and authority. He knows neither ambition nor revolt. He is docile, he is not one of those men who are always patiently awaiting an opportunity and a stroke of luck which never materialize. He makes no plans for the future. He lives from one day to the next, knowing that for him the years hold in store no transformations, no great adventures. He has reached a certain point, he is in a given place, and there he will remain. He sees how men of his station live, how their lives, their deaths, their meager heritage, follow one another. The end of the road can be seen from a long way off. At twenty, many men have reached a level above which they will never rise, a level below which they sometimes find it hard to sink. They are born, live, and die strangled by work. Above them are other men who know only that they will die, while the devious courses they will travel to reach their death are not so clear and pass many crossroads. In the bourgeoisie are men whose destiny may change, men who themselves do not always know what form it will take.

The parents of Jean-Pierre Bloyé were small tenant farmers in the austere and verdant mountains. In the casual course of slow migrations in the heart of his province, somewhere between the ages of fifteen and twenty, he chanced to marry the daughter of a farmer of Allaire, on the borders of Morbihan and L'Ille-et-

Vilaine. On his way home, where his wife and son are sleeping under the eyes of neighbors, Jean-Pierre Bloyé pictures the country of his youth—a great lonely land, sometimes as dry as a bone, baked by the sun along those heights of sharp-edged schists that grate the road beds, sometimes soft and damp in the spongy swamplands, overgrown hollows, and broad valleys of yellow rivers that leave their clay banks between Saint-Nazaire and Damgan. It is a country where men talk little. Jean-Pierre Bloyé is as silent as the others. Bloyé is a name of these parts. There are dead Bloyés in the cemeteries, living Bloyés eking out their livelihood on farms, in the wretched villages. A Bloyé was parish priest of Allaire in the days of the first emperor. Jean-Pierre Bloyé pictures the roads banked by blackberries, the fields enclosed by large slabs of slate set upright, the chestnut groves, his youthful fights with other farm hands. He pictures his wedding with Marie Lesoef in the days when the girls eyed him with quick stealthy glances and whispered among themselves that he was the handsomest boy in the village, with his strong build, his rosy cheeks and clear eyes. He thinks of the day when he left the Lesoef farm, its well-waxed furniture, its images of the Virgin, its big white horses, looking like statues in the dark stable, its walnut trees and holly bushes, the field where their huge wedding banquet was held. Then they left all this for the stations, the signals, the inflexible railway timetables.

Through the years the railroad worms its way to these ends of the world. Kilometer after kilometer, the lines extend their ribbons of steel, their semaphores, their wires over the body of Brittany. Antoine Bloyé is less than a year old when the stretch from Rennes to Brest is opened. For the past twenty-five years all of France has been watching the official inauguration trains go by. The large-funneled locomotives are decked with ribbons and flags, all their copper shining, like the metal of a helmet. The carriages, still faithful to the ponderous beauty of the stage coach, go by, full of invited guests, of newspaper men discovering France and writing it up for the benefit of stay-at-home readers. Women poised on the peaks of huge dresses hold back their little hats with gloved hands and wave handkerchiefs from the carriage windows, framed in green foliage and flowers already wilted, like those on soldiers' trains leaving for the war. In the new stuccoed stations, perched on trestle platforms, mitred bishops, glittering in the sun like horny winged insects, bless the trains. Military bands seated in groves of potted palms play the imperial airs. The poets sing the machines. Even M. Thiers accepts them. "Finistère in its turn has been conquered by steam," say the newspapers of the Second Empire. All over France men in city offices impatiently wait for the magic of steam and the smoke of English coal to transform this immobile backward country. The clatter of the first trains is heard in the heart of the sarrazin fields, at the edges of the moors of Lanvaux, in the echoing countrysides of Brittany. The shrieking whistle sounds through the open cuts, along the dales of the Lorient country, hedged in by forests of oak and pine and hills of apple orchards.

More than one country boy is lured by the snorting of the copper-bodied locomotives, by those metal bees, bumbling across the trellises of new iron bridges that successively span the deep estuaries of coastal rivers, between Vilaine and Penfeld. Every now and then these peasants raise themselves from the crust of earth and straighten the old kinks their muscles have acquired from ploughing, harvesting, and reaping. They pack their bundles and head for the towns which the railway line crosses and connects, the towns where the company does its hiring. They leave the meager life of the stony fields, the penury of the moors, the patches of barley and onions, to train their bodies to other postures, to new forms of weariness, to work for other masters with other sets of muscles, with materials and implements unknown to country folk.

That is why, in the last years of the Second Empire, Antoine

Bloyé comes into the world near a country station, within earshot of the trains. And not, like all his ancestors, amid the heavy silence of field and forest, where his race has lived through centuries that seemed endless before the turbulent era of Guizot, Lamartine, and the Prince President. Field hands, tenant farmers, stubborn, rooted in between their lords and their priests, Royalists who used their hearths to roast the feet of blue-clad soldiers, who died, their backs against their barn walls, shot down by Republican squads (such was the death of Antoine Bloyé's great-grandfather)—the storms of the Revolution had not succeeded in blasting them from their land, from their stubborn adherence to their poor customs. Neither the Empire nor the wrath of the new century had transformed them. The catastrophes of cities do not overturn the countryside so easily. It requires more than this to cast them loose. But in those days of great upheaval that swirled the chaotic stuff of cities and towns, with their prosperous merchants, manufacturers, lawyers, and their poverty-stricken factory workers, mysterious men, in remote counties of England, were sketching the designs of incredible machines and dreaming of putting new mechanisms to work. A man casually watching the use of steam pumps in the coal mines of Northumberland foresaw from afar the great role of nature's new motive forces; a George Stephenson, who had not yet cast his lines over the yielding flatlands, was preparing a complicated future for the long immutable descendants of the oldest soil of Europe. The inventors transform the world and men more than do generals and statesmen. That is why Antoine Bloyé is born in the neighborhood of railway signals that will govern his life. That is why he is completely deflected from the slow tempo of the countryside and the drowsiness of the fields.

3

When Antoine was two years old his father was transferred to Dirinon. He followed the extension of the line from Paris to Brest along the southern coast of Brittany. Even in those days papers with a letterhead mysterious as the bill of lading of a ship, as orders for the movement of troops, dispatched men along the railways in conformity with the requirements of the traffic and the complicated rules governing promotion and change of residence. Jean-Pierre Bloyé, like all his working companions, thought unceasingly of those inaccessible regions whence came the orders that directed his destiny. Like them, he lived a life subordinate to the whims of a line of communication and its masters. He was one of the beads threaded on a long steel wire, shoved back and forth at the will of some far-off inspector, or an assistant traffic manager. For Jean-Pierre Bloyé, as later for Antoine, Pont-Château was distinguished from other towns as the town of kilometer 484; Dirinon was the village of kilometer 759.

But in Dirinon Antoine is as yet many years removed from the game the railwaymen play. For him the railways are still simply the tracks of a terrifying monster. When the trains go by like dragons, he hides his face in his mother's apron, crying with fright. He begins to toddle about on his wobbly legs.

This country, walled in by the highlands around Brest harbor, is a green land of chiaroscuro, pierced by pleasant estuaries that are flecked with grassy mud banks like drops of wax upon the water. It was a favorite haunt of supernatural beings in former times. All Finistère is peopled with miracles. Its woodlands conceal healing and prophetic fountains where young girls run to read their future and the story of their love affairs. The rocks bear kneeprints graven in the granite by the weight of praying saints and hollows formed by the bodies of newborn saints for whose sake the granite was transformed into feathers and wool. You may see the stone troughs that floated on the waters of the sea and brought the apostles of the new faith from Ireland. Chapels hoary with yellow lichen and moss patiently vegetate among the trees. Fountains, mossy sanctuaries, paths hedged by blackthorn and mulberry are dedicated to children's diseases: Sainte Nonne, Saint Divy, who watch over the tender years of childhood and heal the illness of Divy, the sign of which is a blue splotch on the forehead. All the powers of ancient magic are wafted on the currents of the wind. Not for nothing is Marie Bloyé the foster daughter of a sorcerer who could cast the future and dry the milk of cattle and women. She believes in miracles, in the secrets of sorcerers and priests. In the summer months she dips her son in the stone basins of pagan gods, ill disguised as saints of Rome. She makes him drink the icy waters of the fountains and has him sit on the stones of Divy. Antoine Bloyé plays along the edges of the cold waters of the pond of Rouazlé. He grows sturdy, he develops the peasant body of his line.

On this remote extremity of the long European land, on this little finger of Asia, nothing shakes the peace of the country and the peace of childhood. The seasons change; the apples tumble to the grass; the swine are slaughtered, and their cries pierce the autumn; the storms burst, the ruddy stacks of ripened wheat rise in the fields; the hay ricks are hauled inside, the grain is threshed, the trains go by, the children play, the girls get married. In Paris, in Lyon, in Marseille, the last years of the Second Empire roll by. The shells of the besiegers fall on Paris. In Paris the Commune holds the city; its fighters are massacred by the regulars. Men are shot, others are exiled. M. Adolphe Thiers speaks. M. Jules Simon speaks, MacMahon sits on the reviewing stand and his picture appears in farm kitchens with his large red mohair sash across his chest. The Republic is awkwardly installed and the workers withdraw in silence in the cities. But all these events, capable of casting in a definite mold the feelings, the wrath, the simple and impelling aspirations of a child of his class, occur so far away from Antoine that the last dying circle of their waves spends itself at the foot of the divide. He will learn too late that his father belongs to the section of humanity whose last defenders were then falling in the Père-Lachaise district. Jean-Pierre Bloyé likewise knows nothing of all this. No thought of revolt so much as touches this uprooted peasant, whose nose is kept to the grindstone by his respect for the powerful, his ignorance, and his feeling of an unshakable destiny and iron necessity. Marie Bloyé likewise knows nothing of it. She cleans her house, she tends the vegetable patch in the garden. She does the washing. Her mind is drugged by her prayers, by overwork, and by the religious reading matter that the *Pèlerin* provides. She speaks with fright of the Reds, of the Republicans who wage war on God.

Antoine has nothing to do but learn the narrow world around him. He reaches school age. He leaves for school in the morning and comes home in the evening. The school is in another village and he has to walk eight kilometers every day to learn to read and recite the catechism. He walks to school with boys and girls who carry satchels and baskets. Together they learn the shapes and names of plants, the forest life, the ways of animals. They climb trees and bring down nests in their pockets. Transparent tadpoles dart through the ditch water; frogs jump and land with a heavy flop. Birds hop and take flight; the cow dung drones with flies. Sometimes in the middle of the road they find a dead mole with its rosy digging paws upturned, covered with vermin. Or they find the slough of a snake, that looks like parchment paper, like something made by man. They catch the hedgehogs that make the muddy farm dogs bark. They set bird traps. The uncatchable squirrels stare down at them from in between the branches with eyes bright as buttons. One day they find a young owl, lost, blinded by the daylight and heavy with sleepiness, and they take turns carrying it under their shirts to feel against their skin the strange bird warmth. In summer they break off low-hanging chestnut boughs to use as sun shades, and they drink from spring-fed streams. In the fields the peasants reply from afar to their shouts and their questions. On market days they are picked up by carts that carry them along at a bumpety trot, in with the sacks and chicken crates that fall off at every corner. The schoolhouse is an old building beneath the trees. On the walls hang mysterious pictures of imaginary countrysides, collections of plants and animals whose coats are shinier than in nature, and rows of handsome plates depicting weights and measures. Antoine begins to read and spell out words.

Pont-Château is plunged in the night of early childhood memories which are no longer illuminated save occasionally by the bright fires of dreams. Dirinon in its turn recedes down the long aisles of memory. Jean-Pierre Bloyé is now at Pontivy, no longer called Napoléonville. The passing months have already banished the shades of the Franco-Prussian War which so feebly stirred this corner of the world. Nothing remains of its passage save a few forgotten German prisoners at whom the children throw rotten apples through the prison windows, doing their best to aim right between two bars.

Antoine plays with the children of Commandant Dalignac. They are relatives of Mlle Zénaïde Fleuriot. This novelist, with her disgusting moralizing, writes long story books in red and gold bindings wherein this band of children might be encountered. Perhaps Antoine Bloyé served as model for her figure of a poor child well treated by the good rich—those rich whose sons will all go to the Naval School or to Saint-Cyr, as is fitting. One of them, the most virtuous, will become a priest and will marry the other members of the family. But the Commandant's children, at the ages of ten and eleven, have not yet so many ideas in their heads. They play willingly with a sturdy boy of their own age, who is more familiar than they are with the resources of the countryside. Undoubtedly Antoine's parents are under obligations to this rich family. Fairly frequently Marie Bloyé enters through the back way to do the laundry. But Antoine is not old enough to think about these things and be worried by them. He is not humiliated, he does not know how to draw comparisons. He plays. He fights with his playmates, who are rather laxly looked after by a black nurse, brought from the Antilles along with colonial trophies. She is a tall dark girl who laughs and rolls in the grass like a goat, showing her thin legs and heavy breasts, and tosses her kinky hair, badly held in place by a red and yellow kerchief. The entire band camps in a country cave where they cache provisions foraged in the fields and booty stolen from the houses.

They are wrapped in the carefreeness of childhood, which does not distinguish the divisions of time, the mortal accumulation of the years, or the pitfalls of morality. They are a part of nature. Nature is counterpoised to them. With their desires and their games it forms a world where waking is indistinguishable from dreams. The Dalignacs have books which are as much a part of their lives as climbing and running. Together with them Antoine reads the novels of James Fenimore Cooper; along the banks of the Blavet run the last Mohicans, the hunter with the long rifle, and the scalp hunters. Their penknives are bowie knives, the passing peasants are Navaho scouts on the warpath, the streams are the Rio Grande, the Negress Zoé is an Indian princess whom they capture and maul with a pleasure whose source they don't suspect. In the game of "carrying off the princess," these boys, who with the passing years and holidays have attained the ages of thirteen and fourteen, press their fingers against the elastic loins and breasts of the black girl. They grab her round the legs to throw her down and she shrieks because their hands squeeze her ankles under her woolen stockings. Thus they range a universe utterly removed from that of their parents. This wonderful time of adventure comes to all children rich and poor. All little human beings are alike, before this naive equality withers in the pitiless light of incidents and teachings that ill accord with childhood fantasies. Between the ages of five and twelve all people understand each other. When children escape the supervision of grown-ups, childish comradeship neglects all barriers and they play unmindful of sinister idols and family ties.

Long years afterward Antoine will recall his parents' poverty at that time. He will be troubled by the recollection of old sorrows understood at last, and of the years when he was inscribed on the paupers' list in primary school. He will tell his son these memories. It will all come back to him, old scores are never permanently forgotten. But in the fields around Pontivy everything is easy in child's play. All children easily find happiness, more easily in this remote countryside than on the raked walks of public parks where children do not mingle, than in the smoke-choked streets of unhealthy suburbs where workers' children grow up.

Meanwhile the apple trees bloom and the bloom fades away, the shoots ripen into grain. In school Antoine is at the head of his class, the schoolmaster mentions him to the magistrate. The magistrate speaks to the deputy. Influence is brought to bear on behalf of this gifted son of peaceable workers, this anonymous country boy. Exchanges of favors are recalled. Antoine receives a scholarship to secondary school, a scholarship for special instruction, of course. There are special instruction courses at Pontivy. No one thinks of teaching Antoine Latin, much less Greek. Mlle Fleuriot's relatives learn Latin, but Antoine will never be able to quote from memory the first three verses of Virgil's *First Eclogue*, the first two verses of the first book of the *Odyssey*. He will not be a man of culture, he will not sprinkle his speech with bouquets culled from M. Larousse's compendium of *Latin Words and Phrases* or the *Garden of Greek Roots.* Sons of farmers, artisans and minor functionaries receive special instruction. What use would they have for the humanities? The laurels of the liberal arts are not for their brows. Arts of free men? Free men are those who have incomes. In his first year of secondary school, Antoine vaguely senses that he will never command the same stock of passwords and expressions as the sons of Commandant Dalignac, officer and proprietor. But he does not as yet gauge the consequences of this exclusive knowledge, and meanwhile, with the tremendous eagerness of a poor scholarship student, he masters the special knowledge he is offered. Forces whose origins are remote from his ken already impel him toward the well-marked channels of society. He knows nothing of these forces, his thoughts do not range so far. Outside the Lycee he still runs wild in the country. He rings doorbells and breaks windowpanes. He comes home late, hatless and with bleeding knees. He is rough and ruddy, with the movements of a dog. He acquires those childhood wounds whose tiny white marks the grown man still traces on his skin. He breaks his nose, which will remain crooked and swollen throughout his life. One day he bangs his forehead against a tree. He remains in bed with the bitter companionship of fever. Everybody thinks he is going to die of concussion, but he is up in two days. Men of his race do not die so easily.

When he comes home at night, exhausted and bareheaded, his mother shouts, "Antoine, Antoine, where have you been again, you scamp? Where did you lose your cap? I haven't the money to buy you a new one every day of the week."

And sometimes his father gets up from his seat by the fireplace, takes off his big, black, leather belt and whips him silently, grasping the steel buckle in his large hand, gazing at him from his pale eyes. Without undue struggle Antoine masters his feeling of revolt. He knows the price of liberty. He already knows that everything must be paid for, rest by pain, liberty by beatings, love by boredom, and life by death.

4

In 1878 Jean-Pierre Bloyé was appointed ticket inspector at the passenger station of Saint-Nazaire; he became the sort of man who goes away day and night with his bundle and his food and who rouses passengers asleep in their stuffy compartments. Saint-Nazaire is not far from Pont-Château. Antoine returned to spend his youth in the country of his birth. In the town's secondary school, to which his scholarship was transferred, he had companions who were destined for careers more brilliant than his own, careers which he later followed in the *Bulletin of the Old Boys' Association* and the newspapers. Among them was Aristide Briand, son of the café owner, and Antoine often told himself that he might have applied to him, asked him for favors. He never did so; it was merely one of those magic props that obscure men hold in reserve.

The school was not far from the sea. From gloomy classrooms where they learned the things they were allowed to learn—Larive and Fleury's grammar, ethics, Victor Duruy's history, algebra, and English—the students heard the mighty gusts of the equinoctial gale rising and falling. The huge sea monster of the wind shrieked, and their legs tingled with the urge to run down to the seashore. Windows banged, panes fell out.

The children invoked Sunday memories to rescue them from classroom boredom, picturing from afar the flat-bottomed boats rocked on the choppy waves of the bay, and the long greenish-white breakers that cut across the sandy beach.

Meanwhile Saint-Nazaire was growing up around them, growing even more rapidly than the children themselves.

Saint-Nazaire was not one of those statuesque old towns, immobile, dreaming in a corset of walls, ramparts, and memories, where every corner is charged with an antiquity that people recall with pride. Once on these low-lying sands there stood a Celtic settlement. At a later period this spot was the site of a town adorned with chapels by Christian converts, and St. Gregory of Tours mentions this new town. Then this historical beginning disappeared and a forgotten fishing village stood on the dunes and seashells. No inhabitant of Saint-Nazaire took any interest in these vanished remnants that had left behind neither monument nor legend. At the time of Antoine's youth, after centuries of silence, the city was an invention of the Second Empire.

Thirteen or fourteen years earlier the wise men of big trade, the specialists in marine transport, had cast their eyes over the maps of the West. Big trade reckoned that sailings from Saint-Nazaire would cut three days from the long Atlantic crossings, so many fewer tons of coal, so many fewer pay days at sea, and so forth. The Transatlantic Company at length decided that this fishing village on the Loire estuary should become a port for ocean liners, like Havre. This was in the days when the Corps Législatif challenged the ambition of every Frenchman with the pride and the profits of big public enterprises. The Emperor tried to win all hesitant hearts, disarm the last rebels, and dispel the last resentment with promises of epic grandeur and commercial returns. The lively slogans of Guizot were again the order of the day, the "get rich" of the old minister was the Sermon on the Mount of the young sharp-toothed bourgeoisie. The papers began talking of the future city of the South Atlantic; *l'Illustration* published woodcuts more ornate than life itself, depicting the future public buildings. The Paris papers wrote: "Need we be astonished at the strong emotions that thrill the mind when we see Saint-Nazaire, a little village lost in a fold of the Atlantic coast, rise in a few years' time to the rank of one of our main seaports?" From their Louis XV apartments, the financiers of Nantes kept watch over this birth of a seaport at the mouth of their highway, the Loire. MM. Cézard Frères, who at the time held first rank in Nantes, took in hand the future of Saint-Nazaire and founded the General Credit Company.

The Grand Hotel mushroomed up. One day the glass-roofed market started flashing back the white Atlantic sunlight from its myriad panes and their metal framework. Bit by bit the slips gouged the soft shores of the estuary. In 'sixty-nine the steel mills of the lower Loire were built, in 'eighty-one the Loire shipyards.

At fourteen Antoine Bloyé landed in the midst of this town that rose and clamored above the smooth surface of the waters, which multiplied its slate roofs, its houses that bred like coral; over the housetops the masts of steamships and great sailing vessels could be seen from a long way off by Brière peasants on their way to market. A sort of fever drew men seeking work and capital seeking profits toward the quays, the shipyards, and the scaffolding. Between rows of board fences wide perpendicular streets took shape, where the sea wind knocked off the bowler hats of the newcomers from Paris and Nantes. The wind no longer found its former playgrounds and old hiding places. It swirled at the new street crossings, raising clouds of dust. It rent itself on the tops of factory chimneys belching smoke into the once unsullied sky.

The papers went into transports. "Everything in Saint-Nazaire," they said, "recalls the legendary towns of the California gold rush." Antoine lived through this great upheaval from the very beginning. He was swept along by the town's growth. In an era when mature men abandoned themselves to the orgy of construction, the young were even more easily impressed. How could a boy of fifteen resist the industrial fervor that seized grown-ups? Antoine went the way of his compatriots of the Grande Brière who left the poverty, the dreary liberty of their peat bogs and swampy lowlands, the slow traffic of their flatboats on the canals, to seek employment in the factories, whose furnace-glow they saw on evening walks along the byways of their kingdom of shadows. The naval yards at Indret had already drained the Brière of its inhabitants. In all corners of France the machines began to suck in the youth from the fields.

All the concerted movement of industry, the waterways, the railways, and the great shipping lines, conspired to wrench Antoine from the earthy rut where he had germinated and whence he had been shaken prematurely. He was conscious of his poverty; he early experienced the painful ambition of workers' sons who see the doors to a new life open part way before them. How could they refuse to leave the joyless world where their fathers never had their fill of air and nourishment, their fill of leisure, love, and security? The sad part about it is that they promptly forget this world and become their fathers' enemies. At the age of fifteen Antoine was incapable of picturing his future life anywhere save in the shadow of scaffolding amid the clang of steel plate, of rivets and hammers, where steam sirens shatter the sky and tall skeletons of shipyards loom. He childishly pictured himself in the post of manager. The country indifference and passivity, which he had absorbed through all his pores beneath the trees at the foot of the ancient hills of Finistère, passed from him with every engine throb, with every ship that sailed, with every incoming train.

On holidays he would venture off to the shipbuilding yards of Penhoët or Indret. All his powers were attracted by the great game that was beginning. At sixteen Antoine Bloyé is capable of conceiving human action only under the industrial forms that dominate the dangerous age of his youth. The sea that bathes the long nearby beaches, that creeps into the town itself, crowding back its squares and streets, could not wean Antoine from the fascination of the shipbuilding and railway yards. The lazy flatboat journeys across the Loire, the swims from the beach or off the steep walls of the slips, the mail boats from Santander and the Antilles, the parakeets from South America, the Havana cigars and the lead bottles of attar of roses the seamen bring in, and the gold-striped caps of the ships' officers, are for him a source of attraction less compelling than the mechanical forces, the walking beams of steam engines, the belts of the railways, the blast furnaces and the factories with which France is girding its loins. Perhaps, too, he shares the peasants' cat-like feeling of repugnance for the sea. Peasants do not like to leave the reassuring firmness of the ground, to lose sight of land. Antoine follows the example of his comrades to keep from being made fun of, but he admits to himself that he does not like the water.

Besides, Antoine knows what prestige is enjoyed by the men who work the machines. His father, an employee of the administrative service, speaks jealously of the locomotive engineers, of the traction service. The man who counts most is the one who comes in closest contact with production. Antoine is aware that in the endless scale of jobs the engineer holds a rank more enviable than a porter or a watchman. In Saint-Nazaire the magic titles of engineer and chief engineer open every door; these words completely embody Antoine's concept of real importance and authority. He further notices that the engineers live better than his father and better than the sailors and peasants. He is a little hazy yet about the difference between locomotive engineers and engineers, both men of the machines, but he begins to dream of greatness and to promise himself a great future, amid clouds of steam, words of command, and the sleek and oily limbs of engines. He will, perhaps, have trouble getting there, but he feels confident, he knows his own toughness, his capacity for work. On evening walks he tells himself he will make good.

Meanwhile he smuggles the famous bottles of attar of roses past the suspicious eyes of customs guards. They are sure to catch him, the smell goes right through the lead, he imagines himself enveloped in a cloud of rose scent that can be smelt a long way off. But he is never caught. The customs guards say hello to him just as they do to all the boys around the port, whom they know by sight. Jean-Pierre Bloyé dodges customs like his son. He brings through boxes of Havana cigars, purchased from the cooks and stokers of transatlantic liners. He sells them to inspectors, to district managers, to big hotel proprietors, to the stationmaster. Every boat from the Antilles brings money to the house. Smuggling helps make both ends meet. None of the people the Bloyés come in contact with see anything wrong in such normal undertakings. Not till later will Jules Ferry charge the secular schools with the task of teaching the workers to respect the law and venerate the public finances. In Dirinon, Jean-Pierre Bloyé slaughtered pigs for the butcher. Marie Bloyé earned a little money carrying messages at night. She often covered ten kilometers through dark forests, her ears alert to the rustle and scurry of small nocturnal animals and the hoots of owls. She held her stick ready to give a lively reception to phantoms or evildoers. These tramps would net her a franc or two. The smuggling in Saint-Nazaire was more remunerative.

Meanwhile, with the passing years Antoine began to suffer because of many things he saw. . . . For example, because his parents were the objects of disguised charity, because, being docile and respectful, they were presented with old pairs of pants, old dresses that might still do good service on the backs of people less fastidious than the original owners. As a favor, his mother went to do the laundry at the stationmaster's house. One cannot refuse one's superiors such a service. His father received money for little errands that he ran. Antoine needed a good deal of pride to soothe his feelings in these matters. Well-dressed men would stop Jean-Pierre Bloyé in the street. In a loud voice they would ask about his health, then they would avow their purpose: "Say, Bloyé, is there any chance of getting some cigars? My stock is running low."

Bloyé would answer that he had some friends, a steamship would soon arrive, there was always some way of arranging the matter. The customer then told him to watch out for the customs guards, who were not always as stupid as they looked. He feared vaguely that they might become involved in some sort of mess if Bloyé were caught, but Bloyé would answer, "The guard who'll catch me has not yet been born."

The other would laugh as an accomplice who was, after all, at a safe distance. Antoine didn't like the tone assumed by these gentlemen of Saint-Nazaire and inspectors from Nantes who didn't wear uniforms. It made him shudder to see his father salute docilely, and politely suffer himself to be slapped on the shoulder in a presumptuous patronizing way.

"We must respect the men higher up," said Jean-Pierre. He took the words and gestures as they came and never saw any malice attached. He saw nothing wrong in all this. There would always be big people and little people. It's just like war—we aren't the ones who'll change the world.

And Marie Bloyé would add, "Our place in the world is decreed by fortune and the will of God."

Antoine didn't know what his father thought, what ideas might lurk behind his passive words. Perhaps Jean-Pierre accepted things less submissively than his appearance indicated. There were days when he sat meditating with a sort of angry sadness; the muscles of his jaw would contract. But it is not in the nature of things that sons should divine all the thoughts that form in the heads of their fathers like big painful tumors, and sons are never dispassionate judges.

Sometimes ladies whom Marie Bloyé worked for by the day met Antoine in his mother's company. Calling her "Mother Bloyé," they ordered her to come to their houses on such and such a day, at such and such a time, to do the cleaning or the washing. Then they would absentmindedly notice Antoine's presence. They would question his mother, they would ask what she was going to do with her "big boy." Marie Bloyé would answer that it was not yet decided, that Antoine was always hanging around the factories and the railway, that whatever happened she was sure he wouldn't be a sailor. "He is like his father, he doesn't like the water."

The ladies would give advice. He should do this, he should do that. As though they knew everything, as though they could run the whole world from the tips of their hats. Antoine never opened his mouth; what he would do was none of their business—with their long skirts, their nets and whalebone collars. He didn't quite know what to do with his hands, which stuck out a bit too far from his sleeves, sleeves that belonged, perhaps, to an old overcoat donated by one of these ladies. He stared down at his big shoes; the little girls standing by the ladies also stared at his big shoes. Antoine hated the ladies and their little girls.

The days passed. Antoine worked like a boy who has no resources save his own arms and his own head and not the arms and head of others, the head of an uncle or the full coffers of a father. He worked like a boy without a heritage. He learned geometry, algebra, physics, history. He memorized names that meant nothing to him, that were not a part of his everyday life—Athaliah, Andromache. What relation did these heroines of cultured families bear to his father's nightshift duty, to the smuggled cigars, to the steaming blood of slaughtered pigs? What relation did *Le Cid* and *Chimène* bear to the washing of Mme Dubuis and the meanness of the rich? One year he was sent to the Rennes Academy regional contest for secondary schools. One of the questions was to comment on this thought of Pascal: "Truth on this side of the Pyrenees, error on the other." Antoine could play the wise monkey as well as anybody. He received a first mention. In school he took all the prizes that year.

One Sunday he found himself standing on the squeaky boards of a red-carpeted platform. Through his clothes he felt the sun beating on his back. In front of him were the professors in their academic regalia. A man in a general's uniform—the prefect—and a priest. They had just read off the list of prize winners for his class. Special instruction, third and fourth years: first prize in French—Bloyé (Antoine) of Pont-Château, day pupil; in mathematics—Bloyé (Antoine). The prefect handed out green diplomas signed in the corner by the principal. He was talking, but Antoine, half dazed by the light, heard only snatches of words . . . congratulate you . . . hope . . . our industrious population. A man standing behind a table handed him a bundle of books. He turned around; he saw the little ripple of heads and hats surge forward and break gently on the backs of the musicians. Horse chestnuts fell in the morning silence which the crowd did not disturb. An outgoing ocean liner tooted. All of a sudden several people started clapping. In the first row, a well-dressed lady in a purple dress fringed with slightly yellowed lace clapped. Her white hands fluttered like a pair of fleshy wings above the curly hair of the trombone player. They were detached like aerial beings. Further back, Antoine made out his mother in her tight black skirt, neat bodice, and her loose-fitting provincial bonnet. She stared at the platform and applauded. Her round cheeks were rosy with pleasure. Through the black mesh of her net Antoine saw the white strands of his mother's hair—turned white at thirty. A schoolmate, who in turn had received his share of the prizes, gave him a shove. He stepped down and walked across in front of the musicians. The lady in the front row leaned over to her neighbor and started laughing. Undoubtedly she was laughing at him, she followed him with her eyes. He fancied he heard her say "the little peasant."

His father was not present, he was on duty on the Nantes train. The distribution of prizes ended toward noon. Afterward his mother took him to the photographer, who did not neglect to congratulate him. Antoine wore a sort of tight-fitting jacket that wrinkled; he had to pose for his picture with one hand propped on his pile of prizes, placed one on top of the other in a terraced pyramid like a little red and gold Assyrian temple. What was the point of it? Antoine asked himself. From the end of the blue-glassed studio, the photographer pronounced the words of his profession: "Look straight in front of you with a lively and determined expression. Hold your head up, gaze steady, let the left arm hang loose . . . that's right, don't move . . . done."

Antoine asked himself if he really had any right to be proud, if this school success meant anything for his future life. Meanwhile, his father, back from Nantes, told the neighbors about him.

But on that very evening of childish triumph, Antoine suddenly remembers that his mother does not know how to write, that she can read only printed characters, but not handwriting, that she mispronounces complicated words, that she says "translantic," that she uses words from the dialect of her Gallic country, *driver* for *vagabonder, caballer* for *tomber, sia* instead of *oui,* and that these things make city people laugh. She believes in bad omens and good omens. She tells in all seriousness of her grandfather who was a sorcerer in Béganne and who went to consult the dead at night. She believes in the truth of proverbs, of sayings about the weather; her whole wisdom is contained in an old musty wormeaten book that holds all the secrets of Albertus Magnus. And that very evening, as he sits on his doorstep, Antoine awkwardly begins to feel that the world toward which his studies are impelling him, and toward which he is driven by childish ambition, is considerably removed from the world where his parents have lived since their youth. He feels the beginnings of estrangement. He is no longer quite of their kith and station. He is already unhappy as though after a farewell, an irrevocable breach of faith, that very evening of August 4, 1879. . . . After

supper, he tries to read the book he has received as a prize for
scholarship. It is *Le Devoir* by M. Jules Simon, of the Académie
Française; he opens it at random.

"Man is free" he reads, "he is ever aware of his power not to
do what he does do and to do what he does not do."

Antoine reflects on these words and on some others besides.
He ill understands them. Is his father free not to be poor, not to
work nights, not to go where he does go? Is his mother free not to
have her back ache from work, not to be tired out and old before
her time? He himself—in what way is he free? To be free means
simply not to be poor and not always ordered about. The rich
enjoy a form of freedom. People with an income. So M. Jules
Simon's words, too exalted for a worker's son, are understood by
him in a way the author never intended. He is not refined, he
does not grasp thoughts that are too noble, he is endowed with a
simplicity he will find hard to lose. He shuts M. Jules Simon's
gilt-edged book never to open it again.

Meanwhile, they talked about him just as they did before in
primary school. Jean-Pierre Bloyé was favorably regarded by his
superiors. People whom he only knew by sight went out of their
way to give him advice. The stationmaster, M. Dubois, who was
young and whose young wife aroused much envy in Saint-
Nazaire when she sang in a beautiful quavering voice at social
gatherings and charity fetes, said to Bloyé, "Your son is worth
pushing. It would be a pity to let a highly gifted child like him
enter an apprenticeship. He would be extremely unhappy were
he merely to remain a worker, he's already had too much education for that. That sours workers. You might try the School of
Arts and Trades—he could make a good place for himself no
matter where, in the merchant marine service, or the railways, he
might become a railway employee like his father. Many graduates
of Arts go very far in our industry."

Jean-Pierre Bloyé was tempted by the thought of making a
gentleman, a bourgeois, out of his son, despite the further sacrifice

it would involve. A boy who studies doesn't earn anything. He is more of a drain, and the neighbors criticize your ambition behind your back as though you were betraying them in trying to spare your son the hardships of a worker's life. But the road of study had been taken and Bloyé dreamed of the future. He pictured his son at some future date in the very midst of those remote unknown spheres where engineers and chief inspectors move. He had an awe of education, he regarded it as an open sesame that unlocked the gates to freedom and power; its secrets would deliver Antoine from the chains which he himself had had to bear. How could a father hinder his son from escaping unhappiness if the opportunity of escape presented itself? He had often beaten Antoine, but he loved him. For one more year of secondary school Antoine submissively followed the advice his father handed on to him. A son never argues. Furthermore, these plans conformed far too closely to his own plans of power and machines for him to want to oppose them. A day arrived, at the end of the year 1880, when he took the train for Angers unaccompanied.

5

On this trip Antoine was happy and light-hearted, like travelers bound for wealth and adventure. He walked impatiently along the station platform in Nantes, waiting for his connection. He went to the end of the platform as though it were the end of a pier where a boat from beyond the seas was about to dock. All France and all of life east of his native country stretched before him beckoning. He was leaving his province for the first time and the Nantes station was like a frontier post. The country seemed familiar, however, if only because his river, the Loire, followed the railway line. The good company of the river, that swerved from the railway embankment and then ran toward it through half-flooded fields and rows of heavy-headed willows, kept him from feeling totally exiled. It was like a thread that stretched between Saint-Nazaire and Angers, between what he had left behind him and what lay in store for him, his past and his future. Many months later, on free days, as he gazed down at the Loire, he fancied he heard beneath the flowing murmur of the great sandy river the hammers of Penhoët and the sirens of the great ships weighing anchor for Santander.

Angers—'eighty, 'eighty-one, 'eighty-two, 'eighty-three. For three years Antoine lived the rigorous life of the National Schools of Arts and Trades, that train the petty officers for the armies of big French industry.

Everything then encouraged the working-class youth, the ambitious sons of artisans and minor functionaries, to enter the cabal of command. Antoine had been caught up like the others, and he was completely ignorant of the springs of this great undertaking. He did not know that along with many other adolescents of his age he was one of the pawns of the huge game that the supreme masters of the French bourgeoisie were beginning to play. He had simply been told he could escape the poverty and precariousness of a worker's life and these promises accorded far too well with the temptations his city offered for him to refuse to listen. He knew nothing. Far from him, even before he was born, in offices, at shareholders' meetings, in the parliament, in learned bodies, factory owners had for thirty years past been voicing their demands. Industry required new human material. It felt a growing need for men able to read a blueprint, to supervise the making of a part, to carry out orders issued from above, to think up those modest projects and inventions of detail that foster industrial progress and increase production. It was not love of man that on March 15, 1858, had prompted the parliament to adopt the draft of a law on professional education. Specialization was no idle dream in an age when the power of machines, the stocks of raw materials and of finished articles, the speed of locomotives, increased every year.

At the moment of Antoine Bloyé's birth on the borders of his peaceful drowsing Brière, France could boast of 150,000 factories of all capacities, 1,500,000 factory workers, 500,000 horsepower of steam in the service of industry. It took able men to handle these masses of workers. The boards of directors clamored for managers. The shareholders gave the public authorities to understand that they needed specialists, foremen, and skilled workers. General Morin and M. Tresea, men schooled in applied mechanics, on their return from the Industrial Exhibition in London in 1862 calculated that the three Schools of Arts and Trades in Aix-en-Provence, Angers, and Châlons, the Central School for Civil Engineers, the School of Mines, and the School of Bridges and Highways turned out an average of seven hundred men yearly: one hundred diplomas at the Central School, three hundred students leaving the School of Mines and the School of Bridges, three hundred certificates from the Schools of Arts. At the same time, according to their estimate, a modest one, the factories employed 1,200,000 people. Thus the ratio of middle managers to the rank and file was that of 1 to 2,000, meaning very few noncommissioned officers.

Higher destinies are reserved for the sons of the big bourgeoisie, the bourgeoisie of the liberal professions—destinies embellished by the passwords of the humanities. But what tremendous reserves exist among the gifted sons of workers, what an inexhaustible source of faithful subordinates! They are needed; they are enticed with promises of a great future and equal opportunity, the dawn of democracy. Each worker's son has in his satchel the diploma of an overseer of men, the passport of a bourgeois.

Those titanic causes, at work in the great centers where the histories of nations are decided, operating through the councils of the government, have launched Antoine Bloyé along an incline which he perhaps believes he chose of his own free will. He will descend this long incline at a speed which will not adjust its tempo to the nebulous desires of an eighteen-year-old boy, who has first seen the world in the gray colors of station platforms and of houses with dirt floors.

The sugary, hypocritical M. Jules Simon once said: "The Schools of Arts and Trades may, strictly speaking, be regarded as schools of apprenticeship, inasmuch as the student acquires the theoretical and practical basis of one of the following trades: forger, smelter, repairman, locksmith, lathe turner, and joiner. However, these schools go beyond mere apprenticeship, they turn out only the picked workers and chief workers." This is why on October 15, 1880, Antoine Bloyé lands in the empty square before the station in Angers.

Angers drowses with its beautiful trees, its lofty castle with its round funnel-like towers, its memories of King René, its walks inlaid with floral mosaics, its secluded houses with their crumbling façades, its cellars of white wines, its officers and provincial belles, proud of their breasts. On the banks of the River Maine, the shops of the School of Arts and Trades run with the motion of well-oiled machines, turning out their human products. Antoine, with the carefreeness of his eighteen years, absorbs everything the school offers him, nourishment and knowledge, with tremendous appetite of mind and body. He is greedier for earthly things than he ever suspected. He laughs at the professors who look at the youth they instruct as though they were enemies. Almost all the teachers are that way. On the blackboard he conjures beautiful, evanescent edifices of figures and dashes. He uses watercolors to embellish his drawings of machines and cogs. He makes friends; in the third division, which is his division, a hundred and one young men of his own age live at the same military tempo as he does, without the leisure to think of good or evil. They live through their regulated round of daily activities, sleep heavily at night, after evening prayer, wake themselves in the morning with the icy water of the washstands. The shouts of the adjutants who are former soldiers, the coarse twenty-minute meals, the prison, the guardroom, the infirmary with the religious warmth of the stoves and the voices of the nuns, the endless hours of theoretical training, the working hours in the smithy and foundry, brief trips to the outside world wedged between the two ends of the week, with the weekly franc allowed by the administration. The hours pile up: five and three-quarters hours of lectures, seven hours of shop a day. The accumulation of activities, the lack of money, the sharp-toothed cogs of a closely fitted mechanism do not leave Antoine much time for dreaming and getting to know himself. Such leisure belongs only to young people who go from secondary school to the open, free, and leisurely life of the universities. Not everybody has this right. In these years of the 'eighties, who would dream of training a Bloyé to a liberal existence and liberal thoughts? On the other hand, no one tries to deceive him now; no more promises of things that life does not hold in store—such promises were all very well for prize-giving speeches. These young people are not promised a dazzling future. They are taught the tasks to which they will be assigned. They are told that when they leave school they will enter the navy and merchant marine as mechanics, or the railways as skilled workers, overseers on small jobs, foremen; others will sit at inclined drafting boards, carefully drawing plans. A few will outdistance the rest, they will be pointed to; they will be the heads of grain standing above the stalks of the field, the heads which will serve to justify mediocre lives without number.

Antoine attains his growth quite late; an interruption has occurred in his development. After his healthy country childhood, he had become one of the youth of the working-class districts—pale faced, long haired, skinny armed. His three years at Angers give him broad shoulders and stocky muscles won by wielding the hammer in the smithy and foundry. The thin boy who reached the school in the fall of 1880, only to spend the winter and spring months in the stifling sweetishness of the infirmary under the care of the nuns, passing through the ailments and the pimply period of the young who grow too fast, his thoughts fed by memories of the postures of girls, by the motion of the hips of the nice young sister Sainte Marguerite, is no more than a dead brother of the young smith in leather apron who poses behind a forge for the annual photograph of the third division. He has changed his skin. The man within him has been allowed to emerge. At nineteen he is built like the peasants of Allaire who, if ever he went to visit them, would have recognized him as one of themselves by his coloring and physique. He is five feet nine inches tall, his hair is slightly reddish, his blue eyes are set in a ruddy face. All at once he begins to look like his father. A certain power is vested in his big frame, which is vaguely aware of it and controls it rather awkwardly. But Antoine has not the spare time to meditate on the fact that he is endowed with strength and with vast desires he will never be able to satisfy. He wields the chalk, the pen and hammer. He swaps soldiers' yarns and like a soldier he is drugged by fatigue. His strength finds outlets as best it can in student escapades. Fortune denies him any time to waste. In those years when young people learn to know themselves—years which are hard for the mature man to make up for—Antoine does not even have vacations. He spends August and September in Saint-Nazaire at the shipyards of the Loire, working in the smithy. His father tells him, "You need money for the coming year to buy clothes with. I have none to give you. You'll have to earn it, my boy."

He earns it, he works hard for it, thirteen hours a day. The francs of his wages do not amount to a very large sum for the whole year's requirements. From May on he no longer goes out on Sundays in Angers. So much rush, so much effort! The knowledge that the days of poverty will end is not enough. He rebels, he feels so much within himself lying idle, all the forces and desires that long for a vacation in order to vent themselves. He senses that hostile forces conspire to stifle the forces of young men of his class, he tastes anger. There is room for hatred in his eighteen-year-old head, hatred for the slave-drivers at the school, for the shipyard engineers. Whose side is he on? He feels himself seized by working-class anger, yet he is nevertheless standing on the threshold of a life where he knows he will order workers. How shall he find his bearings?

One day, at the shipyard, he jumps up on a lumber pile as the workers are going home and harangues his comrades on the necessity of organizing a strike. He allows his inner spring of wrath to overflow:

"Comrades, we cannot stand things any longer, the management gentlemen treat us like house servants. You cannot feed your wives and children. You work fourteen hours a day, you have to pay fines. Our trouble is that we are isolated. Each of us sticks to his own corner and we drag each other down. The bosses will have no power over us once we are united."

Shouts echo in the yard. The men move off, Antoine walks home alone along the road. All his hatred evaporates. He feels powerless in the darkness. There is no strike; the director calls him in and tells him: "You are a child. I am willing to shut my eyes this time but don't let it happen again. I never would have expected such a thing on the part of an educated boy like you, who may perhaps become a manager in the future."

No one takes him seriously. He is regarded as being a worker only temporarily and his anger bothers nobody. A manager in the future? Jean-Pierre said: "You are crazy to risk spoiling your future by such childish tricks. You may get yourself blacklisted. Is this the way you repay me for having raised you and made sacrifices on your account?"

How is he to see things clearly? Antoine has this rebellion without knowing anything. He has never heard talk of socialism, of trade unions. The time is not yet come when Pelloutier will organize the first central trade union in Saint-Nazaire. Afterward, many years hence, he will recall this speech at the shipyards as one of the important episodes of his life. He does not analyze his hatred. The fact is that since the age of fifteen he has been propelled along a turnless road, with no room for bodily or spiritual relaxation, where there are no crossroads, no interludes of idleness, but only brief halts. In the country, even today, one finds small branch railway lines where time is not highly valued. Between Brest and Ploudalmézeau, the engineer stops along the way to pick flowers, or to give a ride to peasant girls going to the market in Saint-Renan, or to play a game of cards with some friend at a station. But Antoine's life is already like the express trains he will drive tomorrow, impelled by an overwhelming force.

Antoine leaves the School of Arts and Trades and becomes a civilian man among men, a man with a diploma that destines him to years without incident, where almost everything is pre-ordained. His last holidays pass. When they are over, he finds himself on the brink of life, in whose current he is about to plunge without even knowing whether he can swim and keep himself afloat in the stream. In the middle of the year 'eighty-three he prepares to play a game whose rules no one has taught him. He has to his credit youth, ambition without presumption, reserves of strength and anger, and a certificate of graduation bearing the seal of the Ministry of Commerce which informs his future masters that he left the School of Arts and Trades eighteenth out of seventy-seven. First in mathematics and seventy-fifth in drawing.

6

Antoine Bloyé entered the service of the Orléans Railway Company. His entire past, his whole history drew him toward the shiny curves of the railway tracks. He had been offered a job in a shipping company that brought Welsh coal to the piers of Nantes and Bordeaux. He would have been stationed for two years at Cardiff and Swansea. For Jean-Pierre Bloyé and for Marie it was like going to the ends of the earth. How could he embark on a trader's career, fraught with unspeakable dangers, a profession which provides no old-age pension, where you may find yourself destitute between one day and the next because you "eat up" all you earn? His parents said all these things, and they added: "Supposing we should die while you were in England? You can't leave us like that and let us die all alone in our corner like old dogs."

It is hard to resist such piteous appeals. Furthermore, in working-class families in Brittany paternal authority still obtained in those days. Workers' children often used the *vous* in speaking to their parents and never dreamed of disobeying their orders. Jean-Pierre Bloyé told his son, "If you leave for England you might as well stay there. Never again will you cross our threshold. . . ."

Antoine gave in. He was not prepared to fight for a life whose advantages he was not very clear about. Perhaps he preferred to give in. His father's veto spared him from having to decide. His ambitions did not range very far, he simply aimed at rising a little higher than his father. The ambitions of young people often do not go beyond a desire to surpass their fathers. For them this feat requites the petty humiliations of childhood. It was easier for a boy like Antoine Bloyé to picture himself as an engineer on an express train than as director of a big shipping company.

As engine mechanic at the Tours depot, he got to know the black roundhouses with their sooty, broken windows, the boiler shops where they stretch out the carcasses of locomotives, the proprietors of the wine shop restaurants, and the first women of his life. They were hatless women in slippers who glided along the endless walls of the railway yard under the greenish pallor of the gas jets. From their rooms you could hear the trains whistle. They knew the timetables and the shifts; their prices were not high. A mechanic earns five francs a day, and love was scaled to a worker's wages. Thus does love enter the life of many men. A woman accosts you on a rainy night and opens up in a poor room or standing in the dark corner of a shed where the smell of stale urine still lingers. Antoine's previous experience was limited to hugging the little girls of the port of Saint-Nazaire, touching their breasts on summer evenings, passing his hand under their skirts along the soft folds of their ruffled panties.

The age for military service came and Antoine departed. It was the winter of 1885, the Second Regiment of Engineers was quartered at Montpellier. When you have never been further than Tours, how intoxicating it is to discover the soil of Langue-doc, the great salt marshes, the endless horizons, the sparkling southern sea! The colonel in command of the regiment, Baron Berge, ignored the men. It was a peaceful regiment. Of a Sunday, the soldiers would lie on the sand at Palavas-les-Flots and munch olives. They bathed in blue striped trunks and pinched the be-hinds of the inn waitresses. At Montpellier, after the evening meal, they would walk to the end of the Promenade du Peyrou, and stand in the heroic shadow of the statue of Louis XIV gazing out at level vineyards that stretched to meet the endless sky.

They marched along roads covered with flour-like dust. The school for pontoon builders was located on the canal, and the men lolled lazily on the bottoms of the flatboats. In autumn, the brown and red villages smelt of grapes and marc. On farm floors, purple stains of drying pervaded the evening air. Movable horse-drawn stills went from house to house, rocking and spilling, and the soldiers drank liters of heavy red wine for two sous—wine that knocked their legs from under them. In those years, the barracks were not yet the great war factories of today, where youths work to exhaustion, serving deadly machines that prepare death with the efficiency of an electric chair. The Engineers service was a peaceful branch. Antoine led an idle soldier's life; afternoon naps on the hard bunk of the dormitory, when your sleep is scarcely pierced by the shouts of the NCO's that echo through the glare, by the sentry's bugle calling the orderly corporal. He lolled beneath the lovely trees of the town without a thought in the world. In the kitchens he ate long tidbits of grilled red meat. It was like a big dreamy vacation that lasted a year.

When his term was up, Antoine returned to the Orléans line. He was assigned to the Paris depot, first as apprentice locomotive engineer, then as engineer.

The depot, together with the Austerlitz and Orléans stations, formed a noisy little world in the heart of the XIIIth arrondissement. The arrondissement itself was a city within a city. At that time, you could not travel straight from one end of Paris to the other as you can today. The omnibuses sailed along the streets like skiffs, held up at all the locks of squares and crossings. There were people who had the spare time to ride on top simply for the pleasure of seeing the countryside. People went to Auteuil for their vacations. The various districts had little contact with each other. They had their own customs and habits. Antoine was a provincial in a Paris made up of provinces poorly stitched together. When he crossed the bridge to the right bank, he would say, since he was heading toward the Bastille and the boulevards, "I'm going to town." And when on the return trip he sighted the hog's back of the great windy avenues which converge on the Place d'Italie, the dome of Salpétrière, and the belfry of the church of Jean d'Arc, he entered a world as familiar as a village square. Men make more than one native land for themselves. There are some who feel at home in twenty corners of the world, for men are born more than once. This enclosed world was enough for Antoine.

He lived on the Rue de Chevaleret over a little red-painted restaurant where he ate. Mme Decailly tidied his room and took care of his clothes. On each side of the door were painted two billiard cues tied together by a carefully painted ribbon. An inscription proclaimed: Beaujolais Wines, Onion Soup. The billiard table had long since disappeared and the silence of the after-dinner evenings was punctuated only by the sputtering of the gas. The Rue de Chevaleret consisted of a long row of low houses, with alleys and passages between, that echoed all day long to the mallets clanging on the hoops and staves of wine barrels in the depths of coopers' shops. There were dingy laundries in whose doorways rumpled-haired ironers emerged for a lungful of the smoky air, empty lots, workers' hostels. The whole district was full of plank shanties, of the long walls of factories and hospitals. Poverty, weariness, and death overhung these workers' streets. In the blind alleys, hay carts stood waiting, their shafts pointing skyward, just as in the fields. Tree branches, fronds of acacia, overhung an occasional gardener's wall like a forlorn hope.

In summer, whenever he was off duty, Antoine had dinner on the terrace of the Decailly pension behind the dusty foliage of a spindle tree. Nearby, two or three employees from the neighborhood talked of their offices and told stories of women. Masons and plasterers sometimes dropped in after work and held glasses of red wine in their rough hands white as the plaster casts of hands. Coopers discussed their craft. Antoine watched engineers,

firemen, trainmen, conductors, go by on their way on or off duty,
swinging their black lunch boxes, and he said hello to almost all of
them; he was one of them. Pretty pale girls passed, their hair done
up in big knots and ribbons round their necks, their bell-like
skirts drawn tight at the waist, women with listless gait carrying
home the evening provisions in a net that pulled their shoulders
down, white-faced children who slowly imbibed the most loath-
some diseases in the overcrowded rooms of poverty. The last
cabs, the last drays with their strong horses rolled by. The noise
of passing trains from the foot of the hill reached as far as the
scraggy trees of the Rue de Patay and slid along the scaly walls of
the Rue du Dessous des Berges. Antoine would then ponder lu-
cidly enough on the poverty of his neighborhood, on the hunted
look of the women, the sorrow of the filthy houses on the Rue
Jeanne d'Arc where the choked privies flooded the stairways step
by step with a constant flow of putrefaction. He harbored within
him a smoldering hatred that was in his very blood. Antoine
linked the sidewalks of the XIIIth arrondissement with the hovels
of Saint-Nazaire where the metal workers lived. There was anger
in his heart—anger against things unbearable; it would remain
with him, perhaps, throughout his whole life. Nevertheless, he
had already drifted apart from the companions he had grown up
with. There were days when he thought of himself as someone
who no longer shared their sorrow and misfortune. He sympa-
thized with these unfortunates, but already he viewed their sufferings from afar; their misery was no longer his misery. An estrangement had already occurred. He did not suffer with them,
he stood apart, and his sympathy came as though from outside, it
seemed detached from his body. This joyless world was like a
land one is about to leave, and the preparations for the departure
prevent the traveler from giving much thought to its inhabitants.

Among the engineers of the Paris depot, there was a small
group of young men who were there only for the time being, living a temporary life. They had gone through the School of Arts

and Trades; one of them had even been through the Central School. They were there for a few years, riding the engines, as they say. They were five inseparables who seemed firmly united in their bachelor solitude, their community of memories, vocabularies, and references and the certainty of a future which was barely uncertain enough to allow for occasional speculations as to what they would be twenty or thirty years hence. Bloyé, Vignaud, Rabastens, Le Moullec, and Martin were all classmates and they possessed a common stock of images which were set forth like an easily legible text under the title Angers 1880–1883. They rarely had recourse to these images. They reserved them for the time when life, connections, successes, marriages, children, and illnesses should have so separated them from each other and cast them in such different molds that they must invoke all their youth to keep them from being silent, bored, and uneasy in each other's presence.

As express train engineers for five or six years, they patiently learned the rules, tricks of the trade, the customs and the snares of the railways. Their habits were other than those of professional locomotive engineers, the range of whose ambition is confined to the sufficiently remote ranks of chief engineer, assistant chief, or substitute chief. They were all bachelors and they lived in furnished rooms off the Rue Nationale and the Boulevard de la Gare. They were without domestic responsibilities. There were no children waiting for them at home, no listless women, drained empty like shapeless, lusterless bags of skin or swollen with unhealthy fat by nursing, laundering, housework. The women with neither ballast nor anchorage who accosted them sometimes of an evening were neither housekeepers nor mothers of families—women with overdecorated lingerie, as temporary as their lives as engineers. The bonuses of the depot, the savings in coal and oil brought them revenues which they squandered as lightheartedly as sailors. These returns swelled to incredible proportions the fixed salaries they received. In 'eighty-nine, the year of the Exhibition, when country folk flocked to see the foreign wonders on the Champ de Mars, Antoine earned nine hundred francs some months.

Every week the group of friends would dine at the Quatre Sergents de la Rochelle. They would take balcony seats at the theater, and on such gala occasions they wore high hats, rented for five francs. They knew the repertoires of the Ambigu, the Opéra-Comique, the Châtelet. Manon singing opposite the Chevalier des Grieux, pale as a dissipated young priest; the horses at the Hippodrome, mounted by heavy-haunched women riders and racing by on hoofs that moved with machinelike precision; the saints in *Jean d'Arc* floating down from the stage roof suspended on invisible threads; Michael Strogoff passing a trembling hand over his eyes scorched by the red-hot iron, while the postal employee shouted: "Ten kopecks a word! The thread is sundered." On the boulevards were girls decked in feathers and lace, in velvet dull as suburban window curtains. They wore laced boots; they had narrow waists and high breasts, their real bodies were invisible. They beckoned to the five friends, who often took the invitation. Their appearance of luxurious inhuman machines seduced men, more effectually, perhaps, than girls of today, with their dresses that faithfully follow their contours like limpid water.

The five friends would often stroll at random through the Paris streets. The city was silent. A country atmosphere stole into the streets, barely disturbed by the hoofs of a cab horse. At midnight, you could walk down the middle of the street, and the five friends did so. They walked side by side, talking little, mingling stories of the depot with obscene remarks. They crossed the northern part of the city and climbed toward Montmartre. But they did not linger there. It was a region far too remote from their part of the world. They stayed long enough for a drink in a café where every custom seemed alien, long enough to listen to the big phonographs, with red or blue horns spread like sterile flowers, long

enough to gaze at Paris, stretched at their feet, with a sort of uneasiness as though at a sea too turbulent and too broad for them.
The strings of street lamps rose and fell, the trains of the East and
North whistled as they pulled into the stations or departed for the
provinces or the remotest corners of Europe. They felt a touch of
pride at thus commanding the town; from such heights, one always feels like a mountaineer gazing down at the plains from
above. But these young men did not think of the conquest of
Paris. Such dreams were not for them.

Then they climbed down, crossed the bank district, the wool
district, the linen district, and ate in Les Halles at four in the
morning. At all hours of the night, in the Sébastopol quarter permeated by the smell of piles of vegetables, other girls grabbed
them by the arm in the doorways of hotels with narrow uncom-
fortably high façades, girls who still wore the romantic costume of
realist songs. Once they had left Les Halles, the boulevards, the
warmth of the cafés, they were alone in a nocturnal world consecrated to the yellow gaslight and to the hazards of venal amours.
They ambled aimlessly, unreasoningly, for the pleasure of being
together and feeling that all other men were in bed, tossing and
moaning in their sleep like dogs. The squares and the crossings
were as deserted as high mountain glaciers, as the towns that ar-
cheologists clear of their burden of sand or lava. Here and there
men were sleeping on benches, their heads on a sack or a canvas
bag full of rags and scraps. Cats slunk past, sensing dangers which
men are unable to detect. Endless avenues unraveled; churches,
asylums, prisons, warehouses reared their somber walls. Antoine
and his friends felt like the last waking beings of the city, gathered together in a single group, able to do what they pleased with
it. This nocturnal world nowhere bordered on the world of day.
They fancied that adventures lurked in ambush which would give
them the opportunity to assert their prowess, but save for this
hazy hope and the possession of youth itself scarcely anything
came their way.

On one evening only, Antoine and Le Moullec were attacked in the Rue du Château des Rentiers by two prowlers. Holding his bunch of keys in his fist, Antoine felled one with a blow on the temple. The other scampered off like a slippery little sewer rat. Antoine and Le Moullec continued on their way and heard nothing more of the incident, but afterward Antoine would sometimes recall this encounter, saying to himself with a relish that bothered him: "Maybe I killed a man." Another evening, Martin's mistress, whom people called Hefty Marie, came along. They had had quite a bit to drink and they laughed like men who let a trickle of wine slobber from the corners of their mouths. The girl walked unsteadily.

"You do it on purpose, you camel," said Martin.

And Hefty Marie burst into roars of mare-like laughter. They dragged her along, protesting to Martin because they did not like having women with them. On the Boulevard de l'Hôpital, she pulled up her skirts and squatted in a corner. Her companions kept on walking and she shrieked, "Don't leave me!"

Martin retraced his steps. The others told him: "She's your woman, after all, take care of her if she's drunk."

Hefty Marie was relieving herself and Martin said to her, "Hurry up." She could not get up on her feet. She fell back sitting down in her excrement, laughing like a new-born babe proud of the products of its bowels. They picked her up, somewhat sobered. Rabastens said in his Gascon accent, "She sure is a smelly wench!"

Later, when Martin and Le Moullec were decorated with the Legion of Honor, they recalled that night back in the XIIIth arrondissement as the most adventurous memento of their bachelor days in Paris.

Thus the engineers lived a life that imitated fairly closely the expensive pastimes of the sons of the rich, whose exploits they read about between the covers of cheap magazines. Antoine sometimes felt he had better things to do, but how could he resist the pleasure of being able to tell himself, like the others, "We are night owls"? They yielded to the rather sordid attractions reflected from the rich quarters. These evenings also divided Antoine from his brothers.

One day Martin invited Antoine to dinner at his mother's. In a private court between the Rue Bréa and the Rue Notre-Dame-des-Champs, Mme Martin kept a quiet family pension where elderly widowed ladies stayed whose married children lived in the country. The house was full of black furniture covered in red plush. The windows were hung with embroidered curtains, heavy with dust and dampness, held back by gilt-tasseled cords. The parlor was crammed with assorted armchairs, pie-crust tables, low chairs, ottomans, and cushions. The place exhaled a bourgeois comfort dating from the Second Empire. A small painted and varnished cabinet, shaped like a sedan chair, contained little animals and shepherds made of porcelain, dancers of glazed Dresden china, great prickly shells with the names of monsters. Mme Martin would point to them with her mittened hands and say, "These are the strombi, from the Indian Ocean. This is the prickly murex that inhabits the Mediterranean, the *murex mondon,* the delphinula." And you fancied you heard the roaring of the seven seas. Lacquer boxes tied with silken cords held medals from Crimean and Mexican campaigns. Tarnished etchings depicted hunting scenes and trysts of true lovers. An ironwood case contained a miniature grave shaded by a willow all made out of hair. The daughter, Mlle Martin, would say, "This is the hair of my grandfather, my baby brother who died when he was a year old, and my grandmother."

She was no fool. Her smile gave you to understand that she belonged to another generation, that she had her own opinions about her mother. Thus everything was attuned to the quiet of the court, where gates kept out the vehicles and where the little prostitutes from the Rue Bréa made their first appointments of the evening, in front of tiny gardens whose damp mold recalled a neglected cemetery. In the hallway, old ladies passed, nodding greetings on their way upstairs to their rooms. The two white-cuffed servants glided about on felt slippers.

Here Antoine came in contact with a world of small business-men and office functionaries, with principles, traditions, and mannerisms that would have been hard for his father to get used to, where his father would have felt completely out of place. Martin's father had been senior clerk at the Ministry of Public Works. Mme Martin's ancestors were Paris merchants as far back as 1815. Here Antoine learned the rudiments of the very exacting and ancient etiquette of the Parisian petty bourgeoisie. Under the strict supervision of Mme Martin and the bantering eyes of her daughter, he made efforts to master good table manners. He had considerable trouble keeping himself from using his knife to cut his bread. The stiff dinners, the endless evenings in the black and red parlor, with all its snares, compelled him to acquire some of the conventions and finesse of the bourgeoisie. In the light of large standing lamps and parchment shades, Valentine Martin played girlish ballads and waltzes on the piano. Mme Martin told in even tone of evening parties at the Ministry, which she had attended in the days of her husband, who had, she gave you to understand, been an idiot. At ten o'clock, she made Valentine go upstairs.

"Valentine, my child, it's bedtime. Say good night."

Valentine departed. Thereupon, Mme Martin told other stories: the scandals of the Tuileries, the adventures of Morny, the orgies of ladies of quality in the Second Empire, and the balls of the Opéra. There were dozens of names with which Antoine was unfamiliar, names that were part of the bourgeois heritage he had not received. There were thousands of references foreign to him, relating to the theater and concerts which Mme Martin had often attended. They were like passwords he did not understand. He could not enter the world to which they gave access. He pretended to understand; he vaguely sensed that he would always be pretending. Mme Martin undoubtedly derived a sneaking satisfaction from telling young men fairly broad stories. It did her soul good to tell them the scandal of the court, though she censured it with unfeigned indignation. A young woman lived alone in the small private house at Number 7, a young woman who had left her husband. It was known through her housemaid that she received men, perhaps one man; for nights, days, weeks on end the lovers never went out. Such debauchery seemed impermissible to Mme Martin anywhere but in a king's court or in the Faubourg Saint-Germain; she detested it on her street, in the case of a woman of her world.

"That Catherine," she would say, "that dirty woman, it's a disgrace! . . . When I think of Valentine, of this child I am bringing up, shielding her from evil. Men come out of that woman's house as limp as dogs. They say that she gives them opium to smoke. Opium on my street!"

"How complicated these people are," thought Antoine, "so indulgent with the aristocrats, so strict with themselves. It's hard to make head or tail of it. What would happen if I told her that Martin caught the clap from Hefty Marie. She'd probably have a stroke. These evenings are pretty boring."

He was bored, but nevertheless he slowly grew further and further away from the hardship and simplicity of the workers, from his childhood environment. He somehow learned how to behave, as they say. Without realizing it, he cut himself off from his own people in Mme Martin's salon. He thought he was merely bored, but secretly he was flattered at being included. Some forces drew him toward the bourgeoisie; other forces sought to retard his transition. There was the Martin force, but there was also the force of Marcelle.

Marcelle was a stoker's widow who with her mother kept a small café at the end of the Rue du Chevaleret, isolated in the

midst of empty lots. Across from the door the Rue Watt, bur-
rowed under an iron bridge from which water dripped on the
horses' necks. Further off you saw the green embankment of the
railroad, lined by a few scraggy bushes. The café stood on a street
corner like a promontory lapped by the stony waves of the Rue
Jenner, which threaded between factory fences and hills of rubble.

A strange twilight of despair, a despair from which the sun was
shut out, brooded over this crossing. It was like a crossroads at the
end of the earth. Every night on the corner of the Rue Jenner,
along the pointed fence posts, a woman attacked the occasional
passers-by. She did not solicit men, she assaulted them. Without a
word, she rushed at them, her bodice and skirt half open, her
breasts and her loins showing in the feeble luster of a lamp ringed
by the night. She made no sound, she reduced her art to the bar-
est essential, to the most brutal provocation, as though sure of the
irresistible power lent by the shadow, the dampness, the solitude
scarcely peopled by the phantoms conjured up by human sorrow.
She was like the queen of this land, a Hecate of the crossroads.
No one knew whence she came; none of the passers-by who had
followed her ever mentioned her. She had reached the rock bottom of the gulf of misery. Beyond her degradation there was
nothing but death.

Antoine passed on the opposite sidewalk, where she never ven-
tured. But he felt her presence, he hastened toward the café
which twinkled through its red curtains as it had on the first evening, when he had dropped in to escape the horror of the neighborhood, and the temptation of that woman. He had often returned.

Marcelle loved to joke with the men and laugh at them with
her yellow eyes and the full lips of her large mouth. He followed
her with his look. She poised on her haunches between two tables.
He chatted with her; she understood the language of the train
men. Afterward, when the evening's last customers had left, she

came over and sat down beside him on the bench. The gas sput-
tered, flies buzzed. When Marcelle, who was particular about her
person, crossed her legs, he could hear the swish of her fine silk
stockings. He stopped joking the moment he was alone with her;
he kept twirling his spoon in his cup, groping for ways to convey
his desire.

"Drink your coffee," she said, "it will get cold."

She started laughing. He drank and felt himself blush. She
baffled him; she aroused in him strange feelings which other girls
had never aroused, feelings that quickened his pulse. One evening
Marcelle said, "Wait for me, I am going upstairs to change."

And with a light laugh she added, "In fact I am going to take
off my corset, it's so hot."

At the end of the room, behind a red cotton curtain, a winding
stair led to the second floor. Antoine watched her go. He waited.
Marcelle's footfalls made the floor boards squeak above his head.
Something fell with the noise of glass. He heard the patter of the
rain and the damp whistles of the Gare d'Austerlitz. He rose and
climbed the stairs of this wall-less tower. In the light of a kerosene
lamp, beside her red-quilted bed, stood Marcelle, motionless as a
hare. Antoine put his hand on her naked shoulder. She turned and
yielded to his embrace.

"Oh! you," she said between clenched teeth.

The huge shadows of the lamplight scaled the walls, whose
black lines of niello work intertwined like tangled hair.

Antoine gave up the long nocturnal strolls with his companions, he gave up the dinners of the widow Mme Martin. All restraints and shams were abolished. He breathed again. For hours
he sat smoking with his elbows on the table. At the Café d'Orléans, Marcelle acquainted him with movements and sensations
whose power he had never suspected. Her broad breasts, her
ample thighs encased in elaborately embroidered black stockings
exercised an invincible attraction on a man who had first touched
a woman's skin through the stockings of the black woman Zoé at

Pontivy. Her red hair, the splotches of red on her arms, the smell
of her body, her musical laugh, ushered Antoine straightway into
a world that eclipsed all his former acquaintances and first bourgeois temptations. How could the image of the well-brought-up
Mlle Martin compete with a presence so brutal and so warm? His
friends teased him and made fun of his "hearty lass," but he
frankly and unashamedly brushed aside the respectable intrigues
of friendship and ambition and buried himself in Marcelle's
feather bed as if taking refuge in that world of warmth and poverty that suited him best of all. Love for Marcelle struggled with—
the attraction of a solidly planned future. Lying beside the young
woman, he told her of his work in professional words that she understood. With impassioned hatred for the rich, she told him sad
stories of Paris.

Meanwhile, the Seine flowed on, flowed on along the banks of
Bercy and Rapée toward unknown provinces bounded by the sea.
The railroads threaded in between the warehouses and factories
of Bercy and Ivry toward Châteauroux, toward Quimper, toward
still other provinces bordering on other seas.

7

All bridges were not burned. Antoine was a man absorbed in his job. Most of his time he passed in the company of ordinary engineers and firemen; these were his most frequent companions. Men who have been on the footplate for twenty and twenty-five years, men whose habits differed from those of the rest of the world. He met them on the line and in the company depots. He ate with them at the convenience of the timetables, in the small wayside restaurants of Saint-Pierre-des-Corps, of Saint-Sulpice-Laurière, of Aubrais, of Vierzon. He slept near them in roundhouses thick with the smoke of small portable stoves. After his years of apprenticeship, he was assigned to the trunk lines. And so he covered the run from Paris to Bordeaux, from Bordeaux to Limoges, and from Limoges to Paris. He had learned to know freight trains; he had, as the saying goes, made the run from station to station with a long line of cars at his back. The stations expect you in between two passenger trains; the stationmaster and the station employees run the length of the train and turn the switches; the train leaves some of its cars on a siding, and the employees shout to the engineer: "You couldn't come and give us a hand, could you, you loafer?"

And the engineer looks down on them from his perch. You crawl along the track, the expresses, coming toward you from ahead and catching up with you from behind, are far off. When they pass, you pull into a siding to let them through. Your hand on the throttle is lazy. Your eyes take in the countryside. It is peaceful work, speed is slumbering in the limbs of the machine. Along the tracks, especially on Sundays, groups of young girls pass by; you have time to follow them with your eyes and shout pleasantries they do not hear. There are women standing at the crossings. You recognize a gatekeeper. You shout to her: "All aboard! Aren't you getting on?"

And she says no, with a shake of her head. Between shovelfuls, your mate says jokingly: "I'll tell her man you've been making eyes at his wife."

During stops he asks: "How about a swig of red, mate?"

You pull out your lunchbox, you climb out for a drink on the platforms of small stations. Night falls. You steer like a ship toward welcoming lights. But Antoine drove expresses. He scorned the mixed trains that never tear themselves from the attraction of wayside stations in remote countrysides, where the village is miles from the station and there are sunflowers growing in the station-master's garden. On the express engines you burn your life up. Antoine found it rather a good life. In those years, the engineer, the fireman, and the engine were more of a unit than they are today. They remained together for years. The crew and the loco-motive were a little moving world which changed its position in conformity with its own laws, along its own trajectory, with its own customs, language, and virtues. Every engine is like a living being; it has its habits, its faculties, its obstinate streak, and its whims. The chance variations of metal and assembly make up a personality that is hard to get to know. Long acquaintanceship of engine and crew at length produced a sort of loyalty, a wedlock. Patiently you had to fathom this great black and yellow beast, ret-icent as a person. And when Antoine arrived at the depot to get his engine ready, he recognized it from afar, with its copper body, its dome, its whistle, its stack, its wheels that were too high, the general appearance reminiscent of Stephenson's time which the express locomotives of around 1887 still retained. Grand, his

fireman would say, "We must take care of her, it is much pleas-
anter to have a clean engine. She's our house, you might say, we
spend twice as much time on her as we do at home. It's not that
we're afraid of the rules, not at all, but as engine riders we have
our own self-respect."

"That's right, mate," Antoine would answer.

They felt a sort of affection for their engine, like the feeling
sailors have for their ship. They talked about her like a person. As
he fed the fire with the sure motions of a good stoker, with scoops
that lifted plenty of coal, one shovelful to the right, one shovelful
to the left, one scattered all over, Grand would say, "We have to
feed her plenty to make her snort, the hussy!"

On the run to Bordeaux, Antoine and Grand were prouder of
themselves than they would have cared to admit. The indicators
on the pressure gauges danced like compass needles. The engine
gathered speed, rocking and yielding to that corkscrew motion
sailors dread. She would leap upward on the curves, you had to
hang on to the housing to keep from being thrown out. All the
motions that ships undergo in a broad undulating fashion, even in
the teeth of a storm, are compressed, crowded upon one another
when gone through by an engine. The engineer lives in the vor-
tex of tempest. The engine coasts down inclines with the lightness of a runner. She banks on the wide musical curves. From his
stormy perch, Antoine felt the power of the engine throb through
his own limbs, a power that transmitted to his own body the pressure of the steam, the restless racing of the connecting rods. It is
impossible to do much talking in the roar of iron. You must concentrate your thoughts and attention. Your hand moves ceaselessly from the throttle, to the lubricating valves, to the whistle
cord. Your eyes are glued to the track that rushes toward you, the
signals that compose a code of warnings which you must deci-
pher: clear track, go ahead, dead stop, semaphore. Of course,
some signals are not clear. The fireman's motions are forever attuned to those of his mate. The fireman responds to the engi-

neer's least gesture. There is no need for words. The stoker watches the injector, pokes the fire, shovels the tons of coal into the blazing fire box, and each time the fire box door opens, a bath of fire envelops his body. The night lights up the eternal cloud that crowns the funnel.

During stops you can talk. Antoine would say: "Well, Grand, we'll have to warm her up, we lost three minutes at Châtellerault."

Or else: "After Saint-Sulpice, we'll have to speed."

Or else: "They can say they screwed us with lousy coal."

Sometimes, an assistant stationmaster comes alongside and shouts up at them, "You'll find the signal closed at 300 meters, it's out of order, slow down."

Blazing stations fall away in a brief roar and flare. Antoine pulls the whistle cord and the shriek rends the night. He does not see the passing countryside, there is no countryside for the engineer of an express. There are only lines, tautened by speed, to the right and left of the train. The broadest rivers are nothing but a clank of metal. There is only the track, the extreme tension of your eyes, ears, and mind, listening to the deep metallic voice of the machine. Anything can happen—the boiler go dry, a wheel overheat, a connecting rod jump. There are sleeping, reading, talking men and women on the train who do not like arriving late. Their lives are precious. There are the level crossings where people cross as though the expresses had time to let them loiter, and the suicides who loom on the middle of the track when it's too late to jam on the brakes or reverse steam—these tons of metal do not stop as easy as a man walking—and you think you hear the soft crunch of their bodies full of blood and water. Like all the others, Antoine had killed three people.

An engineer cannot resist love of speed or enthusiasm for his trade. Antoine was proud of his difficult profession, and the hours of his run to Bordeaux were the outstanding hours of his life. They were unforgettable. These were hard years, nonetheless.

The company owners paid but little heed to the troubles of their men, and at meals, in the roundhouse dormitory, Antoine took part in more than one outburst of anger. When the engineers and their firemen said, "Up there at the main division," it was as though they were referring to the stronghold of their enemies. Enemies who cared little for their ills. They shunted from one station to another almost without respite. It was like the forced marches of an army. Paris–Tours, 236 kilometers, one hour stop. Tours–Paris, 236 kilometers. At Tours, the fireman barely had time to rebuild the fire. There were days of twelve and fourteen hours on the run. Sometimes, when the crews reached Tours, the depot masters despatched them to Bordeaux. There were days 600 kilometers long. The owners of the line took small note of labor legislation. During holidays, at Easter, at Pentecost, in vacation time, during the Exhibition, the service was doubled. The crews came in and went out. The hours on the road accumulated like sand in a bag and their eyes grew heavy with weariness. Sometimes there were avalanches of pilgrim trains bound for Lourdes, and the engineers angrily watched the priests scurrying the length of the cars like shepherd dogs, showing the pilgrims and nuns the way to the diner or the urinals. They pulled out with their cargo of lupus, Pott's disease, cancer, neurosis, fancied or feigned ailments. The assistant chief dispatchers of the depots were put to running trains. Throughout his life, Antoine told the story of days when he did seventy-two hours duty. The company was experimenting. There were engines which you heated with rubble that burned like paper, and in the watch room the crews computed the shrinkage of their bonuses. There were depot masters who skimped on grease, and during stops the engineers would regard the white connecting rods with a worried air. All along the line the men grumbled.

"This isn't a life," they would say.

They had to answer for everything. Their pride in a profession which they still regarded as the best in the world, this pride, thanks to which their bosses knew how to hoodwink them, ebbed away in their exhaustion, irritation, and anger against traffic managers who were trading on their strength. They thought of their rheumatism, their varicose veins, and their hearts, and they said of the chiefs of the line: "They're afraid to go out when it rains, those fellows. We work our heads off and they walk along calmly with their tails stuck up. But it won't last forever."

But it did last.

Antoine shared this anger. He was one of these men; their experiences were his own. Grand told him of his troubles, of his children's illnesses, his haggard wife. At such times Antoine thought like a worker. Between Marcelle and the train service, he utterly forgot that sometime tomorrow he might be on the bosses' side. He had not enough imagination to picture his future. He lived in the present. He did not think of the morrow. He was an engineer, among all the other engineers. A man subject to every command, lord only of an engine whose habits he knew. He never thought that these years would end—at any rate, not while he was on his engine or in his mistress's room.

8

In the Paris depot was an expanse ridged by hillocks of firebrick and coal, where grass sprouted from seeds deposited by the trains, an area of tracks and turntables, studded with piles of cinders, saturated with oil and coal dust. At one end of this area stood the depot master's house. It was one of those black houses with a slate roof and bands of yellow brick, a long flat building like the houses of every depot—the sort of house that is never forgotten by those who are born in it. It was surrounded by a dingy garden planted with asters, Japanese apple trees, and yuccas, enclosed by a rail fence.

Every day, Antoine passed this house on his way to and from the depot. It reminded him of a big firebrick full of holes.

In this house, which also faced on the Rue du Chevaleret, lived a young girl who pushed back the tufted, green velvet draperies and the tulle window curtains when the engineers passed. She was Anne Guyader, the daughter of M. Guyader, the depot master. Antoine never imagined that a young girl with her hair still down her back, and a figure that had scarcely begun to fill out, spied on his passing and that she asked her father: "What is the name of the big engineer with a reddish mustache, who carries a brown canvas bag and always wears a collar?"

"That must be Bloyé, Antoine Bloyé."

"What a common name," said Anne.

M. Guyader was likewise a graduate of Arts and Trades. From 'sixty-four to 'seventy-one he had been second master mechanic in the Imperial Navy. He had gone through the Mexican campaign. He had had yellow fever and scurvy caused by the rancid bacon the crews ate during the endless crossings of passenger-cargo boats. Stationed off Iceland, he had watched the midnight sun. Gliding through the fogs of the fishing banks his ship had rescued stranded dories. And on shore the sailors had gone to see the geysers and volcanoes. They wandered through the muddy streets of Reykjavik, full of small shaggy horses. He had cruised four years in New Caledonia, going from island to island, from bay to bay, on the gunboat *Caïman*. The Kanakas would bring back escaped convicts slung on poles like dead boars, insects swarming on wounds made by stone weapons. He saw tribal dances round huge fires. He rounded the Horn in the teeth of one of those fancy tempests that embellished the tales of ancient mariners before the building of the Suez and Panama canals. The war of 'seventy had halted his advance. When stationed at Lyon, M. Guyader refused to man the naval guns sent against the Commune insurrectionists. "It's a fight between Frenchmen," he said. He had left a Republican navy that held no future prospects and whose ways seemed strange to men who were fourteen years old at the time of the Crimean War. It was a setback for which M. Guyader did not forgive the Emperor. Amid the depots, stations, and roundhouses, this former wanderer still treasured the magic memories of his campaigns, the long voyages on sailing ships and on the first armored frigates. He looked forward to the years of his retirement when he might embellish the close of a lifetime whose course he had not chosen, with the memories of his youth. At work, in his stuffy office, he was sometimes swept up by the gusts of the tradewinds and again he scudded through a tropical sea or over glassy waters within the Arctic circle. He rigorously performed the duties of a profession he did not relish. This stern silent man brooked no shortcomings. His wife used to say, "He is as hard with others as he is with himself."

He had a large heavy mustache and tufted eyebrows that made his eyes seem piercing. The moment he fell asleep, he began to dream. As soon as he dozed off, whether in bed or on a chair, waves that came from afar coursed through him and his countenance assumed an expression of sorrow. He gave little moans; all his hardness would soften. On waking, he never referred to his dreams, whose substance was seldom derived from the events of his present life.

Mme Guyader talked incessantly. She waddled on her short legs from one end of her house to the other, engrossed in tasks that were not always easy to follow. She carried well to the front her hard distended stomach, swollen from an umbilical hernia. She wore her gray hair twisted into a thin knot on top of her head. Her face was splotchy and yellow like that of a pregnant woman. Mme Guyader had been born in Brest, in a hotel where sea captains and naval officers stayed when on shore. In this fashion she had met the second mate Guyader. Their engagement lasted four years. The letters they received from each other were never less than six months old. In those days the crossing from Brest to Nouméa required one hundred and ten days. The campaigns dragged on forever, and the sailors' wives awaited their husbands for years under the drizzle of slippery streets and the Brittany fog. And so, in the days when life was slow, ties were formed which few people had the courage to sunder and which utterly changed men's destinies. A kind of honorable loyalty had kept M. Guyader from breaking with his fiancée when she ordered him to choose between the adventures of the sea and herself. Though she had grown old, frugal as an ant, irritable, and sententious, she retained the value of a woman to whom you have sacrificed yourself. How many women have only this one asset! You cannot let yourself feel you have sacrificed yourself for nothing. So M. Guyader exalted his wife's domestic virtues. But this man who, like many others, had renounced the only future that might have suited him, was not a happy man.

Antoine was invited to the depot master's house. M. Guyader hoped to marry off his daughter. He considered that his best engineer would necessarily make a good husband. He weighed men only by the weight of their trade. Like Valentine Martin, Anne Guyader played *Estudiantina* and showy, rather stale variations of *Faust* and *Le Désert* on the piano. Her parents said, "A young girl should be versed in one or two of the gentle arts."

All their friends said so too. She was a well-brought-up young girl. These evenings would have been very much like those at Mme Martin's, had not the little parlor been pervaded by the atmosphere of the railway, brought in from outside by M. Guyader and his friends. Furthermore, only a few feet away from the house the express trains thundered by, engines maneuvered and shunted to enter the roundhouse, hissing steam through their cylinder vents. The painted Quimper plates rattled on the walls. Mme Guyader often recalled that the wire of her mother's picture had broken one evening when an express passed. The whole house awoke with a start. It was a very bad omen. Happily, her mother had already been dead many years and the omen was inapplicable.

M. Guyader told Antoine of his experiences on the railway and of the various opinions he had formed.

"The chief trouble," he said, "is lack of education. Sometimes engineers from the ranks are appointed depot masters. It's a job they can't cope with. I know of one engineer who became depot master whose reports were written by his wife. When she died, he asked to be put back on the footplate. Such things should not be allowed to happen. I ask myself how it is that some of them, having got to the footplate, didn't stay put. Our profession becomes more complex every day. All depot masters ought to have been through the big schools. I don't like this leveling that still exists among us. Workers are workers, they should keep in their place. It's enough if their sons get ahead."

M. Guyader hated the workers, whom he described as lazy and greedy. Under Louis-Philippe, his father had been a worker at the Lorient arsenal, in a pitiless time when a daily wage of sixty centimes could not buy bread for seven children. With a feeling of mingled hate and shame, M. Guyader remembered the extreme want of his childhood and the huge plates of rice which served as substitute for bread in the time of the Crimean War. He had pulled himself out of the hard life of a worker, and was proud of the fact. He still said: "You can always get somewhere by working. But it can't be done in a day. It takes one or two generations. It takes patience and saving. Today the condition of workers has improved enormously. Much has been done for them. I can't understand what they are still clamoring for. When I think of how they lived when I was young! And yet, they weren't in the ugly mood they're in now. They were patient. Today they all want to be bosses."

M. Guyader hated priests. A sister of his had been seduced by priests, and having taken the veil, she died at twenty at the mission of Tahiti. He viewed religion as the source of human ills. He admired Voltaire, who fought against "superstition." That was all that was left of the rebel in him.

At the other extremity of the railway pyramid were the Big Engineers. M. Guyader judged them as he had formerly judged the frigate captain in command of the *Danaé*. This "big-shot" officer was ill acquainted with the needs of a boiler and the laws of an eccentric. M. Guyader still made angry references to this "incompetent." The "big bosses" were often quite unfamiliar with the modest details that fill the days of a depot master. From afar, they saw nothing but the general outline. To M. Guyader so much unavoidable negligence seemed the height of stupidity. He gave Antoine to understand that he would never be directed by anyone but idiots. Between the insolent workers (you should be glad that you yourself have escaped from their station; the others had the same chance; they were even encouraged to imitate you) and the bosses, remote and absorbed in their world of dreams and unintelligible plans, the only ones who really counted were the people of the golden mean. They were the ones who made the world go round.

Thus, to those young people for whom he had sufficient regard to transmit his experience, M. Guyader preached the pride of an industrial petty bourgeoisie punctilious in its duties, ill rewarded for its domestic virtues—men on whom their masters bestowed little grace for having left and betrayed the workers.

Mme Guyader did her bit. She liked Antoine's manners: he spoke to her so respectfully and listened to her opinions. His appetite also suited her; a good housewife is very much flattered by guests who take a second helping of every dish. Antoine felt a web of tranquility and future certainty being woven around him. He was mellowed by the warmth, by the drone of voices.

"Who takes care of your linen, my poor boy?" asked Mme Guyader.

"You are not ambitious enough, Bloyé," said M. Guyader. "A boy of your ability should aim rather high."

"Do you like children, Monsieur Bloyé?" asked Anne.

An insidious calm began to creep over him. It was like the rising tide with its gentle lapping seeping over the sand. After dinner he felt slightly drowsy. This drowsiness was not without its charms. Anne would eye him furtively; she would blush when he spoke to her. She would tell him of her experiences; there wasn't much to tell. This young girl with her long braids and narrow waist had danced with her schoolmates on the well-waxed parquet of the Ursuline convent at Quimperlé. The convent had a lovely garden that ended on the terraces. Under the beeches over the river, you saw the sloping gray roofs, the trails of smoke from the Brittany trains. Some young girls had considerable authority; they were the "little mothers" of the younger ones. There was a nun with a hearty laugh, who blushed after laughing. The chaplain would tap the little girls lightly on the cheek. They were shown the box studded with huge nails where they put those nuns who needed to do penance. Several girls in the dormitory were coughing, but the doctor, being a man, was not allowed within the cloister. There was the ghost of a nun that wandered through the corridors at night. There were the mulberry trees in the park, the blue ribbons and clusters of flowers in the chapel. Antoine listened. Over his head, where the assistant manager lived, people were walking about with a ratlike patter, the noise of a conversation could be heard, the fire crackled. The world was shut out by the walls, the tales, this warmth and corroding security.

Anne belonged to an entirely different world of feeling from Marcelle. Antoine asked himself, without much clarity as to the issues, if the ardent kingdom of women without a future and without reservations was not a greater prize for a man than the virginal sweetness, the chaste artifices of bourgeois virtues. To answer this required a wisdom which Antoine Bloyé had not yet had the time to acquire, which he would acquire too late, which he would perhaps never acquire.

M. Guyader would tell him: "Bloyé, you are no longer a boy, you are twenty-seven years old. Don't you think it's time for you to make a place for yourself? Why don't you get married? One of these days, you'll be appointed supervisor. It's a post well suited to a married man."

His father wrote him: "You must get married. It seems to me high time you settled down."

All the "duties" that people throw up to him and the wiles they use! He must either give in to these inducements or resist and take his stand decisively on the side of Marcelle's life. Antoine has the external attributes of strength, but for all that he is hesitant and weak. The smallest struggles leave him disarmed. He tells himself that he is made for big struggles. This is how men console themselves for their weaknesses. To go with Marcelle, to throw over his career, is to take the windward side, a difficult path. To go with Anne is to choose the sheltered side of the world, the cottonwool of peace and calm, to earn the good wishes and approval of his father, his employers—to take the side of order. Anne possesses the attractions of all young girls, he can take to her, after all the women he has known. He dwarfs her with his stature. She comes to him with an air of seeking protection. Mme Guyader says, "A wife must look to her husband for strength."

He also feels that by marrying Anne he will "rise" in the world. He persuades himself that he loves her, it's just as though he loved her. One can love almost any young girl. All would be well if he did not have a certain feeling of remorse when he thinks of Marcelle, whom he is neglecting. His conscience is not quite at ease.

In the course of dinners, anecdotes, conversations, hesitations, Antoine became engaged to Anne Guyader. Their engagement was fairly long, as is the habit of prudent families who know the ways of the world and do not lightly commit their children's future. They were waiting until Antoine was off the engines, until Anne had attained her growth. On Sundays they went to the Exhibition, where the meringue buildings, the fine metal trellises, and exotic pavilions had won the hearts of Paris. Eighty-nine was a good year, full of social fetes and civic orations. It was like one long Fourteenth of July. The Parisians ate beneath the overhanging trees at Robinson, and President Carnot commemorated the centenary of the revolution at Versailles. There were balls, the phonograph began to prevail, the mayors of France held huge democratic banquets. Lighted fountains played. Women shrieked when jostled in a crowd. It was hot. An atmosphere of a bourgeois wedding prevailed. The cabs were weighed down by bridal trains. In the town halls, civil marriages were performed to music. The Republic had bigger breasts than ever before, the mayors bigger beards. Caryatids groaned beneath the weight of bronzes and balustrades.

Antoine was introduced to the cousins. He held strange children on his knees and Anne would say with a sigh, "How well that suits you!"

He thought of Marcelle, he felt guilty and undoubtedly he was guilty. He felt that his marriage would cut him off completely from people of his own kind. It would be his first social rise, his first mutilation. His declassing. . . . Not all declassings are downward.

In June 1890, Antoine married Anne at the town hall of the XIIIth arrondissement; then they went to Notre-Dame de la Gare for the church ceremony. This virgin presided over the birth, life, and death of many a railway employee. A cousin of the Guyaders, who was a parish priest in Brittany, made a speech which Mme Bloyé kept all her life, which she reread from time to time as its paper yellowed, as its creases fell apart.

"Monsieur, my dear child.

"A priest is for everyone the dispenser of divine grace, and never does he perform his office without feeling. But there are circumstances under which this feeling becomes keener and his prayer more earnest. Thus it happens when he becomes the channel of divine beneficence to members of his family.

"I left my humble village to convey to you on this solemn occasion the blessings of both priest and relative.

"There is no need, monsieur, for me to dwell on the virtues of your fiancée. Allow me to tell you that Providence has directed well your choice in placing your hand in that of a young girl with a Christian upbringing under a good mother's guidance. Her worthy father, thanks to an industry whose first beginnings I saw, has won for himself an honorable and elevated rank in the hierarchy of work. You too, monsieur, likewise working on the railway and guided on this path by an excellent father, are called to the same success. Religion, despite all rumors to the contrary, approves all the progress of the sciences and arts and blesses them.

"And you likewise, my dear child, give thanks to Providence which has given your hand to a spouse whose intelligence, courage, and Christian sentiments are on a level with your own. The union you are to contract is a covenant holy as the altar which is its repository. Having both been raised in the school of faith, convinced that religion must preside over all great acts of life, you have come here to the foot of the altar to vow the love, the inviolable fidelity your hearts have already promised each other. From this holy vow flows the constant, faithful, and Christian love you shall bring to each other.

"You, monsieur, shall love your bride who shall become your choicest earthly possession. You shall act as her guide and counselor, you shall be her strength and staff alike, in days of joy or adversity of your earthly pilgrimage.

"You, my child, shall love your husband as your master and your support. You shall reward his care with your devotion, your wish to please him, you shall share his sorrows as he shall share yours.

"And now, let us pray to the God of Isaac and Rebecca, of Jacob and Rachel, of Tobias and Sarah to bestow on you his most bounteous blessings. Your families and friends are gathered here around you. All together we shall ask the good and merciful God, through the mediation of the sacred Virgin, patron of this church, to accord you the prosperity that makes for happiness and the grace that makes for saintliness. With even step you both shall tread the path of honor and virtue. In the future, as in the past, you shall continue to be the hope and joy of your worthy parents, so that, if it pleases divine Providence, you may later receive the same reward from your own children, measure and prelude of that reward which God holds in store for you in heaven."

One felt all the guests restraining their desire to applaud. Anne was sobbing under her white veil. M. Guyader seemed transfixed. Anne was very touching, and Antoine watched her out of the corner of his eye. He knew that he himself was not so very Christian, not so very taken up with heavenly thoughts; it had been ten years since he had last set foot in a church.

Thus, everything was arranged and established; there was no appeal. There was only the pang people feel when they set forth on long journeys. Marcelle receded softly to that shadowland of interdicted thoughts where human strength founders. She was not dead, she would rise to the surface in time along with many other dormant germs, many other idle forces. It was over. He had told her that he was getting married. She had laughed. She had not been angry; she had said, "All right, go ahead and marry. It was bound to end that way."

Antoine had asked, "Are you sore at me?"

She had answered, "Not at all, don't dream of it. I don't hold it against you. You will hold it against yourself. You are leaving the world where we were together, you will become a gentleman, a bourgeois. You will be bored, Antoine, you will have a household, you will have children."

"Well?"

"Well, good-bye."

So it was bound to be. Marcelle had watched him go. She had stood on the threshold of the Café d'Orléans like Ariadne under the sun of Naxos watching Theseus vanish over the sea.

After mass there were congratulations in the vestry. The wedding party took a landau to Robinson for lunch under the June trees in that lovely year 1890. That evening, the newlyweds left on their honeymoon. They went to Sète, Montpellier, Marseille. The bright sunlight frightened Anne. Everything frightened her. The oil, the olives, the women, the men from the Orient who strolled along the Old Port, the dust. She thought of her mother. The waterfront smelled bad, people talked too loud. She was still somewhat frightened when she was alone in a room with her husband. The honeymoon lasted fifteen days, then they returned to Paris. And amid the stifling summer of the tracks and stations, Antoine Bloyé and his wife started their new life.

Part II

9

The years went by like unmoored boats borne on a river current. Antoine and his wife passed through different towns, each with its characters and customs. But they made only a cursory acquaintance with each, and no town ever succeeded in claiming their affections for good. They always lived provisionally, they did not settle down. They squandered the days of their youth without even realizing it. They moved in, learned to know the ins and outs of each new house.

"There aren't any street signs," Anne would say.

And they would get used to the proper names, accents, climates of new provinces, and then leave. Anne always would have liked to take root, settle down for the rest of her life. She was a woman of settled habits who disliked a nomadic existence. In each new place she would tearfully say, "Don't try to persuade me, I know I shall never get used to it."

But she adapted herself to the new life; with the sureness of an insect she restored her shattered cocoon.

Antoine Bloyé was following the trails blazed through western France by his company's lines. At each move he went up one step in the hierarchy the Breton priest had pictured to him on his wedding day. He was, as they say, getting ahead. Supervisor of traction in Paris, assistant depot master in Brives, in Aurillac, in Montluçon, in Limoges, supervisor of equipment and traction in Angers, depot master in Tours. He followed the long inflexible path of the traction division. At each post, to the former activities, to the former decisions were added new activities, new decisions which he had to master promptly. At each post he felt the growing weight of responsibility placed upon him by his bosses, hidden away in their offices at the main division, the engineers of the "Forty-One." This burden drew him toward them. It signified that he had made his entry into that once mysterious society of which he had often dreamed before, when strolling on the waterfront of Saint-Nazaire, the society of men who command. Each year, more and more engines and workers were subordinated to his will, and he was not held accountable to those beneath him.

As the years fell away into the past, consigned to oblivion— and he did not notice their fall, it takes plenty of leisure to notice the passing of time—his arms, his hands, and body knew idleness but he used his brains more and more. The timetables, the calculations, the graphs, the route charts, the tryout reports multiplied in his head. Every year the service extended, the locomotives grew more complex, the depots included more engines, more running and repair crews.

Over the railway network of the world, the traffic rose like a temperature curve. The momentum of capitalism drew along willy-nilly the men and machines that worked for it.

Unawares, the men of Antoine's generation had crossed the dividing line between two eras. From the year 1900 on, the railways entered a new age, coinciding with the spectacular arrival of the turbulence of the twentieth century. An age which began with the first run of Stephenson's Rocket from Stockton to Darlington gave way to the age of bogies, compoundings, and high pressures. The speed and the load of trains had grown to keep pace with the traffic's requirements. The power of the locomotives had grown to meet the requirements of speed and weight. Between 1890 and 1910, the average speed of passenger trains increased 25 percent; the dead weight per passenger between 1898 and 1908 rose from 350 kilos to 916 kilos. For the "AT 5" cars on the Paris–Bordeaux line, it was increased up to 1,120 kilos. In 1909 the giant express engines weighed two hundred tons. A year later four hundred. In 1900 the Orléans company possessed 1,430 locomotives with a total of 692,000 horsepower; in 1910, 1,826 engines had a total of 1,381,079 horsepower. In the course of eleven years the power of the big locomotives rose from 1,000 to 1,600 horsepower.

The steam pressure in the new types of engines was a source of consternation to old engineers and to depot masters on the verge of retirement. When Antoine saw his father-in-law, M. Guyader would be skeptical of the figures his son-in-law quoted; he resented these increases like so many insults addressed to him, for they told him that the time had come when he would be deposed and set aside as too slow for the force of these new momentums. This man who had seen the stage-coach lines in Brittany give way before the onslaught of the railway would say with a kind of anger, "But those boilers of yours will blow up under such pressure!"

"Oh, no, they won't," Antoine would answer, laughing, "they won't blow up."

Antoine followed the trail because he was one of those men who lived through this crisis of growth without leaving the sooty world of the stations and depots, just as self-contained, as unique among all the other different worlds composed of fragments as the world of ports, harbors, and docks that the sailors never leave. He was one of the active participants in this industrial metamorphosis, one of the men whose heads were ceaselessly filled with worries about the engines and their drivers. In keeping step with the rapid time of this dance, such people never thought of allowing themselves the leisure to ask what they were doing on the earth, what they were good for, which way they were heading—what the whole business of life meant. They amused themselves little, badly, and seldom. They never cast the log in the all too foamy wake they left behind them. Antoine did not turn round, did not

stop to ask himself questions, he did not relax. He simply did his
"job." There are thousands of ravenous machines that thus involve men in their rotation: the banks, the mines, the big stores,
the ships, the railways. Scarcely anyone has time to catch his
breath. It requires too much attention to work as swiftly as their
cogs work, to avoid their driving belts, their motors.

Antoine was caught like an insect in this quivering web of railway lines, surveyed from a distance by calculating, abstract spiders. He was tied to these thousands of kilometers of rails, which
pierced the heart of Europe through the loopholes of frontier stations. Everywhere was this maze of single, double, and quadruple
tracks. Everywhere the trains moving day and night, magnetized
by the figures of the timetables, with their engineers straining for
the glimpse of signals, their grimy stokers lighted by the fiery
mouth of the firebox and their conductors taking their turn at the
icy vigil in the brakeman's cabin. Everywhere those glittering
points of communication, the stations lighted by their constellations of arc lamps, the turntables, the luggage carts, the switch
capstans armor-bright from the friction of steel cables, the double
inclines whence the cars coasted smoothly down toward the radi-
ating tracks, the switch points more alert than the captain's bridge
on a ship, the smoky roundhouses. Everywhere men sat engrossed
in gloomy offices that shook when the express trains went by,
their walls adorned by red, green, and blue designs of air brakes
and cylinders—thousands of men living, toiling, dying for the
service of the lines, nameless men.

Antoine was one of them. He loved the concatenation of their
jobs. He understood them. He was at the center of it all, a pris-
oner of the ramifications. Like many railway officials, he had his
professional pride. A man must have his self-respect. He lived
surrounded by the symbols of his calling. On his desk stood shiny
photographs of Consolidations and Pacifics; for paper weights he
used broken fragments with their flaws still showing, slivers blue
from the strain where the lathe had cut them. For years he kept a

reddened fragment of tubing on his night stand lying on his copy of *The Life of George Stephenson*. He thought almost incessantly of his engines, racing like black steeds day and night over the main lines, those huge fiery beasts which had taken on new shapes. And he dreamt of his early days, of his years as engineer, when they had not yet acquired the somber supercilious bearing of the compounds and of superheated engines. As the "300" engines that had hauled the expresses from Paris to Bordeaux in ten hours and two minutes were successively relegated to the locals, the freights, the shuntings, he felt his youth ebbing with them, away from the main lines, and he would say, as though to justify his youth, "All the same, it was those engines that made the most money for the company."

The maps of the lines, the charts of the service, the reports on the routing of his engineers, the game of substitution and reserve turned in his head like carefully calibrated wheels. Even at home, he lived haunted by time, always in a hurry, racing with the clock. At night, his wife would wake up sometimes and listen to the words that escaped him from the depths of a dream: engine and train numbers. In this period of all too rapid changes the depots were short of supplies. The station would ask the depot for engines when not one of them was in condition. But the trains left just the same and they were not 500 meters from the platform when Antoine started to worry, always uncertain whether they would reach the end of their runs in safety. He was afraid an engine would collapse, overcome at last by weakness, by age, by the wearing out of some organ, like an old man who falls at a single stroke. He felt the uneasiness of people responsible for human lives and for equipment. What distresses them more, the loss of equipment or the death of a human being? They end by loving metal as much as man. At lunch time, Antoine would go to the kitchen and impatiently pull back the curtains. He would ask the servant, "Have you seen my Bordeaux express pull in?"

At length the express would appear. He would see it race along the wide curve of the track, banking like a cyclist, with its smoke scattered over the rooftops, and he would hear its whistle blast, long and drawn out like the train itself. He breathed then. He would say, "You may serve the food now."

He harried the men who were under him by his worry over work. The subofficials on night duty would see him suddenly push back the doors of their office at midnight or two in the morning.

"I have come to see if everything is going all right," he would say.

He did not forgive weakness or shortcomings in the work. There was one temporary assistant master, a small dark Gascon, who would climb down in the pits to inspect the engines without dirtying himself, because of his small stature, and Antoine would shout at him: "You've inspected the new compounds? Yes? Really! You walk along hunched over, you're afraid to get yourself dirty. Not a drop of oil on your back. You call that work!"

There were days when there were not enough engineers. Antoine would take the place of the assistant masters; the assistant masters would work as engineers on the line. Antoine would be left alone with the care of his hundred and fifty engines. The trips were speeded up. Connecting rods and wheels overheated, and the engineers at the other end of the line asked for replacement parts, waiting with their engines in strange depots. The wives came to the depot to inquire after their husbands. The joints of connecting rods would break loose at full speed. Antoine awaited the return of his engineers, their reports, their explanations. He thought of the questions which would come down from "up there," from the main division.

In the evening, after sixteen or seventeen hours work at the depot, Antoine would suddenly fall asleep on the dining room table, his head on his arms, exhausted like a child who has overplayed. The traction division men played a man's game that did not allow for distraction or neglect on the part of the players.

Thus did old age accumulate in all the recesses of their bodies.

M. Guyader said to his son-in-law, "You are killing yourself, my poor friend. I cannot understand why you take such pains for the Company's sake. You know you won't get the least thanks for it."

"And what of it?" answered Antoine. "There's never any harm in doing your job well."

In those years, Antoine stuck to his profession. He was in the prime of his life, doing what had to be done without gaps or letup, capable of holding in his head all the branches of his activities, without lapses or omissions, finding, without hesitation and without dreaming, solutions that met the problems of every hour—repairing a water tank, a connecting rod, raising derailed wagons, a report, replacing a crew, dividing a train, dispatching reserve engines. Derailments occurred and the tracks had to be cleared; crew members, cleaners died, their chests crushed between two buffers; there were calls for help from firemen, repair workers, and assemblers; there was the arbitration of quarrels—a man's problems. At Aurillac the snow had to be cleared from the track. He drove the emergency engine toward Vic-sur-Cère, toward Murat, and a kind of exhilaration filled his lungs because of the snow and the wind that lashed his face, leaning out as of old over the flight of the tracks. At all hours, he had to score small victories—against time, against fatigue, machinery, absences, and the men. The great machine of the railway system was less well oiled, less inflexible than today. It sometimes allowed the initiative of its men to enter into play. When Antoine explained the difficulties of his job to the inspectors, the engineers of the traction division, they would answer with a wink: "The company lacks people and supplies. We know it as well as you do, Monsieur Bloyé, it's a hard time to weather. What do you expect? We muddle through. You will manage all right."

The precision and knowledge his decisions and activities required completely absorbed Antoine's life and prolonged the intense period when he himself had been an engineer. His language was still full of an engineer's turns of speech. He said of a man who drank, "His injector works well."

Of a pregnant woman, "She has bulged her boiler plate."

These souvenirs of the lingo of the machines were his ties with his youth. They also showed the engineers under him he was a man of the profession who knew the ropes and who could not be fooled. Thus the survivals of his youth served to strengthen his authority. Everything conspired to make him successful. His long practice with engines, and his knowledge of the workers who ran them, gave Antoine an effective grip on the men. He made them give the best that was in them, he carried them along with his own activity.

His wife, who did not in the least like these memories of an era where she played no part, said, "Good heavens, Antoine, can't you talk the way everyone else does?"

But he would only laugh. He laughed willingly in those times, for he was active, he felt strong despite the hours of weariness. He had no qualms about his language or his life. At least he thought he had none. Everything seemed clear enough. His trains had to run, just as ships must reach port. A man like Antoine was too simple to ask himself the why of this necessity. It seemed to him as natural, as matter of fact as the necessity that water flows and night follows day. The trains leave, the men must work. That is how it is. It is part of the scheme of the world. The trains must run on time and the men must do their job.

Antoine sought no further. He was content with this certainty. For the time it sufficed to keep him from feeling like a stranger on earth. He scarcely doubted the justice of his world even in the hours of overweariness when he longed for the warmth of his bed with the yearning of a wounded man, in the hours when accidents on the job, despair among people he loved, warned him that all was not running as smoothly as a piston rod. But these doubts vanished in the too-smooth swiftness and eagerness of his life. He forgot them and allowed them to sink into the background of reserve thoughts that can wait a long time for the day of their victory.

One night, while he was assistant master at Aurillac, he was awakened. A derailment had occurred. He dressed in the cold of the unheated room and crossed the little town. The torrents from the round snow-covered hills flowed with the ceaseless sound of fountains toward the waters of the Jordane, murmuring over the pebbles.

The station hummed faintly in the night like an animal dreaming of its daytime activity. It was in the empty hours after midnight when an occasional express rushes through making the station roof tremble. Bells ring forlornly in the stationmaster's office. The men on duty wait for dawn and have a hard time fighting off sleep at two in the morning. Alongside the first platform an engine emitted puffs of steam. Two employees were running the length of a string of freight cars, swinging lanterns. The stationmaster, half awake, rubbed his hand across the night's growth of stubble on his cheeks and told Antoine how it had happened. It was one of those accidents of everyday occurrence. One of those minor derailments that do not attract the newspapermen from Paris, or special inspectors from the traffic division. The derailment of freight trains, of engines concerns only the railway men.

The engine and the emergency car left the depot. Antoine was driving; he never drove now except on days when derailments occurred or if a snow plough was needed, but he felt that the engines still obeyed him, that he had not forgotten their ways. The accident had occurred not far from the depot. There were four cars off the rails, as well as the locomotive and the tender, their wheels in the air. The brakemen shouted and ran about. On the network of tracks covered with thin snow, frozen by the night, the engine lay upside down. You could see its black belly, its crushed pan whence glowing cinders issued like fiery blood.

Steam escaped from the twisted tubing with a whistling sound.
The plates were staved in. In the chaos of metal the steel pieces of
the connecting rods stood straight and shiny. It was like a shapeless corpse whose human form is torn to pieces, but where one
naked leg, whole and white, still stands out like a piece of marble
in the welter of torn flesh. The coal of the tender had caught fire,
blue flames flickered, melting the snow and laying bare the black
coal-saturated earth, the cinders and ties.

The gatekeeper gazed at his small triangular garden devastated
by the last car, which had landed in the cabbages and strawberries. This huge wooden creature was utterly alien to these
plants; it was incongruous, fallen from another world, like a mete-
orite that falls in a wheat field.

The section chief swore between his teeth; apparently the accident was due to the bad condition of the tracks. But the depot
master felt no qualms. He was thinking: "I shan't always be the
one to get hell. It is high time maintenance got what was coming
to them."

And he jotted down some notes in a square ruled-paper notebook bound in black canvas with an elastic band around it. Each
page bore the imprint of an oily finger. Antoine distributed the
contents of the emergency car. There was no time to lose. The
trains must pass. On the line, the passengers put their noses to the
window and protested against the delay. They went to the front
of the train to pester the engineer and the head conductor. The
jackscrews, the Stroudlay engines worked in the light of flares.
One by one the cars were righted. Soon a crane arrived, blindly
swinging its great arm above the debris, like the tentacle of some
deep sea monster.

The bodies of the engineer and the fireman were laid out on
the ballast. Sheets borrowed from the gatekeeper covered their
mangled faces. The depot master said, "Bloyé, go and break the
news to the wives on my behalf. I don't enjoy doing it. Excuse

me for leaving you the dirty job. No, no, there's no need to come back, you can then go back to bed."

Antoine left with two stretchers, their bearers silent. They went on foot. In the depot at night you have to watch where you put your feet. The ground is full of traps and pitfalls, switch heads, ditches, and engines under steam, a tiny wisp of smoke coming from their stacks. Antoine was thinking. He did not take to such deaths very easily. People said, "Accident at work." And they tried to make you believe that work is a field of honor, while the company provides the widow with a pension, a niggardly pension, it parts with its pennies like a miser, it thinks that death is always overpaid; later it hires the sons of the dead and all is said. . . .

Nothing is said. Every morning Antoine still saw on his arm the scar made by the explosion of a water gauge when he was an engineer. It dated from yesterday, this severing of a radial artery. He was "off the foot plate" too short a time not to feel close to men who die on their job from the blows of their profession. Engineers, people who give orders from afar, administrators, die in their beds more frequently than do the men of the train crews, firemen, conductors. General staffs rarely fall on the fighting line. How does one get reconciled to these things? Already there were so many stretchers in his memory, smashed chests, figures mangled like charred wool. He knew the life of the men who run the trains, their joys, their work, their code of honor, and their death, and now he was going to announce the final episode. It was a boss's mission, the bosses announce the deaths and injuries. The bosses send messages of condolence. The bosses sometimes experience the uncomfortable feeling of guilt.

The stretcher bearers and Antoine arrived before the engineer's house and then before that of the fireman. Antoine climbed their dark stairs, stifling his breath and muffling his tread as though to wake each new-made widow as late as possible, to delay the moment when he had at last to face the cries, the stammering of a woman blinded by the pepper of pain, befuddled by the coils of sleep. It was nevertheless necessary to knock and await the woman's cough, the shuffling of her slippers, her fumbling with the latch. The door opened and all the warmth and security of the rooms evaporated. He entered the quiet semi-darkness as a thief, as a demon. And he spoke at first of wounds; he said, "We have brought him home."

Then of severe wounds, then at last—and the wife had understood from the beginning—of death.

"Be brave, madame. It is a fatal accident."

It left an unforgettable impression on his memory—the hastily lighted lamps, the plates on the oilcloth beside the wine bottle, the rigid bodies heavily borne to beds still warm from the women's bodies, a dazed child standing in a corner, the widow's wrath.

"You take away our men from us, you bring them back in pulp. Company of murderers!"

That night, Antoine discovered death. A certain death that he could not forgive himself.

To lay out the driver's body on the bed, he had taken it in his arms. What terrible weight a dead man is. Besides the seventy-five or eighty kilos of his flesh, bones, and blood and all his fluids there is the weight of death itself, as though all the years the man had lived had suddenly accumulated in his body, weighing it down, coagulating like lead grown cold. A wounded man still knows how to make himself light; he has the magic warmth of his breathing, of his blood circulation, but this dead man was as rigid and motionless as marble. This dead man no longer looked like a man. Only his clothes were like all other clothes. Antoine held him tight, he embraced this body fraternally. Living men do not clasp each other thus, their bodies do not come into contact save through their hands. Embraces are decently reserved to love; men scarcely venture to touch each other. So it needed death for him to embrace this man.

Antoine could do nothing for him save stretch him out, and the weight of the dead man drew him toward the bed. He felt like saying to him, "Come on, old boy, help yourself a bit."

He wanted to ask for forgiveness as though he had killed him with his own hands.

How much harder this job was than the job of merchant or bureaucrat. Its stakes were life and death. Why then do men die? Antoine was rather proud of his profession, of his ability, of his professional integrity. But how about these workers who died? One should at least die for aims that are worthwhile. But to die because the track was not in good condition, because there was a rotten tie, because a joint had sprung; to die for the shareholders, for men who know nothing of the railways save the stations, the tickets, the first-class carriages, the de luxe trains, for the Baron Rothschilds, for small investors and bondholders, for the pools of buyers and financiers? There was a machine that quoted a certain price on life. And the shareholders thought that all was well and the bondholders undoubtedly thought that it was expensive. When you did not die before retiring, you received a bronze or silver medal, a medal stamped with a locomotive, hung on a tricolor ribbon, like a life-saving medal. You received a letter: "In return for your good and faithful services."

Live and die for a medal, for nothing.

But he, Antoine Bloyé, who commanded others, who transmitted orders from above like an adjutant—and soldiers can also be killed in peacetime, in target practice or on the march, by a stray bullet, or by sunstroke—but he, who was not the enemy of these men, was he then their enemies' accomplice? In vain did he try to defend himself, telling himself that it was the fault of the track maintenance division, summoning to his aid the thoughts of the functionary. He knew full well that he had passed to the side of the bosses, that he was their accomplice. All his efforts, all his memories, altered not one jot of his complicity. He thought of his father, who was one of those who took orders, of his comrades in the shipyards of the Loire and in the railway depots who were also on the side of those who serve, on the side of life without hope. And returning home in the icy Auvergne dawn, he repeated to himself a phrase that held good for the whole of his life, a phrase that he forced himself to forget, that only disappeared in order to reappear in the time of his adversity, on the eve of his own death: "So, I am a traitor."

And he was.

10

Amid the hubbub of the engines, in his narrow sphere of action, Antoine had no time to go through human motions other than the motions of his work. Like many men, he was impelled by demands, ideas, and decisions connected with his job; he was absorbed by his profession. There was no opportunity to think about himself, to meditate, to know himself and know the world. He did no reading, he did not keep himself *au courant*. Every evening, before going to sleep, he opened his *Life of George Stephenson* and, having read through two pages which he had got to know by heart, he fell asleep. He glanced at newspapers casually. The events they told of belonged to another planet and did not concern him. The only publications he took a vital interest in were the technical magazines with their descriptions of engines. For a space of fourteen or fifteen years, there was no man less conscious of himself and of his own life, less informed on the world than Antoine Bloyé. He was alive, no doubt; who is not alive? To go through the motions of life all you need is a well-fed body. He, Antoine, moved and acted, but the springs of his life, and the drive of his actions were not within himself.

Will man never be more than a fragment of a man, alienated, mutilated, a stranger to himself? There were so many elements lying fallow in Antoine's personality, so many things aborted and thwarted by his marriage, by the Company that devoured its "agents" with such a ravenous and impersonal appetite! Nor was

113

Antoine totally unaware of these gaps. He suspected that he might have been what he was, and done what he did, and something more besides, something that was lacking. He allowed to go to waste an internal strength that was greater than he imagined, a strength that came from his own body, like all real strength and real power. At thirty-five, Antoine Bloyé had muscular limbs covered with a ruddy skin that faded to white on his chest and on his back. He carried sacks and heavy weights easily. He could hold out for a long time against exhaustion and lack of sleep. He had a well-ordered head. He did a tremendous amount of work, he moved with the suppleness and ease, the naturalness of an animal. His workers said, "In fairness you must admit that he is not afraid of work."

And they nicknamed him the Thoroughbred. But his strength was being spent on the grindstone of alien work, he was not putting it to his own account. He was not using it to further his own human development, he used it up for the profit of the people who paid him, the anonymous shareholders and their abstract interests. Such is the ill-fortune of many men.

One has to earn one's living, one has to do one's job, he thought. He had always been taught these things as truths that no one under the sun had ever thought of questioning. But everything he might have been slipped through his fingers like the sand one sifts in holiday idleness: all his work only served to hide his essential unemployment. Thus he sometimes felt a slight dizziness, as when in a dream you climb an endless winding stair. He felt that complex forces conspired to prevent him from standing firmly on the ground, as a man should by rights. He was troubled by such doubts on short Sunday walks, or during his brief relaxation at home. These forces existed. They were doubtless fully as real as objects with weight, shape, and tangible dimensions. Perhaps they even had names and human faces. But he did not distinguish them. He could not, he dared not lift his hand against them. There were times when he would have liked to quit the life he was leading and become someone new, a foreign someone who would be more like his real self. He liked to picture himself utterly alone, lost, like a man who has left no address and who does what he wants, who breathes freely. One day he was offered a position in China, as he previously had had an opportunity to go to England.

"You'll go alone if you insist on going," said Anne. "As for me, I shall not leave my country and my parents to go and live among savages in a country where we don't know anyone, for a position which provides no retirement pension, for an adventure!"

So many ties would have to be severed, so many little battles would have to be fought, his own secret timidity would have to be mastered if he were to make a decision that would turn the future on a new course! He would have to revolt against the shell of his present life in order to set free the other self imprisoned there. He feared a woman's tears, and the breaking of habits; he cringed at the thought of being called a "monster," or impossibly odd, no longer like the run of men. He lacked self-assurance. False is the courage that waits for big occasions, extraordinary dangers that never materialize. Real courage consists in daily overcoming little enemies. Like many men, Antoine lacked this real courage. For a time he thought over this opportunity he had been offered to transform himself, then he pretended to have forgotten it.

"How wise you were to listen to my advice," said Anne.

"Yes . . . I dare say. . . . Anyway, don't let's discuss it, it's a closed incident," he answered.

One more defeat, like England, like Marcelle. It does not take many defeats to down a man.

These moments of uneasiness, these impulses of restlessness, were only flashes. They were doused by the waters of common sense. Whenever his father-in-law saw Antoine preoccupied and uneasy, he would say, "Don't let things rankle, you take things too much to heart. You must be more philosophical in life."

To be philosophical meant to accept anything, to take life as it came. It meant falling into the deepest rut. Antoine lived in a world where the word philosophy meant laziness and cowardice. And thus the rest of Antoine's personality failed to find an outlet. Many elements unknown to him lurked in the background of the picture. Antoine was a man with a trade and a certain physical makeup, and that was all. That was all a man amounted to in the world where Antoine Bloyé lived. People speak of a nervous merchant, a full-blooded engineer, an irritable worker, an ill-tempered notary; they say these things and think that they have characterized a man, just as they say a black dog, a tiger cat. A doctor had once said, regarding Antoine with the air of arrogant assurance of his professional vanity, "You are nervous and full-blooded."

When Antoine was downcast and wore a troubled look, his wife would say, "The doctor said so, you are nervous and full-blooded; easily discouraged, easily restored."

So there you were, the last word had been said. Anyone could manipulate him like a classified article. He moved among other articles. What a life! In the foreground were the engines, the routine of instructions and actions suited to the work: the engineer's plane. In the background were grouped the hazy outlines of characters dwarfed by perspective, in the hazy landscapes of family and free time: the plane of nervous full-blooded men.

The chief engineer of traction and equipment would say, "I know men, gentlemen, Bloyé at Tours is one of our best depot masters."

Anne said, "Antoine is extremely conscientious. Overconscientious. One shouldn't do so much!"

The engineers of the depot, the cleaners, said, "The boss is pretty shitty sometimes but he's a cart horse when it comes to work."

Antoine would say to himself, to give himself confidence and courage, "What am I? I'm a man who knows his job."

But later, when he was old, Antoine one day whispered to his son, who turned out to have the same physique as he, "You know, I don't think I've given my full measure."

Is man no more than a driver of machines?

What is a wife, what is love, for a man utterly taken up with a man's work? Women and love—the false duties of blind work eclipse them, together with all good things in life. Old couples tell their children with pride: "We lived for thirty-five years together. We had our bad moments, or quarrels, like everyone. No one is perfect in this world. But we had a pleasant life of it all the same."

What fidelity! How many Philemons and Baucis's there are among the functionaries and tradesmen! They die within five minutes of each other like two clocks that were set going at almost the same time. But they have not been with each other even a quarter of the faithful time on which they pride themselves. Once the hours of work, of sleep, of appointments, of silence, of trips, have been subtracted from the twenty-four hours of day and night, there remain very few hours consecrated to a woman and love. These hours are themselves eked out. Neither the men nor the women love. Love is a task that requires too much patience, too much companionship, too many common goals, too much friendship. They invent sorrows and sudden tragedies for the sake of their cowardly illusions, in order to excuse their indifference through ill luck. They are fond of saying, "Paris was not built in a day . . ." but they apply this proverb only to careers, to fortunes, to houses, to progress.

Woman's world, man's world. A deep gulf divides them. A man and his wife do not seek to bridge this gulf. Such a venture over the unknown frightens them. In the first days of marriage there is the sport of youth, desire easily taken for love, laughter, the novelty of a bed where you are never alone at night, where you no longer can freely spread the compass of your legs, as when you slept alone. A new existence limits your every move, your every thought. How many gestures a man would make alone which anyone's presence prevents. He would scarcely attempt them before a mirror. His reflection is already another being that judges him. It requires a love that is almost completely inhuman to lose all inhibitions, to risk the gestures that only action in a dream allows. A wife prohibits her husband from ever forgetting himself. Indeed, this form of politeness and discipline, these repressions play an important role in the beginning of a marriage. The least sensitive are thus obliged to watch themselves. The domestic services a husband performs for his wife, the guidance of a superior he renders her in petty-bourgeois society where wives are nobody, make him important in his own eyes. He finds a source of pride in these cares which give him an exaggerated idea of his protective power. Thus is love imitated.

Like other men, Antoine was absorbed by these novelties. Anne was very young, her youthfulness was ignorant of everything. Brought up behind the barriers of a society that held young girls closely tethered, Anne had much to learn from her husband —the acts of love, the meaning of certain words and the titles of certain books, the refrains of certain songs. This "initiation" is easily clothed in the semblance of love. But love is not this tawdry collusion.

Besides, Antoine very soon had "other things to do." Together with his wife, he embarked on the life that is the most common pattern of human lives. A couple constitutes a single being on the outside. Married people say, "Now we are one," and they confuse love with their unity of interests, of income and expenditures, of economies and opinions, of cut-and-dried sayings. They so easily acquire the habit of this false unity. They tell themselves so glibly that they are like two fingers of a hand. But two fingers of a hand are not so intimate, nor so simple. Their acquaintances say, "What a united little household!"

United because they do their bookkeeping together! Their parents are touched by the sight, and say, "How they love each other!"

And the couple embrace just to please their families. Each of these two individuals brought together by chance, by the circumstances of a society that hates love, by a brief moment of desire, or merely of tenderness and weakness, soon becomes for the other no more than a material presence, an object only slightly more mobile in space than houses, trees, furniture, and household utensils. This fleshy object speaks, it makes signals that are easy enough to comprehend, words bereft of mystery and charm. In the case of most couples, around five hundred words suffice for all their life and all their love, all their companionship, though there are tens of thousands of words. They put in an appearance at certain hours, like the little manikins of famous astronomical clocks. What worries are caused if the clock is slow! There are no hidden secrets; every gesture, every glance is transparent. This transparency gives the impression of security; they are, after all, like everyone else. A household is rarely the place that great human events choose as their setting. One married person never thinks of the other as of someone hard to fathom, worthy perhaps of living a human life, capable of living. They are not going to explore the mysteries that serve man as a covering.

"I earn the money for the household," say the men.

"I run my house well, I raise the children," say the women, and they think that everything has been said, that earning money, waxing the furniture, warming the water for the laundry, setting the table, the Sunday cakes, family parties, children's shoes are the whole of life.

Barely do they interpret the moods born of the body. A good husband knows that a wife who is having her menstrual period is irritable; a good wife knows that an overworked man talks little at table and gets angry over trifles. And they force themselves to be indulgent. They "make concessions," as in a little war.

"I know him so well," says the wife.

But this is the way one knows household utensils and domestic animals.

Antoine rarely thought of Anne as a separate individual. Perhaps in reality she was not, but who would dare assert that another being conceals nothing? He lived with her, five or six hours a day, that was all. Their married life was an exchange of phrases and services, where the only human undertaking was undoubtedly their nocturnal copulation. The most ridiculous inhibitions confined them to the prisons of the night. These adventures of the shadow involve movements, pulsations stronger, far more real and warm than the icy ceremonies of meals, walks, anniversaries, children's lessons, weekly accounts. Men take no part in all this, and get nothing out of it.

These wise animals standing on their hind feet, so proud of their vertical station, say: "We are not dogs," and they furiously throw buckets of water on dogs in heat when they get stuck. Their ears do not twitch like those of rabbits. They are quite proud of their thumbs, which can be opposed to the other fingers, and of the fact that their feet are not prehensile—"We are not monkeys." These wise animals blush over the animal nature that reveals itself so shamelessly beneath the warm tents of beds. They have been taught to be ashamed of deep waves that stir them. They console themselves for so much shame by exalting the false poetic love of songs and books, by murmuring the phrases of a false tenderness. They flee from true union like priests. This is the secret of the prostitute's appeal.

"You don't treat your wife like your mistress," they say with proverbial wisdom.

"You must respect the person you love and respect yourself too; we are not animals."

Anne Bloyé mistook for love the banal amenities of *Grande Marnière* and of *Roman d'un Jeune Homme Pauvre*, which she read in the Tours public library. Antoine thought briefly, as fleetingly as possible, of Marcelle's room and of the secrets of that young woman who on that last day had promised him boredom. He remembered those afternoons when Marcelle looked at him darkly and said, "Kiss me."

He had renounced that world of scandal, he was a respectable man.

One day, on a trip to Paris, he passed the Café d'Orléans. Perhaps Marcelle was standing by the door as of old with that faraway look of hers—she would not have aged, she would be wearing the same dress—but there was only a big dark woman sitting and reading and a man in a blue apron rinsing glasses behind the zinc counter. It was impossible to imagine the place where Marcelle had ensconced herself, the place where he might have made a second start.

With the passing years, the Bloyé household more and more patterned itself after the usual type of "respectable" households. It was a union where the force of going through the same motions, the necessity of keeping up appearances, the slowly acquired habits, imitated love. Antoine came home in the evening, Anne waited for him, having spent an unexciting day in the company of the little maid whom they paid twenty francs a month. She had embroidered, she had made pastry, she had seen this or that lady, the wife of the assistant depot master. The concierge of the depot had forecast the weather for the morrow, she had read a novel, *Femme de Trente Ans*, a biography, or the *Petits Secrets de la Femme*. Antoine rang the doorbell, Anne came to open the door, embraced her husband, and said: "Tell me."

"What do you want me to tell you?" he answered. "Nothing has happened. Everything is as usual."

Antoine took off his coat. He asked, "What have we got for dinner?"

At table, they discussed stories of the depot, the station. Little anecdotes of the service, rivalries, advancements. It was rumored that the wife of the district chief was deceiving her husband. Sometimes Antoine scribbled figures on the margin of his newspaper. He was a man with the cares of a narrow budget. Then they went to sleep.

Time was consumed in the round of such activities.

In 'ninety-seven they had a daughter. She burst in on Antoine's life like an unexpected intruder. He had not wanted her, he had done all he could to keep his wife from having a child.

"We must take every precaution," he said, "you are far too delicate."

But he thought to himself—it was a thought formed in a recess more remote than thoughts that are ever expressed in words—that a child seals every union. Without children, no marriage is final and indissoluble. A door always remains open to liberty, to a new departure and a new chance. Without even suspecting it, Anne knew how to defeat this hope. With all her being she longed for a child that would chase away her vague boredom, that would keep her company, that would fill the keenest of her needs. It was the hunger and thirst that wells from the depths of many a woman's body.

"The children I have had," she said later, "I can truly say they are my children. It was I who wanted them."

Thus Marie Antoinette Bloyé was born of the intrigues of the marriage bed. She was born, and six years later she died.

She was pale-eyed, like her father, with hollow temples. When she cried, and later when she ran, her lips became blue. The doctors kept saying, "There is really nothing to be done. This child cannot live. She will never get beyond the age of puberty."

"Everyone has his cross to bear," said Anne.

During the six years the child was alive, the Bloyés were carried beyond themselves by their struggle with a calamity which they knew was in the end inevitable. They lived in unrelaxed anxiety, a state of mind that never yielded. It was a war full of stratagems against the death that hovered around their daughter like a wasp bigger than an eagle. They defended her, under the doctor's instructions, with their own anguish. Every day won seemed to them a victory, every night that passed without a crisis, without suffocation, every meal she swallowed. All the mechanical tawdriness of their life receded before this struggle, this active and tender protection; the Bloyés attained a life that was almost heroic.

Almost every night they thought the end was at hand. And they never slept more than a light sensitive sleep. The child would cry suddenly, would choke. They had to give her medicine, and carry her up and down for hours on end to quiet her. And she stared fixedly at the lamp like a grown-up with a fever, whom nothing can dazzle. During all these years Antoine stole many hours from his sleep, walking his daughter up and down, and he left for the depot in the morning in a daze with his sides aching, and twinges through his back.

"When will I be able to get some sleep?" he thought.

The ailments that merely graze most children would prostrate Marie on her blue-and-white bed, her nostrils pinched, her cheeks hollow like those of the dying. Convulsions and missed breaths would lead to fainting spells. Anne would rub her, and from the other end of the room Antoine would ask timidly, without daring to look in his wife's direction, "Will she come to?"

Her heart resumed its beating with flame-like spurts, with long pauses that made her parents hold their breath, like an almost empty lamp that does not want to light and sputters and smokes. There were times when, in order to bring her to, they had to plunge her in mustard baths; her mother thought, "I'll never bring her out alive."

Marie was endowed with the thoughtful watchfulness, the disturbing gaiety of sick children. She followed grown-ups with severe eyes that accused their powerlessness to aid her, to free the way for her to breathe. She felt the big sponge of her heart swell against her ribs. When she was able to walk, she did not explore the little world around her. She remained for hours seated in her chair, on her cushions, husbanding her strength with the miserliness of an old invalid. Then she talked, and her parents could scarcely bear to hear her words. Anne had to avert her head to keep from crying. The childish sayings that fathers quote with pride to their friends at the café, that mothers mention in their letters, the opinions, falsely wise like poetic inventions, the plays on words that childhood makes up, cut them to the quick. In Marie's mouth they expressed a wisdom that was too profound, nourished by forces and forebodings too uncanny not to alarm the simplicity of the Bloyés. How could one stop her from doing anything when she had the ready answer: "You must let me do as I please, you know quite well the doctor said I mustn't be crossed."

She guessed that she would not live long, that one day all would be black around her. Death, unknown to most children, was for her like an inner companion. "When I am in heaven," she would say, "I shall give you anything you want."

With her eyes she followed the other little girls who ran, skipped rope, played games and swung, like beings of another race, from another world almost, like cats and birds. In summertime her mother worked in the garden of the depot house with the wife of the assistant depot master who lived on the floor above, and Marie would sit listening to the conversation of the grown-ups, the stories of servants, tradesmen, cooking, of ladies' work. The grass on the lawn, the yuccas with their sharp strands, and the Japanese apple trees were covered with soot, and the children who rolled in the grass would get up black. The engines passed behind the house; you heard the soft whistle of steam and the pounding in the shops of the depot. Birds flitted through the sky, insects chased each other, Marie listened and looked. Sometimes pieces of soot fell on her hair like the tail end of a rain of cinders from a volcano at the other edge of the world. When the other little girls came to ask her to play with them, she would answer with a certain pride over not being like everybody else, over harboring in her body a deathly secret, "I can't run with you, because of my heart. It is forbidden."

Everything was forbidden, by her parents, by her own exhaustion that overcame her so quickly, her palpitations, her pain. A thousand weights, a thousand invisible strands held down her limbs, weighted down her birdlike movements. She could only play quiet games, going shopping, going calling, housekeeping, cutting out paper dolls. She had sudden tantrums and outbursts of anger. When another child went near her mother or touched her skirt, she would fling herself toward it screaming, "I won't let you. That's *my* mother. Go away, go away, go find your own mother."

She had all the delicate graces of little girls doomed to die. You could see the veins beneath her skin.

"Mamma, look at the rivers," she would say.

For hours on end, sitting at Anne's feet while Anne was sewing, she would sing tunes she made up, with words her parents could not understand:

> When Mammas were dead
> Daddies did everything to their children. . . .

Or else:

> When birds are killed at night
> the blackbirds turn to rain. . . .

Her mother bent down to listen to these songs that were akin to the words of poetry or of madness. She felt uneasy before the world of childhood mysteries, and in the end she would say, "Keep quiet for a bit, child, you tire me."

In the end Marie had a cerebral hemorrhage and died. During her illness she moaned like a woman in labor, "It hurts, it hurts."

And thus she gave birth to her own death.

They buried her. Antoine spoke to none of the people present. Tears trickled down to his lips and he caught them mechanically with his tongue. It was perhaps twenty or twenty-five years since he last had cried. He took it badly, but he controlled himself. He made himself force back the lump that rose in his throat, the feeling of nausea. Piercing noises made the most sensitive parts of his head ring. He hunched his shoulders like a man attacked—would he defend himself or take flight? For men exert their bodies to shake off their sorrow just as they do to enter into full possession of their joy. One sees happy men stretch their arms and expand their chests, or run. Unhappy men tremble like small animals that feel the cold. They contract the area of their bodies as much as they can.

The bearers came down the stairs; the corners of the short coffin where Marie lay amid her toys, her cutouts, her dolls and blocks like the dead of Egypt, tore the tapestry and scarred the plaster. The stairways of houses are not designed for dead children. Once they set out, Antoine completely forgot his wife. She could go cry in her own corner. Grief cannot be shared, grief cannot be carried by two like a double-handled basket; her sorrow concerned her alone. No one helped him, Antoine; men are strong, no one consoles them, no one tries to ease their sorrow with words of comfort. He did his best to keep from crying. One must not forget one's manners, one must know how to behave both at table and in mourning. A man who cries commits a breach of etiquette. Each time he saw an unevenness in the pavement he felt certain he would stumble; the pavement bulged like a mole hill. He could no longer measure distances, he no longer controlled his muscles. He moved in a dream where the least stone or hollow was a magnet that dragged him down to the red cobbles. He stared at the coffin and its little yellow-fringed canopy. The bearers marched lockstep behind their leader with slow measured tread; their legs remained suspended in the air and touched the ground softly, without making any noise. He would have liked to see them trip, with their damnable precision; any sort of incident that could break the funeral spell, a clap of thunder, a burst of laughter, a passerby who would refuse to take off his hat and someone who would pounce on the bad patriot of death. But the crowd shuffled along behind him in silence. The sky was clear, the inhabitants were polite. Not a single woman forgot to cross herself. They passed the square where the members of a traveling fair were putting up a merry-go-round with wooden horses. Marie had never ridden such a merry-go-round because of her weak heart.

But everything came to an end, Antoine experienced a kind of terrible relief.

The following morning he awoke with the heavy head of dissipation or of great sorrow. He felt crushed, ideas raced through his mind like clouds. The house was in the disorder of death; his wife slept, red-eyed, with her mouth open—obviously she must not be wakened. He again saw Marie in her coffin with her blonde hair, her curved lids, her waxen skin. Marie in the garden, sick, gasping, leaving for school in the white frost of the one month when she wanted to go to school in order to be like other children.

Men do not understand death right away. Antoine kept imagining that she was still breathing in the neighboring room. He only knew he would never see her again, as one knows that winter comes again every year. Lie down, sleep without waking for several days, wake up at last entirely cured, utterly forgetful, with the wound completely healed. His every movement seemed useless to him. The departure of a being whom one loved, who will rot away, takes all the meaning out of life. Every gesture reawakens grief, that enemy which should be consigned to motionless slumber wrapped in sloth and subterfuge.

Nevertheless, he washed, shaved, brushed his clothes, rolled his first morning's cigarette—you should not smoke on an empty stomach—the first one always tastes best. He walked to his office, he bought his newspaper. The papers, the records and charts were waiting on his table, the shunting engines glided before his unwashed windows, and their huge shadow passed over him like a hovering cloud. A mechanic or one of his assistants came in; he answered their questions. The day's work rose before him like a little pile of excrement that must be cleaned up before evening in order to clear the place for the next pile of excrement. He must do his job. All his life he had accepted, as a matter of principle, that work came first. He had always been told that work came first—by his father with a leather strap, by his school teachers, by his counselors. There was no duty other than that of doing one's job. There was no greater sin than falling down on the job. There was no greater heresy than to ask if work had any sense.

Nevertheless, that day Antoine did his work as though it were an act of treason to his daughter, Marie, who lay cold and damp like a drowned cat in the mold of her little grave, among her wooden and cardboard toys whose colored paper was already starting to peel in that starless night. Doing his tasks was like lifting a terrific weight, for he struggled against the powerful attraction, the powerful lingering temptation of love for the dead. He was already struggling with the beloved shade of Marie. And together with him the stubbornness of living men at war with death fought his fight. His entire moral code bade him work, his entire moral code bade him overcome grief that spoke within him in the name of death itself. He worked because sorrow and death are slothful and the whole of his wisdom consisted simply of obedience to work. He never suspected that within him were other inclinations to laziness, other temptations besides death, opposed to work. He was a man who scarcely ever recalled the nightmares and dreams of triumph he experienced at night. His trains had to run just as ships must reach port—the trains leave, the men work, and the trains must run on time and the men must do their jobs. . . . You can't go wrong if you do your job well. Work is liberty. . . . Marie shared the fate of all the dead. The simplest arguments of social life slowly began to crowd her out as they crowd out the whole of man.

They came to fetch Antoine to go and inspect an engine brought into the depot because its injector functioned badly. He went out, every step he took was a triumph over his desire to sit down and let go of himself. But work that will not wait, the affairs of men drew him with all their force. He would never have the leisure thoroughly to indulge his greatest sorrows. Passing near a locomotive he heard the fireman say to the engineer who was greasing the axles, "Life is a fight even so, you know . . ."

Coincidences of this sort almost make you believe in magic, in mysteries. It was one of those chance phrases you catch in mid air during the great crises of life. They have an inexplicable connection with the event that concerns you, they seem charged with a warning and a meaning.

A fight against grief, against work, against death, against love, a victory that would count as long as there was room for victories, until the final defeat, until death claimed him too. Antoine passed the two workmates, shrugged his shoulders with the gesture of a soldier adjusting his knapsack, and asked the mechanic what the trouble was before going down into the pit by three steps covered with a paste of oil and dust.

11

Thereafter, the Bloyés lived like convalescents. Little by little they relaxed, like weak men after a fit of anger. They let themselves go, after having lived all those years at the highest pitch of tension and anguish. With the patience of a lower animal, they reordered their life that had been mutilated by the loss of their daughter. They thought unceasingly of her first gestures, of her first words, of her illness and death in a year when even in the winter the weather was so fine that it seemed impossible to imagine children dying—like invalids, like criminals, like old people. At first they never spoke of her—an animal caring for its wounds licks them in solitude. It hides them, it seeks privacy. Each of them retired to his own corner and ruminated with a kind of hostility toward the other. Grief is, perhaps, the most animal-like of human feelings.

But one day, without even suspecting that it was the beginning of their recovery, they started exchanging their memories, memories which were not the same, which did not recall to them the same dates, the same hours. Anne cherished many images that Antoine never even suspected. Men work; men are less familiar with the lives of their children than their wives are. Antoine felt a sort of envy in the face of this memory richer than his own. He needed his wife to complete the picture of his daughter. He was not satisfied with knowing that Marie resembled him physically. This half-jealousy, the yearning, the exchange of memories, the years it was impossible to erase, during which they had for the first time carried out a common task—there were no arguments over the child's upbringing, her heart disease had placed her outside the quarrels that parents foment around the questions of catechism, lessons, lay schools and church schools—when apart from the false unity of the household there had been between them a profound understanding, a community of worry and love as though they had labored at the same task with a single impulse and a single will—all these elements of sorrow at last created the bonds of a real love between Anne and her husband. There existed between them a bond, a complicity more potent than all household habits. Their marriage acquired a true strength and solidity, as though it had been founded on a great purpose, on a great passion. Antoine felt himself tied down, as though despite himself, by a fidelity that could never completely vanish. He was enchained, he was set in marriage. The whole of the future was clear to him.

Antoine and his wife knew they would never forget the brief life and death of their daughter, but they never guessed that in time this bitter memory would acquire the likeness of an old love, that this great loss would in the end have for both of them the very charms of youth. No desert in human life is so dry that the grass cannot grow over it, no wound so deep that the flesh cannot heal. The Bloyés turned toward new hopes with the unity of purpose they had acquired by habit around Marie's bed. The observance of their mourning each day underwent a defeat. They made plans for trips, for vacations, for the future. Or rather, Anne made plans to which her husband docilely agreed. He was tied to her. Many hidden paths, many avenues to other people in his life thus closed before him.

Anne was an exacting wife, one of those good homebodies who are far more "fatal" to men than the fatal women of legends. There are thousands of such women among the petty bourgeoisie. These spiders crouch in the depths of detached provincial houses and envelop their husbands in webs that it would take an effort, an heroic intent, to tear asunder. They secrete a saccharine slavery. They hate "loose women" because they feel themselves threatened by these impudent accomplices of male freedom. Their domestic virtues protect them. How can any one rebel against them? Such a rebellion would be aimed at order, at morality, a whole menacing edifice, a great ship of which they are the figureheads on the bowsprit. Anne was one of these women. Had anyone accused her of tyranny, she would have burst into tears, misunderstood, struck in her most sensitive spot. She thought herself good; she was good, after the fashion she had learnt from her mother—her mother who was "not always agreeable."

The cooking was good and on days when Antoine invited a colleague, the guest took a second helping of every dish. The parquet floors were shiny and by the outer door were felt mats on which you could slide over the slippery waxed floor. The recesses of the Henri II sideboard, the moldings of the cupboard hid not one speck of dust. There was no woolly fluff under the beds; the laundry was ironed every Thursday; the accounts were kept up to date; the medicine cabinet was never without iodine, sterilized cotton, antipyrine.

Men should find their houses in order. Anne took pride in her house, she adorned it with curtains, doilies, and antimacassars. She copied embroidery patterns from the women's magazines. She never went out, she had the nesting instinct. In a few year's time the young girl she had been was transformed into a woman identical with Mme Guyader. Mme Guyader had loomed very large in her daughter's life. She forbade her to do almost everything. Anne said: "When I married, I scarcely knew how to fry an egg! Mother never let me set foot in the kitchen."

She took her revenge. She had wanted to outdo her mother, to be more frugal, more tidy than she. She had succeeded fairly well. And when Mme Guyader came to see her, she compelled her to feel as idle and useless as she herself had felt. She let her mother know that she was mistress in her house and Mme Guyader wandered around her daughter's apartment emptyhanded, her glasses pushed back on her forehead, two knitting needles stuck in her smooth, tightly held hair. What virtue! Anne flaunted it proudly. None could ever doubt or overlook the sacrifice of pleasure and amusement that went into her housekeeping. She demanded much in exchange, without anger, without issuing orders. Anne was not, as they say, an "imperious" woman. But one had to be on the spot. Her husband's latenesses she regarded as an insult, as proof of estrangement. On such occasions he saw her waiting for him on the threshold and he quickened his stride, feeling guilty. He had had a glass and a chat with the assistants or with some of the passenger service employees. Anne would say: "Good heavens, Antoine, you still smell like the café. You've been drinking beer though you know perfectly well you can't stand alcohol."

And she cried, in the name of her wounded "sensibility," of her need for "affection" betrayed. It was like a little thrust at the heart which Antoine felt himself powerless to parry. He tried to win forgiveness for things he had not done. After all it was true: she never went out, she did not have a very gay time of it, cooped up within the four walls of the house. She waited for him; he should feel sorry for his thoughtlessness. There could be no interval of respite between work and home, friendly get-togethers, idle conversations between men, manly pleasures. From his office, from his engines, he plunged straight into household trivialities. There was nothing else on earth. How much courage he would have needed to fight back! Anne made of his slightest gesture of rebellion the act of a "monster." Few men have the courage to be monsters, to stand the tears of wives who cry at the least provocation. And he stayed put, he did not stray. The cocoon woven by Anne enveloped him. However, little by little he lied. He lied for no good reason, without mystery. There was "nothing to hide." He had no adventures; he was not unfaithful to his wife; he did not conceal from her any of the money he earned. He lied quite disinterestedly about unimportant things. When he had been to the café, he told her the name of some other café. When these lies succeeded, he experienced a sort of pleasure, a feeling of victory. Hardly aware of it, he was preparing himself a retreat for the days when he would have to lie with a straight face about important matters. He defended his life by seeking to hide it. He protected himself against the total invasion with which his wife threatened him. He kept avenues of escape open for himself.

And the memory of Marie presided over all his scheming.

12

In 1905, for the second time, a child was born to the Bloyés. This time Antoine had wanted a child as much as his wife, in order to complete their common recovery. It was on a midwinter day, a day crowned by the black smoke which the north winds blow back over the depot and over that section of Tours covered with cinders and soot which is called Beaujardin.

Antoine, who has taken the day off, watches a bundle of red flesh stir on the pillow. He stands in the corner where the midwife has placed him like a useless domestic animal butting into the midst of important human affairs.

"Stay there if you like," says Mme Guyader, "but don't move, don't bother us."

He vaguely distinguishes the puckered features of his son, the lips, the puffy eyelids, his skin creased like a new leaf. He listens to the shrill cries that issue from this new flesh. A new man delivered from the maternal warmth and fluids learns to breathe in the open air.

Mme Guyader, who has come to help her daughter, walks about the room; with little groans she bumps her distended stomach against the corners of furniture and the bed frame. She gets swaddling clothes and a package of gauze. She departs on an errand with which the midwife has commissioned her, which she alone is capable of performing: boiling some water, finding a lemon for the eyes of the newborn. She emits a sort of joyous humming; she leans over her daughter, who is stretched on her back, tired, drowsy, content, and famished, like a swimmer floating in the sun.

"My daughter, my daughter," she cries, "how handsome he is! You have really borne a man!"

She leaves the maternity room, murmuring between her teeth, "Poor little *magaden*."

When Mme Guyader is excited, she invariably reverts to the Breton words of her childhood.

Antoine stands apart and the women ignore him. He is cast aside like a drone bee. He feels superfluous, but deep down inside him great hopes begin to shape, hopes which he would not dare mention to anyone in the agitated hours of childbirth. The defeat of his daughter's death is erased and is followed by a victory. He takes stock of things with a measure of contentment that he did not experience at his daughter's birth, his daughter who had tethered him to the cropped marriage pasture. His son's birth can change many things. He will no longer be alone with Anne. A future companion has just been born. A being with the same functions and gender as himself. A man loves a daughter, but warily, as a future woman, with reservations. Between him and his son there are no mysteries. A son's birth brings with it the promise of the greatest manly pleasure on earth. A man senses that if he goes about it properly, if he does not waste the fleeting opportunities, his son can give him the opportunity of knowing the simple and exalted sentiments of friendship better than any friends. He feels that a son will require less tact than a daughter, so many fundamental things can be tacitly understood without danger between two men. Many a father feels awkward and secretly irritated in the presence of his daughter, whose ways announce the studied gestures and little artifices of the woman. Antoine had sometimes experienced this awkwardness and uneasiness before Marie, even though she was only a sickly child, a little flickering flame.

Thus, in the inconspicuous corner where he tries to make himself as small as possible, Antoine, who has not many companions, promises himself a friend. He shall wait ten years, he shall wait twenty years, he shall wait all the required time; he shall wait till his son has built him a manly frame and they shall be happy together. He shall help this being devoid of strength and knowledge in every way he can, he shall clear the boulders from his path. He shall save him from frustrations. He shall allow all the subterranean thoughts that course through the depths of every man to come to the surface. It suddenly occurs to him, "My son will avenge me."

For Antoine is a man with scores to settle, a man who has not enjoyed life to the full, who knows that he will never himself get even with life.

Antoine is allowed to go over to his wife, whom the midwife has finished tending. He embraces Anne with a kind of gratefulness that is quite unlike love. She wants to talk. She is about to make one of those inappropriate remarks that would spoil his contentment. He makes her a sign to keep quiet with an impatient little wave of his hand. He tells her in a low voice, although he feels like shouting, "Keep quiet, keep quiet. Do not tire yourself, the doctor has forbidden you to speak. Tomorrow . . ."

He does not dare embrace his son. He looks at him and finds him curious and ugly. But he takes the fist of the newborn between two fingers as though to transmit a current of power from his body to this body without strength. Thus the child touches the paternal soil and takes courage after the great anguish and gasping of his coming into the world. He quiets down and a deep calm prevails.

In the midst of this reverie Antoine hears the noises of the world that begins on the other side of the velvet curtains, windowpanes, and walls. He listens to a train whistle calling for the right of way. Mechanically he pulls out his watch—6:17, the Brittany express. At this moment, a moment he will remember, between the sounds of his trade and the signs of this knowledge, and the short gasping breaths of his son, are contained all the resources of his life; he takes possession of them.

What commitments are involved in the advent of this little soft blind animal! You can see the bald skin of his cranium throb. You could kill him with a finger stroke. For years he will require the warmth of well-covered beds and even room temperatures. He will fall; he will catch diseases; he will hurt himself. He will have to be shielded from death. He must be well armed. He must be given the heritage, the armor of secrets that men pass on to each other. Antoine wants this child to have a fuller, "juster" life than his. This is a hope and a pledge.

Antoine is not a meditative man. His thoughts rarely range far ahead. He focuses only on the most immediate, but this evening is an evening of idleness and contemplation which he can devote to projects that will perhaps be smashed, that will perhaps end in nothing. Antoine suddenly thinks of his own death to come and he regards this son of his, who is nothing as yet, who may betray him, who may hate him perhaps, or may die, as the great force that shall deliver him, that shall save him from death. He tends the coal fire in the grate to keep the child and its mother from catching cold. He stares unseeingly at the marble mantle, the Limoges vases, the clock, and suddenly these objects detach themselves, stand isolated. They are no longer part of the room's furnishings. He asks himself what they mean. He sits in the armchair and calculates. There are such days of leisure and reverie when men start reckoning.

"Three years of school, seventeen and three make twenty. Twenty years. If I live to sixty that makes a third . . . I still had two-thirds of my life ahead of me. One year at Montpellier, twenty-one years. Six years of the railways, on the engines. At twenty-seven, I married. My daughter died when I was thirty-five. We are now in 1905. I am forty. Next month I shall be forty-one. Terrifying. If I live to sixty, I still have twenty years, one-third. Nothing has ever happened. Something was always about to happen but nothing ever did happen and nothing more can happen as far as I am concerned. Now it is too late. . . . Twenty years . . . as long as from my birth to my leaving school, from my leaving school to the present. So quick. I have lived two-thirds, four-sixths of my life. And nothing has ever happened. It could all be told in three words. Every day the same thing. There are twenty-four hours in a day, it is now four o'clock in the afternoon and the day ends at midnight, at midnight I die. Midnight equals sixty. At four o'clock, you start thinking about dinner, you feel the day is over, you think about having to go to bed soon. Between eight o'clock and midnight, hardly anything happens, you sleep. I might even live to be a hundred. . . . Impossible, people don't live to be a hundred, only sometimes in the newspapers. . . . To eighty . . . to seventy . . . that is more likely. Forty-one. . . . If only I were just halfway."

He sees himself stretched out on his deathbed. Forty-one, this whole weight of years bears down on his shoulders. He sinks deeper in his armchair. He sees himself on a height whence he surveys his son with the clarity and penetration of those about to die. On the one hand, death to which he will inevitably be delivered, and on the other hand this budding life that will fight against death, that will perpetuate a line of men. He thinks of his future as though there were no one besides his son and himself. All else is lost sight of; he forgets his wife, the barely extinguished suffering that made her groan, the events of the earth, his friends. He undertakes to found the edifice of the years that remain on the uncertain survival of a child, on the relationship of father to son.

The child cries suddenly. A first nightmare? The midwife opens the door, gathers up the baby in her arms, soothes it back to sleep with a song of her province. Antoine's thoughts are swallowed up like a wine drop in the sea. He drowses in his mingled anguish and contentment listening to the elusive words of the song:

Som som som
Beni beni beni
Som som som
Beni beni don

Such is life of a winter's evening, with the charcoal lamp glowing beneath its water-green glazed paper shade. You will die, but you have sons. After all there is no reason to regret being a man and being alive.

13

In the lives of men there are years that seem poised in equilibrium. They hold themselves upright, they have the assurance of a firmly established being that moves forward confidently with arms outstretched. Or else they run like water courses, and the days flow into them like rivulets that finally make a river. Some flow over stones; they are born of the gradual constant melting of glaciers. Others issue from a water table under a hillside and they follow the slope of the roads. The tributary bears them to the river and the river flows into the sea as years into life. But the sea is never full, while every life reaches its repletion. It evaporates all at once, it rises like a sudden mist, like the smoke from an explosion. All that remains of the vanished landlocked sea are faint traces soon obliterated. This is what men call death.

Antoine was not at this point. He was still quite far from this sudden evaporation of his life; he floated easily along the current of his river, freely fed by days and hours that came from many sources, from work, from rest, from home, from hope. A kind of idle peace reigned over this invisible current that coursed through the streets, houses, shops, and landscapes of one of the most peaceful provinces of France. Possibly this peace was no more than a veneer. But Antoine knew nothing of this.

His life did not occupy a very broad area. And it was not exposed to the public view. Antoine was one of those men whom the provincial papers briefly mention when they die, when they

141

have children, or when they are decorated. His existence contained very few events, it would fill a very meager chronicle. It
had the well-ordered pattern, the slowly rising curve of the lives
of functionaries marked for advancement. It was not upset by the
mishaps of the world. In those prewar years, the French bourgeoisie bloomed in great calm and contentment. It was securely
established, no ills could befall it. No catastrophes hung over its
head. It rejoiced in a power that no force seemed to threaten. It
did not read the papers with the panic it experiences today, on the
eve of its death.

In Antoine's mail, there arrived at intervals letters from his
company's central office. They informed him of changes in his
position and residence and of salary increases. They announced:

Monsieur,

By decision of the Board of Directors of the Company, taken at my
instance on . . . you have been appointed . . . .

Your salary is set at . . . beginning . . . .

Accept, monsieur, the assurance of my regards.

> For the Director of the Company,
> *The Chief Engineer of Equipment*
> *and Traction*

Whenever these letters announced a salary increase, there was
an extra sentence:

I took pleasure in prompting this decision.

Thus by printed formula did the men who directed the game
casually remember the pieces they moved. These letters marked
the stages of life. The commentaries made on their terms and
their figures, on the hopes they raised, filled many conversations
and many hours. What reckonings it took to apportion the few
hundred francs that they added each year! What a host of desires
to pick from—new wallpaper, a piano, new armchairs for the living room, more life insurance. All life is woven from such ele-

ments. These printed slips with their blank spaces filled in by the careful writing of an office employee with a beautiful hand are the only traces of the worldly trek of obscure men. They are rediscovered at the bottom of a chest or a cupboard after the death of the addressee.

Up to August 1914, when his life will be forcibly speeded up, when he will cease to be sheltered by bourgeois peace, the entire duration of Antoine Bloyé's life could be condensed by an observer unacquainted with Antoine's aims and passions into one yellowed report page, into what the administrative division of the railway terms an information sheet: repairman, journeyman-locomotive engineer, engineer of the fourth and fifth class, traction supervisor, assistant depot master, supervisor of equipment and traction, depot master, manager of the shops. In 1888 Antoine Bloyé earned 1,800 francs, in 1894—2,700, in 1904—4,200, in 1909—6,000, in 1914—7,200.

These titles, these monetary symbols expressed the entire social shell of Antoine Bloyé's life. At his death, coupons deposited at the company's pension department, on the Rue de Londres, will take the place of memoirs, which men of his kind are not given to writing. The whole substance of his life was hidden in these lines—all his encounters with other men, all his loneliness, all his moments of enthusiasm and discouragement, all his pride, all his sorrow, work, leisure, weariness, deceit, his encounters with death and what Antoine, like his fellows, submissively called duty. The duty of doing his job, the duty of being faithful to his wife, the duty of raising his son, the duty of making the workers move in their rut, the duty of being on the side of the bosses, the duty of accomplishing "his task" before dying. But what task?

During this period of calm his house and the town around it occupied the foreground of his life. As he earned more money, each house he leased was bigger than the houses he had lived in before.

He could allow himself a fairly high rental. How small his rent had been fifteen years earlier, on the Rue du Chevaleret, in Paris! Anne Bloyé never thought of those first lodgings without a vague feeling of shame.

"We lived just like workers," she would say.

Around 1907, life was not expensive in a new provincial town. At the Hôtel du Commerce et des Postes, you could eat *foie gras* and game; rooms rented for two francs fifty, and on market days the wealthy farmers who came to lunch there paid for their meals in kind. A cab cost one franc fifty an hour. At last Antoine could draw up his family budget without worries, his new appointments allowed him to see his way clearly, he was no longer uneasy about the morrow.

The town they lived in was not far from the Limousin. When you take the steam tramways from the Place de Francheville, you notice a sudden change in the color of the furrows, the smell of the fields, the dampness of the air; the hillsides are studded with groves of oak and thorn tree, half-ruined villages stand on the hill-crests; the shepherds knit. You watch for the first boundary mark to read the name of a village, for the pleasure of saying, "Look, we are already in the Limousin."

If you go southward from the town, you find yourself in real southern countryside—tile-roofed farmhouses, grapevines that climb the trees, great hazy horizons crossed by rivers, plane trees growing on the squares, the big derricks of the wells, and palm trees planted in the courtyards of the houses. People who have traveled are reminded of Lombardy. It is a mellow country free from coarseness, where it seems as though it would not be hard to be happy.

The town is circled by a ring of hills, winds that sweep down from the mountains do not ravish its secrets. The town is close huddled, as though hoarding its own self. It feels protected by the forests of beech, walnut, oak, and chestnut. It has a history, of course, like all towns, but this history plays no part in the life of

its citizens. Out of the 31,973 inhabitants in 1906, only a distinguished minority recall with considerable pride that the founders
of this city were the men of the Four Armies and worshipped
Vesuna. Only the members of the Archeological Society, who
meet once a month in the dungeon of an ancient feudal castle,
glory in a past whose dust they disturb. Antoine Bloyé was one of
those people not the least concerned with the glory and antiquity
of towns. He was not an amateur historian. He lived in the
present, without family traditions, and he was periodically trans-
planted from town to town, like all the men who made the railways run. The country of his birth had little hold on him after so
many years; he crossed it only once a year, when he joined his
wife and son at the far end of Morbihan for the holidays.

In this town, Antoine settled down. He took to its comforts
and its customs. The enforced wanderings that he had endured
for so long, that did not leave him the time really to make acquaintance with the towns and their inhabitants, the succession of
temporary homes and the hardships he had known, gave way to a
permanent home. For the first time Antoine became like other
men who feel a sense of ownership in their town. Clustered
round its prefecture, its bishopric, its Masonic Lodge, its municipal theater, its law court, this departmental seat was more of an
agricultural market than a factory center or a junction of the big
lines. And there still prevailed a rural atmosphere, as in almost all
French provincial towns. You often saw peasants in blue overalls
and straw hats go by. In the streets you came across herds of goats
and cattle, ox-drawn wagons, hay carts. This setting had nothing
in common with the previous surroundings of Antoine's life.

The Bloyés lived in the most newly constructed section of the
town. The routes leading thither, when they walked home from
the center, gave its inhabitants an agreeable impression of their
earthly station. They could choose at will the Rue Lamartine and
the Avenue de Paris, or else the long Rue Louis Mie; but whatever the route, on reaching their own district they always expe-

rienced the sensation of plunging into an independent world. It was set apart from the streets and squares devoted to commerce, around the public buildings whose ruins, two thousand years hence, will denote the contours of the town—the market, the town hall, the post office, the court house, the Banque de France, the new arcade. There in the center the merchants lived, behind the windows of their stores, absorbed even during their meals in the arrangement of their displays, keeping watch over their cash drawers constantly threatened by the pranks of tough boys from the lower part of town. Any moment a customer might push back the door and start the bell tinkling. He was welcome, you made a pleasant face, you tried to seduce him with smiles and carefully chosen words; it was like a masquerade. Antoine's neighbors said: "In business you are really much too much of a slave. You must always be on the go, forever at the customer's disposal. You have to be pleasant even when you are not in the mood for politeness, you are dependent on the wishes of others."

In the center there still lived people of the liberal professions, who slept and ate next to their consulting office or study. The headmaster of the Lycée, the assistant headmaster, the bursar lived right in the school, like the pupils.

But the inhabitants of the new quarter were privileged. Their existence was divided, it had two faces. It was partitioned into two worlds that did not communicate, where you entered by openings as dissimilar as the ivory door and the horn door of the prophetic dreams. One of these worlds contained professional cares, the worries of the job, the motions, the annoyances, the routine of the daily task. It was the prosaic world where you earned your livelihood, it was permeated by the smell of shops, the dust of offices, halls, and munitions stores. There you heard the noises that a free man must know how to forget in the bosom of his family: hammering, sirens, drills, circular saws, the bang of drawers being pushed back into place, the rolling of the corru-gated shutters, the rustle of commercial correspondence, the machine-gun rattle of typewriters, bugle calls, the clatter of harness and gun butts on armory floors, telephones, orders, speed, smoke, work. Almost all the heads of families were engineers, functionaries, employees, and junior officers.

The second of these two worlds held the peace and relaxation proper to emancipated men who have finished their task for the day and take their rest awaiting the coming task. Each evening they came into possession of that domestic quietude that is the privilege of men whose job ends every night. No one called them to account, their responsibilities ceased the very moment their work was over. Big silent engines with their belts disconnected, and empty offices where all the drawers were closed, awaited them far from their beds.

The streets they passed through on their way home likewise set them apart from the Toulon quarter where the workers lived at the gates of factories, the most important of which is the railway shops. The workers were aroused at daybreak by the first call of the sirens. They were constantly steeped in the echoes of work, disturbed by the traffic of the main line, the whistling and coupling of freight trains shunting about at midnight under the arc lights. What a feeling of satisfaction you derived from not being mixed in with the workers, from feeling divided from them by such a goodly distance, by so many steps!

They also sought to derive satisfaction from the fact that they did not "reside" in the southwest district, situated well above them in an urban hierarchy that no one sought to question. You reached this lofty region after passing the Place de Francheville, where the fireworks were set off on the national holiday, and where the civil and military parades, the military drills, and the livestock market were held. This shapeless, measureless square, sloping like a hillside, resembled the areas voluntarily demolished, the heroic deserts that peoples threatened by invasion establish between themselves and the enemy. And in fact, in summer months and on Sundays when the people of the east and north part of the city went walking with their wives and children, they hesitated before this vast treeless emptiness, gulched by the storms, baked by the July sun. They receded before the repelling force of this bulwark and turned their steps toward the Bordeaux road. Following the blue shadowed strip of sidewalk, like a stream bed, they moved off toward the river and the garden of the Lycée. If, later on, they landed in the quarter of the rich, it was after a long detour, a flanking movement that permitted the beleaguered to bolt all their doors and herd their animals and children within their walls. They arrived like conquerors in a deserted region. In these well-guarded streets, in houses of handsome stone shaded by *portes cochères,* lived the industrialists, the wealthy investors and the big merchants, the senior officers of the Thirty-Second Artillery Regiment and the Fiftieth Infantry, the nuns of Sainte-Marthe, and impoverished noble families who in springtime moved to estates they still possessed on the river bank.

As in every French town, the streets of the center bore the abstract names of institutions and regimes, of great men and public buildings: the Republic, the Bank, the Market, Victor Hugo, Louis Blanc. The aristocratic streets of the southwest section owed the names on their signposts to the most remote memories of local history, to the glorious remnants of the ancient city. In choosing their names, recourse had been had to the Middle Ages, the Gallo-Roman deities and the monuments built by Rome. There was the Rue Bertrand de Born, the Rue de Vésone, the Rue des Arènes, the Rue Romaine. One wonders what scruples had prevented them from going back to earlier periods, from naming a Boulevard des Eyzies or an Avenue Quaternaire. The streets of Antoine's district bore the names of more modest celebrities, Lagrange Chancel, Louis Mie; they kept traces of a recent rural past. Antoine lived in the Rue Combe des Dames.

The Bloyés' neighbors preferred not to envy the rich section. They made a pretense of believing that people there led restricted lives, subject to iron laws, to traditional restraints incompatible with the notions a provincial French petty bourgeois has of the pleasures and freedom of life. Making the best of things, they sought gratification in feeling themselves equally remote from the workers, of whom they were suspicious, and the big bourgeois, whose strange customs provided them with endless reasons for not coveting more power or wealth than they possessed.

They said that rich people were badly brought up because they did not have the same rules of polite behavior they themselves had. They indulged in innuendos and slanderous remarks that pictured the southwest quarter as a glittering world of license, debauchery, and disease. They spoke of its adultery, drug fiends, decadence, and vice, and believed their own words. All men greatly exaggerate the vices, cares, and sorrows of those who are placed above them. It seems to them that evil grows with wealth and power. Nothing is astonishing on the part of the "big shots" because they are regarded as capable of anything, as exposed to everything in their extravagant world of tragic figures and useless heroes. It is the world of Andromache, Ajax, of the Atrides. And irate destiny directs its blows against these beings so surfeited with pleasures, wealth, and pride. Each scandal that breaks, each drama, each death, each ruin confirms this naive belief of the petty bourgeois who wants to feel so virtuous, hard-working, and wise by comparison. Thus the inhabitants of modest streets defend themselves from social jealousy and justify their lack of glamor. Their bursts of indignation, their righteousness avenge them. Thus they console themselves for the frustration of their dreams of power, pride, and wealth. They teach their sons and daughters that they may not aim too high for their station, the wisdom of the just middle, the modesty of violets, the philosophy of honesty and the golden mean.

Toward 1910, in the provinces all things were ordered; society had its levels, and rarely in the course of those lazy years did a man make a sudden leap to the summit of this solid edifice. The only way of rising at a single stroke was through winning in the lottery. With a half smile to salve their consciences, to show they were not fools, the family heads carefully followed the Communal and Land Loan drawings. They sought to justify the beauty, pleasures, and virtues of an obscure estate which it was hard to rise from, but which was, after all, far more attractive than the downtrodden and precarious life of a worker, a manual laborer. When the inhabitants of the Rue Combe des Dames reached their homes, they experienced, in fact, a bodily relaxation, a relief from tension that they prized very highly. They imagined that these pleasures were unknown to their richer, more important fellow-citizens, ever anxious as they were to rise higher, to live up to their station and offer to the eyes of their children, servants, and friends an impressive picture of their mien, of their "importance," their presence of mind; forever taken up with a large exacting role which demanded that they never forget themselves.

At seven o'clock, while waiting for dinner, and after dinner at nine, during the months of good weather, they gave themselves over to pleasures that are today forgotten by their equals, who, like the workers whom they still mistrust, are now tormented with anxiety about the coming weeks and months. They chatted with their neighbors over prickly shrubs, clusters of sunflowers, thickets and hedges of laurel and syringa, in garden strips behind "detached" houses. They strolled down their paths as though they were intending to pull weeds, fumigate a peach tree, keep the slugs out of their lettuce with a line of quicklime, or spray their grape stalks; but they soon ended by leaning their elbows on the dividing fences, for you must look the man you are chatting with in the face. They discussed how their vegetables were sprouting, what the prospects were for their creepers, for they were all gardeners, and talked of the important seasonal dates and world events, for they were all meteorologists and politicians. And all through those years that preceded the war, there were many events of every kind, many topics, figures, and changes that they discussed at length, without ever for a moment suspecting that many of these things were slowly, imperceptibly, propelling their little crystal world toward the brink of adventure. Agadir, the gunboat *Panther*, the dividends of the big companies, the struggle for world markets. M. Joseph Caillaux, the strikes, the exploits of the Bonnot gang, the dramatic death of Garnier, the defense of Adrianople, the passing of Halley's Comet—people in Japan committed suicide to flee their terror of the end of the world—the Paris floods—you could go boating in front of the Gare Saint-Lazare—the bloomer craze, automobile races, the first aviation meets, famous actresses, the death of Lantelme, plays, catastrophes, famines, wars. The submarine *Pluviose* sank and nurses sang their children a melancholy ditty:

> Le *Pluviose* a coulé
> Très léger . . .

The cruiser *Liberté* blew up, as the *Iéna* had done before. Cyclones on land, visits of royalty, cannons decorated with streamers, pictures of reviews at Longchamps, the Sarajevo assassination, the outer shell of the world beneath which forces are at work that no one is aware of, not one of them.

At the time all these bits of news were commented upon by hundreds of men in their shirt sleeves in the gardens of many French towns. They discussed them with detachment, with indifference, as though from lack of anything better. They were all deluded into believing that the world's events, the very cataclysms of their planet, were no affairs of theirs. They felt utterly apart, wonderfully secure and sheltered, and all these things happened for their diversion and amusement, to provide subjects for their game of comments and opinions. Weeks when scarcely anything had happened, they would say as though they had been robbed, as though fate had cheated them on a bargain, "There is really nothing to read in the papers, they are utterly empty."

When Halley's Comet was announced—and at the time the papers declared the earth might be threatened—they said: "That damn comet! You can't get a moment's peace these days. So it's our last evening today. Maybe we'll wake up dead tomorrow. These newspapermen have a hard time making things up. Is the end of the world possible? What? All of a sudden? So long until tomorrow, if we're still alive. Anyway, we'll have a good night to die in."

And they laughed, and they did not know that the star of war was already closer than any comet and that the end of their world was approaching.

They believed themselves wise, they believed themselves stable, they believed themselves happy. They were capable of the greatest anger, the most reckless courage to defend the wisdom, the stability, the happiness of their small exacting lives against all change, all forces. They thought with deepest hatred of revolutions, of the workers who would make them. They were the kind of men who loved the gendarmes. And Antoine lived among them, he was one of them. Month after month, he sank deeper into this soothing languor of habits. He dozed, he no longer thought of his frustrations, his old dreams, his ancient hatreds. Perhaps, like his neighbors, he believed himself wise, stable, and happy. How could so much apparent security and self-satisfaction fail to win over and corrupt a man whose life had been hard and uncertain, a man who for years had not mingled with the life of a group of humans, ever since the time when he was on the engines among other men? The cotton wool of bourgeois life kept him from feeling the wind. Thus he spent his evenings.

Meanwhile, the wives and servants were busy in the kitchens and dining rooms; you heard the clatter of plates and glasses. Later in the evening they cleared the tables and put the children to bed upstairs, the shutters banged, the lamps were lit.

On days when the weather turned to rain, the men bethought themselves of their power of the ballot and complained of the stench that came from the cheap gasworks. M. Baud, who was division head at the prefecture, said, "That plant is a permanent outrage. Its smell of rotten eggs ruins my evenings for me."

They would discuss municipal decisions and pass critical judgment on their prefect and deputies. But they never touched forbidden topics. They never spoke of the Lodge, of the politically minded priests of the Cathédrale Saint-Front, save in an undertone. They never exchanged comments on the other inhabitants of the Rue Combe des Dames for fear these might spread beyond the vegetable beds and sow discord among the garden lovers. They were men who knew how to live. It was not in the peaceful atmosphere of these evenings that evil rumors originated and spread. Out of their own charmed circle, in town, the neighbors knew how to accuse each other with all the venomous meanness that was kept in check in the evenings by their selfish desire for quiet. Thus the petty bourgeois, isolated like islands in the sea, made efforts to lead a social life that was barely interrupted by winter and the rainy end of autumn. Perhaps this meant that they were further removed than they suspected from the popular fellowship and unity of the workers' districts. Even the officers who would live on this street until the day when an additional stripe would give them the right to cross the town did not think it beneath their dignity to put on an old tunic without stripes and take part in the intercourse of civilians and confide to them across the crisp smell of the lettuce, in the scent of lilac and syringa, that France was strong, that nothing could catch its armies unprepared, because the Fiftieth and the Thirty-Second at any rate were ready, and you could judge all the other regiments from them.

At the same time of day, the workers of the Toulon district likewise conversed from door to door or gathered at the wineshops or along newly opened streets, where children in the black smocks of the public schools splashed in the puddles left by the torrential rain. But the crowds of the Toulon district were less certain of the morrow and of peace than the over-tranquil tribes of the Rue Combe des Dames. In their discussions there were accents that the powers of the Rue de la Cité and the Rue Bertrand de Born sufficiently suspected to be uneasy about them. The people of the Toulon district saw signs of change in the world. The anger that sometimes roused them, the hardships of their life that they mastered through the strength of brotherhood and the hope of a new world, infused their days with a warmth and a stability unknown to the placid petty bourgeois of the Rue Combe, whose even tempers concealed their loneliness, their envy, their mistrust, their intrigues, like panicky little rodents.

Day after day, night after night, Antoine lived this life. It permeated him with its ease, its thousand sources of indifference and forgetfulness. He let himself go, he no longer struggled. He was settled. He would say, "Everything has worked out. How calm you become as you grow old!"

He told himself these things because he had need of such assurances, because he was not so sure, after all, that they were true. But god knows where he might have landed if he had not kept repeating to himself the most reassuring words he could find.

The calendar pages, with their historical anniversaries, their jokes, depended on the year—"This year I'm going to choose a funny calendar," Anne would say—the calendar pages with their schedules of the moons, the tides, the rising and setting of the sun, were torn away one after another. The months differed from each other only through changes in temperature and the seasonal vegetation, only because your skin was sensitive to changes in the outer world. Everything seemed so well ordered that Antoine speculated on all the projects that came into his head.

"After I have retired," he would say to Anne, "I shall buy a house at Palavas-les-Flots."

Anne hated the south, ever since the short trip they made there on their honeymoon. She would never go and end her days in that country of oil and strong wine. She knew she would have the last word and these plans were nothing more than a game she allowed Antoine to indulge in. He ended by picturing to himself the height of his ambition. He thought he would be completely satisfied if he succeeded in becoming engineer of the shops.

Each morning he went to his office; he hung up his umbrella or his overcoat. Winter came and then summer; first the season of derby hats, then the season of straw hats, of panamas. He sat down, lit a cigarette, and went and opened the door of the neighboring office as soon as he heard the sounds of a man, coughing, footsteps, a slight whistle, snatches of humming, the heavy sound of a body depositing its weight in an armchair. This meant the engineer had arrived. They exchanged the phrases that inaugurated the day, a few anecdotes, some witticisms, the first phrases of the day's duties. Antoine pulled back the soiled tulle curtains. Before him stretched the buildings and the long central avenue of shops where men in overalls went to and fro. On the sidings stood lines of cars with whitewashed hubs and the high traction wheels of locomotives. Along the brick walls and grimy windows of the foundry and boiler shop stood stacks of joists, boilers rusty as the hulls of freighters, piles of reddish scrap iron, copper and steel shavings. To the left of the office grew a little spruce, and some days, when he felt tired, it was enough for Antoine to look at it in order to regain his strength. From the shops issued little jets of steam. The big stack of the central shop belched its shimmering column of black smoke. From his overheated office Antoine heard the factory air full of noises: whistle blasts pierced a confused curtain of metal clangor, vibrations, reverberations like a measured drumbeat—the deafening and angry sound of the big steam hammer of the forge. The foreman arrived, the assistant shop heads, like subalterns reporting, and immediately after Antoine would plunge into the din of the shops. He went to "make his rounds" in the forge, the foundry, the boiler shop, the assembly shop, the car department; sometimes he even pushed open the

door of the shop where the files were resharpened. He inspected
the wooden shed where they sandblasted the boilers, and despite
his big respiratory mask little fragments of silicon would tear the
lobes of his lungs. In the nickel-plating department pieces of steel
bathed in vats of a deadly solution, and the men of the nickel shop
were often hollow cheeked. These were buildings that Antoine
did not enjoy entering very much, buildings where his conscience
was not entirely easy.

The big shops were the world where he was powerful, the
world whose secrets he knew. He walked among the machine
tools like a peasant among his animals. Machines have their personalities just like living animals. There are some you can love because they are not dangerous to man. The great double-wheel tire
lathes revolve slowly and the advancing cutter scales thick spiral
strips from the surface of the steel. They only need to be
watched, they do not bite. There were other machines he detested, deadly machines that carried men with them in their whir-
ring speed, and the hands of their operators hovered over the controls like quick and wary animals who know where the traps are
set. The only peaceful thing about these machines is the little
trickle of water that falls on the parts. The milling machines, the
turret lathes and the presses arouse hatred and defiance. But
cruellest of all are the lumber machines. This was how Antoine
regarded the cast-iron and steel organisms in the lumber shop. A
white light came through the windows, a hospital light; saws and
planes sliced the boards with fits and starts of the motor, the saws
slid through with the rage of a propeller that breaks water on the
crest of a wave. The blades turned with terrific greediness. In this
shop many hands were not whole, many fingers were lopped off,
like so many splinters of wood. Antoine inspected the safety de-
vices. He was accountable for fingers and hands as well as for machines. He thought that the machines were never adequately protected. He must be able to face the workers' delegates, the union
officials, without any qualms.

In the boiler shop, in the assembly shop, sick locomotives stood idle like ships in drydock. Pneumatic hammers rained furious blows on the white-hot rivet heads. The sides of locomotive fireboxes, newly riveted, shone like bronze doors. A boiler moved forward suspended from the overhead traveling crane. Antoine went his rounds. Sometimes he would stop behind a worker, pondering the fact that he had reached the point where he watched the hands of others work. His job consisted exclusively in giving orders and making plans. He calculated, he jotted things down in his notebook. He supervised the progress of tasks that he himself had formulated and that were translated by charts and blueprints. And when a task was delayed he called the head workmen, the foremen, to account. At the forge he would sometimes operate the steam hammer to show how it should strike the object. It was less for the sake of giving an example than to feel his body go through the old motions. He told himself that this was an act outside his functions. A factory head should not bother himself to demonstrate; that is the job of the head workmen. But he could not resist this pleasure which allowed him to escape from his own importance, from his office. He would tell himself that he knew how to command and that he knew the work and the men, but . . . that it was utterly futile to have to write out reports and projects! Why write so much! Everything you wrote outside of formulas and figures boiled down to etiquette, to sheer rhetoric. He returned to his office and told the engineer, "I've made the rounds."

And he plunged into his reports and projects. How many days would it take to repair the tube-plate of the firebox of Engine 3635? How should he begin his report to the chief engineer on the breakdown of the upper cylinder of the 300-ton press? How should he decide on the plan for rearranging the machine tools in the boiler shop? He formulated all the answers and put them in their proper sequence. The plant functioned, the repaired locomotives left the shop bright with paint, their rods shiny as the muscles of cyclists. When Antoine saw them roll away along the tracks, he told himself he had something to be proud of.

He would further tell himself that no one would "put any spokes in his wheels." The engineer of the shops never bothered him. He reserved for himself the administrative functions and rather looked down on the technical side. Antoine had a certain contempt for M. Huet. He was a small man with watery blue eyes as motionless as though they were made of glass. He seemed to have an air of mystery and secrecy about him. In reality, however, there was no mystery; M. Huet was merely an alcoholic. At forty he still derived a childish pride from having graduated from the Polytechnic, from being a member of the powerful confraternity of masters of mines, bridges, big railways, ship building, and the learned professions. M. Huet was a member of the big bourgeoisie, with family traditions. His wife's relations included a general and an ambassador. The prestige of these connections raised the Huets to a rank above what would ordinarily have been appropriate in this town to the engineer of the shops. M. Huet seemed like an exile in the grimy offices amid the coarse tribes of the railways. He sought solace in the modest glamor of provincial cafés. At night a traction inspector, who could hold any amount of liquor, took him home. He knew Latin and he quoted Barrès and Nietzsche. He made Antoine feel that he would always lack this culture, that he would never enter the circles of the big bourgeoisie. M. Huet kissed the hands of the provincial nobility in salons where the Bloyés were not invited. But Antoine's ambition had never aimed so high.

Thus the days took their course. Many threads were woven into a firm fabric, a cloth that grew steadily longer, the whole of life.

14

Antoine Bloyé would have been completely lost and anonymous in one of the big industrial capitals that flourish and smoke along the river banks, near coal fields and iron deposits. But as the head of the company shops, which was the largest enterprise in the town, he acquired importance. For the first time in his life he passed beyond the circle of his workers and immediate neighbors. He could come in contact with the people who ran the petty affairs and politics of the town. He escaped from the narrow environment of his job, which had long confined him to the railway neighborhood as to a little closed world apart from towns. He mingled with the bourgeoisie, he could share the bourgeoisie's consciousness of its own social weight. He belonged to those whom the local papers referred to as "distinguished citizens." The newspaper *Le Combat* had promptly announced his appointment.

There were fewer men in a position to force things on him and he could at last afford to be more particular. There were fewer counselors whom he was impelled to listen to for the sake of advancement or from fear of disfavor. He witnessed the fulfillment of his early dreams of power. What a record for the son of Jean-Pierre Bloyé, obscure employee of the passenger division! Fifteen hundred workers under him, so many machines repaired per year, so many coaches. Industrial activity flowed in channels he had mapped. He felt his own strength and professional knowledge.

In the railways, there exists a sort of hierarchy of the various branches of the service. Each profession judges its various specialties, it has its values, the things it admires, the things it looks down on, in short, its moral code. The division of tracks and buildings, and the division of supplies, are scorned. The divisions of equipment and traction are placed far above them. The rather broad witticisms that the dispatchers shout through the carriage window to the gold-capped stationmasters are overheard with a measure of secret satisfaction by the engineers and depot masters who do not belong to the passenger division. It rather irks the passenger division to be patronized by the traction service. It is fully aware of its own importance; the stationmasters of out-of-the-way stations regard themselves as masters of the railway and try to put in their place the agents of the other divisions who are dressed like civilians. They earn the funds spent by the equipment and traction divisions. They recoup the money the others waste. In the heroic age of railways there was a stationmaster at Angers who said, as he gazed at the engine, "This engine costs *me* 50,000 francs." And the traction division contemptuously denounced "this impudent falsehood."

Jean-Pierre Bloyé had been one of the most insignificant cogs of the passenger division. Antoine measured his own rise by recalling how his father had lived, in his station employee's uniform. He was aware that he belonged to the aristocracy of his profession. Undoubtedly, there were posts to which it was vain for him to aspire. They were reserved for the graduates of the Polytechnic. There are few instances of a graduate of the Arts and Trades becoming chief engineer of equipment and traction. And Antoine realized that many of his schoolmates never got beyond managing a depot or the title of inspector. His father-in-law had gone into retirement as inspector of traction. How could he avoid being satisfied with what he had become and what the future seemed to hold in store for him? How could he continue to put questions to himself, how could he fail to yield to the soft bourgeois contentment that encompassed him? He knew nothing more. Why should he think of the world and the things he had given up, his old comrades, the memory of Marcelle, the days of Saint-Nazaire? He behaved as though all these forces were dead.

The Bloyés had the leisure time to get to know the townspeople. They made connections. Up to then they had been anchored to the line, living in the depot house, a smoke-blackened station annex in a corner of the railroad workers' district. Their only acquaintances had been people connected with the railway and their families. But their new position gave them greater scope. Antoine lived a well-ordered life, just like the employees and officers. They were no longer housed by the company. They had taken their places among the regular city dwellers.

Anne had chosen a day for "at homes," the second Friday of each month. For her this ceremony marked a stage in her social progress. There came a year when she had enough money to think about having a salon, a year when she still had money on hand after paying the insurance premium, and after buying the City of Paris bonds. Her husband's salary permitted her to rent a house with a de luxe room where, a few days out of the year, one could live a life detached from daily cares, a life subordinated to fatuous rules of etiquette and form. When a bourgeois household can add a reception salon to the rooms devoted to eating and sleeping it feels it has made a step forward toward honor and respect. It glories in receiving its friends in a setting specially designed for the purpose. In the rigorous postwar years, ill-fortune often compelled hostesses to surrender this glory; giving up the salon seemed to them a bitter defeat.

The Bloyés' salon was done in Louis XV style. The chairs, the armchairs, the divan were of polished oak covered with green patterned velvet. In the corner was an Empire card table in mahogany with gilded copper inlays, bought at a sale. Antoine never passed in front of this table without being reminded that he could play neither chess, nor backgammon, nor whist, but only rummy,

which he had learned in the depot roundhouses. The floor was
carpeted. A crystal chandelier was suspended from the ceiling.
On the walls hung several pictures with over-heavy frames, a porcelain mandolin, a big Limoges plate on a background of garnet
velvet. On the mantel stood a black marble clock flanked by two
Gien porcelain vases. The draperies had large crocheted insets.
The armchairs had antimacassars, the flower vases were carefully
draped with green velvet covers. Anne Bloyé's friends would tell
her, "What nice taste you have, madame!"

And Anne would answer modestly, "It's quite natural, I am so
fond of my own home. I really don't deserve any credit."

One afternoon a month, five or six ladies would gather in this
room and talk about their husband's careers, their children who
went to school or had scarlet fever or the whooping cough, the
rumors around town—all the topics reserved to women. There
was the wife of a traction inspector whose manners were rather
casual, but who was "so witty," the wives of a division head of the
prefecture, of a lawyer, of a captain, of an engineer in private industry, of a businessman. They were haughty women who spoke
very patronizingly of the "lower classes," the workers; they regarded people below them as "ordinary" or "common." They
wanted to set themselves apart, to be "distinguished." The word
"common" seemed reprehensible to them, they used terms of
horror to describe the common run of people, the ordinary
women. They regarded themselves as a rare species; their children did not attend the public school but the Lycée, or the Institut Saint-Joseph. Their houses played a large role in their lives.
They said, "There is nothing more unattractive than a home
without a personality, a home where you don't feel the woman's
touch."

They took an interest in their servants' love affairs, regarding
them with mingled patronage and irony when they were legiti-
mate and "justifiable." Their servants' loves were touching; they
did not take the same kind of interest in them as they would in

the love affair of an engineer or a member of the Chamber of
Commerce, so serious, so pathetic, so shocking. They talked as
though they were dealing with the habits of a species of animals
unlike themselves, a less rare species. They hated workers, who
were never satisfied. They somehow sensed that it was harder to
laugh at workers than at peasants, for instance. Peasants are so
comical, but a worker does not make you laugh, a laborer on his
job would not let himself be stared at by these ladies as though he
were "some strange animal." They had their charities; they went
to the Toulon district to give advice and show the mothers of
families that they needed the guidance and enlightenment of
bourgeois wisdom. Philanthropic activity permitted them to while
away many fatuous hours; it gave them an exaggerated idea of
their own abilities, their talents, their mission to the poor. They
were born to give guidance to the poor, to teach them; they were
wise for their sake.

"Those people are incredible," they would tell each other.
"They go through life like children. If you only knew how disor-
derly those women are, how unsanitary. Good heavens, what
would they do without women like us to give them guidance!
One sees the most revolting scenes. Can you imagine, I landed
among one family in the Toulon district where the husband
called in his older children when . . . exactly, with his wife, and
he told them: 'It's about time you learned how you were made!'
What horror! What degradation! They live in animal-like prom-
iscuity."

Anne told her husband these things. He felt seized with a sort
of anger whose source was not quite clear to him. The insults that
these "respectable" ladies heaped on "the people" seemed to him
aimed at the most vital part of himself, directed against his own
father and mother, who had been among those the ladies gave advice to. How could he share their opinions without completely
betraying his own childhood, the men and women he had loved?
But wasn't he himself ranged against them, didn't he order them

from above? Such thoughts were very perplexing. They carried one too far afield, they must be repressed. And sometimes he stormed. "Don't tell me all about those prudes! I know what a worker is and I can tell you he doesn't need any advice from those ladies. Do they expect him to be grateful in return for their antics? They make me laugh with their talk of degradation! I'd like to see Mme Brun live on a worker's wage. The workers are worth a hundred of them!"

He fully realized that such protests were inadequate, that they did not compensate for his own desertion to the other side of the fence. It was like a timid gesture of futile goodwill that leaves the world as it was. He forbade his wife to take part in the charity work. She gave in, but she thought regretfully of the fact that charity work would, nevertheless, have allowed her to rise one rung higher in the social ladder, to "see" the noble ladies who directed the charities, to be received by them on the pretext of charity work. And she would say, "Really, I cannot take on any charity work. I am so taken up by my husband, my son, and my house! I know it may be selfishness, but you will excuse me, won't you?"

"We are extremely sorry," replied the ladies.

And Anne would seethe with inward indignation against Antoine. She would tell herself that he would never shed his first skin. She thought of that coarse formula which she would have blushed to say aloud: "The barrel can never get rid of the smell of herring!"

So the Bloyés climbed no higher. Antoine had a kind of internal resistance that prevented him from overstepping certain limits. At the peak of the social pyramid there remained a group whose secrets and games he did not share. But he was by no means an outcast; he was not snubbed by anyone. He received invitations to the annual Chamber of Commerce ball, to the ball given by the Union of the Women of France. When Mme Blanche Toutain came to town to play in *Le Voleur*, by M. H.

Bataille, on the evening engaged by the Chamber of Commerce and Industry the Bloyés sat in the second row of the orchestra stalls, behind the senator and the prefect. On Sunday, when they went to listen to the band in the Allées de Tourny, they exchanged greetings with many people—magistrates, storekeepers, teachers—people whom Antoine did not know intimately but with whom he could exchange a few amenities after Mass, at a garden party, at the pastry shop, with the agreeable feeling of a certain community of interest. These little satisfactions helped him fairly well to forget the men among whom he was born and who continued to walk in darkness.

One year a strike broke out, a strike that one could see coming a long way off, that was born in all corners of France, wherever there were railwaymen. All summer it gathered like a storm and the boards of directors waited for it to burst. All the demands, all the grudges had finally crystallized into a form that was simple and clear to stokers, depot cleaners, and station porters alike. The secretary of the national union had said, "We want a raise and we are going to get it." Those five francs a day, perpetually promised, perpetually postponed, fired the men with a purpose where the money was not the only stake. In autumn, events came to a head. The strike broke out. The Compagnie du Midi raised wages twelve centimes a day. The North stopped working completely, then the Paris-Loire-Midi line, then the East. M. Briand had twenty-one railway workers arrested. M. Briand called up the reservists among the railwaymen for a period of twenty-one days. The strikers thought they could hold out for fifteen days. M. Briand had the premises of *l'Humanité* searched. At the Saint-Paul riding school Jaurès spoke before eight thousand men amid threats of martial law. Jaurès asked, "Will the police run the trains?"

Jaurès denounced the illegal transformation of workers into soldiers. Lépine's police ruled Paris.

In town, Antoine and the engineer waited for the strike to die. First there had been clusters of men in the court, where the workers conversed in low tones, clusters that slowly broke up whenever an inspector or Antoine approached. Then the strike had set in like a sickness. The foremen paced through the shops with long idle steps, under the white glare of the skylights, where the machine belts slumbered as at night. Antoine wore a red armband decorated with four gold stripes. It was like a war. It was indeed a war, in which he had the feeling of having deserted to the enemy. In town, people asked him, "Are you sure, Monsieur Bloyé, that there will be no trouble?"

"Everything will be calm," he answered.

"An eye should be kept on your hotheads," added the frightened merchants.

Soldiers had stacked their guns in the shops. It was like a staff headquarters in wartime. Gendarmes arrived with messages. The police commissioner and the prefect appeared suddenly.

"Just let them try some sabotage!" they said.

These men were prepared to kill workers. Antoine hated them, but he gave them advice on how to break the strike without violence. "I am my own enemy," he would say to himself. His division against himself, the splitting of his life, the chasm that divided his youth from his maturity, were unhappily brought home to him during these conferences with the police.

Antoine lived at the shops; a camp bed had been set up for him in his office. He was unable to sleep. Propping himself on his elbows, he could see the tip of his blue spruce swaying in the October night. But the blue spruce did not console him. He was obsessed by thoughts of the strike. At dawn, when he returned home through the streets of the Toulon district where the powers of the strike still slept, the women opened their shutters, banging them against the walls. Antoine felt their eyes following him as they would have followed a spy. The women conversed from their windows.

"They won't go back this morning," they said.

One evening, the strikers demonstrated. Leaving the workers' quarters, they marched toward the center of town, where usually they only went with their families on Sundays. They were singing. Their song rang through the town. On the boulevards, the coffee drinkers slithered away, hugging the walls. The column entered the Avenue de Paris. The crowd was not choosing at random any street where it might show its power. It was a single being following a definite plan.

"They are going to Huet's house," Antoine told himself, watching the demonstration from a distance.

And in fact that was where they went. At the corner of the Rue Lamartine and the Paris road stood the Huets' handsome stone house. It was a smooth haughty house protected by a fence. All the shutters were closed. The crowd surrounded it. The *Internationale* ceased. There was no sound save the voices, the shuffling feet. The crowd was like a cloud. Shouts burst from the cloud.

"Death to Huet! Death to him!" the workers shouted. A stone struck the house, then two, then a volley of stones. The *Internationale* pealed forth again. Inside his house, the engineer fled to the cellar, shivering with mortal fear. From the crest of the Paris road, the gendarmes swooped down. The strikers booed, a few stones fell in the direction of the blue-clad soldiers and the police. The demonstration turned back toward the Toulon district. Antoine watched it surge back, singing. He was alone; the strikers held the secret of power. These unimportant men possessed the strength, the friendship, and the hope that he was denied. On this evening Antoine understood that he was a solitary man, a man without fellowship. The truth of life was on the side of the men who returned to their poor houses, on the side of the men who had not "made good."

"They are not alone," he thought, "they know where they are going."

The strike ended. The railway workers returned to the shops and depots, to the tune of the *Internationale*. The last flames of the strike were dying out. In their prison cells the thoughts of convicted strikers turned to other battles. The soldiers went back to their barracks. The police drew up their reports. The day of their return, Huet watched the defeated workers pass. He drew back the curtains in his office and said to Antoine, "We've whipped them, the scum."

Antoine made no answer, for he was this man's accomplice. He experienced difficult and mixed emotions. He shared the joy of having defeated the strike, the joy of a strikebreaker. He was amazed by this joy. He hated the workers because secretly he envied them, because he knew deep down inside him that there was more truth in their defeat than in his bourgeois victory.

Eight days after the strike, Antoine ran into an old workmate who had been his fireman for six months in Paris.

"What's become of you, mate?" asked Antoine.

"Fired, fired because of the strike."

Antoine blushed. He felt awkward, like a guilty man. The fireman departed. Antoine never saw him again.

15

Pierre was growing up. First he learned to read, then to write. His bright sayings were quoted at his mother's Friday at-homes. In the evening, he stood by the green garden gate that led to the house. He ran toward Antoine noiselessly on his sandals.

In 1912, he entered the Lycée in the eighth form and he received first prize. He played in the garden, always alone, with the ingenuity and resourcefulness of an only child. While he was going through the paint shop or signing papers in his office, Antoine would recall that today was Thursday and that his son was out of doors, running and shouting; perhaps he was treading on the lettuce, on the strawberries. He collected stamps, he asked for marbles and cap pistols. He had the best games in the world. Alone in the cellar, he played Fantômas; they were showing the film at the Jardin de Paris. In the evening, Antoine made him recite his lessons and told him, "You should never learn your lessons at the last moment. Study them in the evening before going to bed. After you've slept on them you'll find you know them. Your memory works for you while you're sleeping."

Sunday arrived in due course. When the weather was good, Antoine took his son for walks.

"This child does not get enough exercise," he told his wife. "You wrap him in cotton wool. He is only too willing to bury himself in his books."

The two Bloyés would go off.

These walks, which Antoine had first regarded as a part of his paternal duties, grew into a habit that he did not give up until many years later, when the time of his decline had come.

Almost all the roads they took to leave the town wound toward the hills. Only the main Bordeaux road followed the river valley from the point where it begins to widen into the plain. On sunny Sundays between Easter and All Saints' Day and on dry white Sundays in December and January, they went to villages called Chancelade, Champevinel, Campniac, Port à l'Anglais. They cut across through forests of oak, chestnut, and walnut, they crossed the crests of uplands planted with juniper trees and tall thickets of blackthorn. There were vineyards, orchards, ploughed fields. Sometimes the earth gave off the heavy steam of rain; sometimes it was dry as a cliff. In autumn, the wine presses were set up in farmyards or in the barns; Pierre gathered burry chestnuts. Antoine pulled up juniper bushes, hart's tongue, maidenhair, by the roots, and packing the earth around them, he wrapped them in pages torn from newspapers that he carried in his pockets, of which he never read more than the headlines. Such plants can be set between the stones of artificial rockeries, which are a great addition to a city garden. Father and son set out on voyages of discovery, each on his own side of the road. The child could run; as yet there were not many automobiles on the roads. They stopped, they started out again, they shared each other's discoveries.

Sometimes they headed toward the plain where stretched fields of tobacco with their lofty salad leaves, rows of artichokes that the wild hogs trample in the autumn. At the end of the season, bundles of tobacco leaves dried along the dusty roadside, under sheds, exposed to the wind. In springtime, the wind bent the graceful wheat stalks. In damp places, narcissus and wild hyacinths bloomed, and crowfeet with their shiny petals.

A huge elder grew on the Bordeaux road. Some Sundays, when his son returned from high Mass, a package of cakes dangling from his throbbing finger, Antoine would say, "Come on, old fellow, let's go and cut down the elder."

There were hills to the left of the road; on the right the river wound through meadows. Among all the roads that crisscross over the countryside, the main highway was best suited to the steps of two men unafraid of the world. Five kilometers from town stood the elder, and Antoine, who still retained from childhood the lore of little matters, of bird traps, of stone-throwing, of windmills, of slingshots, made his son a pea shooter out of the twigs. Later, they returned in the cool of evening and Antoine would carry his son on his shoulders. He sang the refrains of marching songs and felt happy, a sound man, free from contradictions. When he later recalled those years in the south, that in relation to all the others seemed so secure, like birds gliding on outspread wings—those years when he was tempted to think he had succeeded in life, that they had not lied to him when they said he would make good, that he would become somebody—the first picture that flashed back to him was the picture of his hikes along the southern roads with his great stature dwarfing the child at his side. He again experienced the feeling of strength he had had and then lost, as in the times when he strolled with his engineer comrades from the Paris depot, as in the times when he was a single unit with his traveling mate on the engine.

From the height of his own importance Antoine did not look down on his son's childishness; he treated him as an equal, an ignorant equal who needed lessons. He explained certain matters to Pierre in order to help him find himself in the world. He told him the things he knew, the right time to plant small peas and hoe the Milan cabbage, he showed him how to hold a spade and a hammer, how to throw stones and how to skip them over the water. He also told him that it was hard to change a brace or a front housing plate, that it was hard to bring an express in on time when there was poor coal in the bunker and the injector worked badly. He taught him to like a job well done; a good piece of work always retains its worth. The best thing men do is work. You have your task before your eyes. You can look at it, you have a right to be proud. You bring it into being before you, like a creation. You are not afraid of either man or nature, you can conquer everything. One day, there was a salvaging job to be done in the Creuse. A locomotive had fallen into the river. It seemed literally impossible to raise it, yet he had turned the river, he had salvaged the engine. The grass along the water's edge squirmed with vipers, and the workmen wore rubber boots. He remained whole days with his legs in the water; in the evening, exhausted and frozen, he had attacks of vomiting. The workmen and he were a single being fighting the river. How proud he felt the day the engine was back on the rails. They had all gazed at it as though it were a living being. They had conquered the weight, the current, the mass of metal, the time of year.

"That was a fine piece of work, old fellow," said Antoine.

Pierre listened, all ears. Men are full of secrets and children expect a great deal from these soothsayers, these masters of wisdom. Antoine sensed that he should teach his son to build toys and to like pieces of work well done by head and brain. He also taught him the signs of the weather.

Some Sundays Anne accompanied her husband and son. She had gained considerably after Pierre's birth; she was heavy and hated long walks, so they would barely reach the edge of town. Antoine loathed the emptiness of those countryless Sundays. He found that only the mornings were to his liking—what with getting up later than usual, the idle pottering to and fro between his room and the bathroom, his cigarettes, the paper, the hot water for his shave, Pierre scampering on the stairs. Most of the morning belonged to him, for Anne and Pierre left at ten for high Mass in their Sunday best and only came home at noon. Antoine sat reading in the dining room, he heard the servant moving the pots and pans or bumping her broom against the baseboard in the salon. He went out into the garden to see how his plants were getting on. He passed the time of day with a neighbor. Sometimes he dressed and set out to meet his family. On days when the weather was fine—days when you look at the sky at seven o'clock and say, "It's going to be a fine day," and by eleven the heat haze has risen and there isn't a cloud in the sky, when the whole town looks more Italian, more Roman than ever—they would take a carriage, one of those wedding vehicles called landaus covered with a white fringed canopy like English baby carriages. They would go along at a trot; sometimes they would get out, stretch their legs, stop for a drink in a village café. Lindens shaded the towpath that bordered the canal. The reflection of the branches in the water was unruffled by a single ripple; to the right, beyond the gardens, the river followed the canal along the foot of wooded hills. It was a deep olive green, almost black, with a strip of sunlight. There was no other sound save the noise of the wheels and the horses' hoofs. Now and then the notes of a bugle came from the barracks. Birds beat their wings in among the reeds of the canal. Magnolias and palm trees grew in the yards of the round tiled houses between the canal and the city.

"What weather!" said Anne.

And Antoine, who was melting in the heat—the cloth of his vest seemed on fire in spots—softly echoed her as though human life were indeed good, utterly clear, utterly simple and devoid of uncertainty.

"What beautiful weather."

At Caesar's camp, on the other side of the Campniac ferry, Anne picked crocuses, meadow saffron, and eglantine in season, but her black dress and her hat with its over-fuzzy ostrich plumes, brought from Aden in metal tubes, took all the meaning out of these country jaunts. Manly conversation, the intimate companionship of men, was lacking, and both father and son felt more constrained than usual.

16

Every year Antoine went to a little village of Morbihan for his month's vacation. Anne and her son left sooner, the day after school closed, and he would join them the first or the fifteenth of August. He almost always went by way of Paris for a taste of the atmosphere of the main division offices, like a sailor who between two voyages visits the home offices of his company. He would see two or three friends and then leave from that same Gare d'Austerlitz where formerly he had come with his engine to hook on to the head of so many trains. He crossed the depot whose every corner he still knew. Between the dome of Salpêtrière and the bridge of Orléans-Ceinture stretched the setting of his 'twenties, beyond the palings rose new buildings, erected since his time, that faced on the Rue du Chevaleret. Every stone, every sidewalk of the XIIIth arrondissement was charged with memories, and that young man in a cap, walking under the left bridge toward the Rue Watt, was himself on his way to the Café d'Orléans, to Marcelle, to that other life that might have taken the place of his actual life, that would have been utterly unlike his life as it was. Then the Brittany express, having crossed the main suburbs, the royal bridge of Juvisy, the big ramp of Etampes, and the ridges around Brétigny, began to glide over the surface of the Beauce; the train and Antoine lost sight of the last stone houses, the town's last piles of scrap iron, the Beauce stretched before them like a sea, steeples rising like ships' masts. The weather was almost invariably one of those fine days of the west in summer; washing hung out to dry in the farmyards, big dogs chased their own shadows; at grade crossings and before the laurel bushes of wayside stations, groups of children, young girls waved at the passing trains. The Touraine caves yawned in the tufa cliffs and vineyards striped the rounded back of the Anjou uplands. Between Angers and Nantes, around Champtoceau, Ingrandes, and Oudon, great sheets of water stretched over the fields. Loire flatboats were moored along the embankment's edge; square nets were hung on racks to dry.

Antoine measured the hours by the length of the rails, by the periodic clack of the bogies. When he took a night train he reached Pont-Château at sunrise. On the square, facing the freight station, stood the big flour-mill building with its inscription. Antoine had never gone back to Pont-Château. Who would have recognized him in his native town? He was completely cut off from his childhood. He knew every station of this country. Drefféac, Saint-Gildas des Bois, Saint-Nicolas de Redon, Redon, where his parents still lived. At Redon, you knew by the color of the fields, by the feel of the wind, that the train had entered Brittany, and soon after you arrived at Vannes and Auray.

At Auray, he took a little train where old colorless cars and the company's old copper engines ended their days. This line passed through Belz Plœmel, through Plouharnel-Carnac, through Kerhostin, through Saint-Pierre-Quiberon; it rolled on like a river through gorse-covered heath, fields of buckwheat, and groves of coastal pine. No one was in a hurry to get there, and on either tip of the peninsula, at both ends of the branch line, they spoke the same dialect, wore the same headdress. Along the track grew fields of onions with large purple heads; piles of grass burned. Through open windows came the smells of the tide, of resin, and of the pitch burning in the distant gravel pits at the edge of the cliff. Gusts of wind struck you in the face like damp washing. At Saint-Pierre, Antoine got off. He followed the track by the plate layers' path till all at once he came in sight of that long stretch of windswept coastland, with all its villages, Kergroix, Kervihan, Kervidenvel, Kerbouleven, Kerniscop, Manémeur, that clustered around him every summer. The gulls, cormorants, and petrels flitted about and he recognized them from one year to the next. Amid the birds of the south, he had not forgotten the shape of their beaks, the color and arrangement of their plumage, their manner of flight, cutting the air with the blade of their wings and buoying themselves up on it like swimmers. They flew high to make known that the good weather would last.

The first evening of vacation, Antoine, dressed in loose summer clothing, would leave with Pierre for the waterfront. Fishermen walked along the quay moving slowly, hard to budge. The fishing ships rounded the breakwater in silence with only the creaking of their pulleys, like Flying Dutchmen tamed by these still waters. A brig or a schooner was moored to the jetty and the men were cooking their supper. A wisp of smoke rose from the blue or green painted galley. Sometimes on the square in front of the low customs building, girls danced to airs of mingled sadness and restlessness like tunes from Asia. The blows of a hammer on the hull of a sardine boat that was being caulked suddenly ceased, and a profound peace settled over the evening. At such times, Antoine would forget the noise of men and factories. He would spend in leisure one month torn from his life of work.

The peninsula was a narrow stretch of land almost unbroken by hills or dales. It was studded with villages that all faced in the same direction so that only the gables of their houses were exposed to the seawind. Each of these villages contained little gardens pinched between granite walls, full of fig trees, tamarisks, virgin vines, hortensias, morning glories, and hollyhocks. At the peak of the peninsula stretched a long forest of coastal pine where the cracking of trunks rang out like vegetable fireworks, punctuated by the dull thud of the cones falling on the needles and dwarf eglantines. The sky grazed the tops of a clean countryside girdled

by the sea. Antoine showed his son the fens where vipers hid—
once they saw one as they were walking along the road—the bull
pen, the farms.

"Next year," Antoine kept saying, and he might as well have
said, "In twenty years, in a hundred years."

For this month passed in security and Antoine forgot the future; was there such a thing, need he reckon with it? He conjured
neither cares nor plans. He was completely on vacation, vacant, at
nature's disposal, endowed with liberty which was not gainsaid
by the fullness and the friendliness of the season. It was a truce,
an interim. All the fetters of industrial life, of bourgeois life, all
the fetters of vanity were broken, all conflicts were suspended.

For sixty francs a year the Bloyés rented a gatekeeper's house
which stood alone on the sea cliff. From the attic you could see
the whole peninsula, the glittering half moon of the bay, the
grassy forts, the signal tower at Kerbouleven, the mills. At night,
the lighthouses flashed their warnings through the darkness and
the long luminous arm of the light of Belle-Ile-en-mer revolved,
throwing its brief flash on the bedroom walls. Of a Sunday,
groups of people walked along the road toward the town; you met
dump carts laden with corn stalks, sometimes a burial procession
descended toward the church of Saint-Pierre: a drowned man
being brought back to the mainland, being returned to earth on a
cart covered by a white cloth, drawn by two cows. In time Antoine learned the names of all who went by, and passed the time
of day with them. Only the strangers, in white trousers and
yachting caps, escorting women in light dresses, huge straw hats,
and white tulle veils, stopped to ask the way to Port-Blanc or the
time of the train to Auray, with considerable haughtiness and insolence.

Along the track amid the reeds and blackberries grew wild
hay, ferns and fennel, flowering plants, mullein, borage, and mal-
low, shepherd's purse, and plants that grew from seeds scattered
by passing freight trains.

In a triangular plot of sandy soil, beyond the level crossing, Antoine grew his crop of potatoes and toward the beginning of September he dug them, he churned up the powdery earth that ran through your fingers. He retained a last link of kinship with the soil. He had not completely forgotten the peasant gestures of his fathers. Vaguely he was finding an outlet for the instincts of the farmer he might have become, instincts that were not completely dead within him. Seldom does the instinct of the soil die out entirely in men of the west; the strolls of Parisians in the Paris suburbs, the little workers' gardens that cling to the outskirts of cities, the taste for nature testify to its presence.

Thus time flowed on, unobstructed by the barriers, the dams that industrial pursuits and city calendars raise in its course. From morning to night the sun alone marked the passing hours. Antoine lost the mannerisms of the Rue Combe des Dames, of a prominent member of his community, in the farmyards where the hired hands carried newborn calves on their shoulders, wrapped around them like a horse collar. How could you think of anything but the animals, the crops, the sea? You were glad to be rid of city folk, who are hard to know, hard to understand, with their reticence, ambitions, hates, and schemes. Antoine did not care to think that hatred and defeat, master and servant, were known to the fields as well as they were within factory walls. For him at any rate there was no conflict, no travail. Anne, resting from household duties, was never cross, or worried; she never got irritated for imaginary reasons. She also took walks; she embroidered. She would sit with her husband and son on the deserted beaches, and the ships of sand that Pierre fashioned dissolved in the rising tide like the schemes of man.

The weather was fair enough for you to go to sleep without a qualm. Sometimes it was so quiet you could hear the distant strokes of the long oars of the fishing boats, the creaking of the pulleys as the crews set or reefed their sails. Over the horizon, the masts of a steamer rose, then its smokestack, then its hull; the

earth was really round. Some days, Antoine went fishing on the
bay with sailors from Saint-Pierre. The red-sailed smacks of Port-
Navalo or Arzon drifted by. At midnight, the bells answered each
other across the bay. Hazily the thought would drift through Antoine's mind that it was easy to be happy. What a truce, plunged
in oblivion of fret and weariness and war, in this little rounded
world that ended at the isthmus of Penthièvre, where there was
nothing but the road and the tracks! This area was enough for a
man who settled down among its sands, its pastures, and its winding shores strewn with sea shells, swept by the long gusts of the
breeze, which bore the smell of resin and iodine. Perhaps this life
was real life and the life of the factories an irreparable mistake
that no one had discovered.

But toward the fourth week of vacation the summer began to
wane; the parched tops of the potatoes in the fields showed the
turn of the year. They had to go inside earlier in the evenings.
Anne would say, "The days are shortening. Did you think to
bring the coats?"

And about this time, Antoine began thinking of other things.
The images of his work, the faces of the men on the job rose in
his mind. The country and seaside world softly receded; a new
world arose softly in its place. Antoine experienced a longing for
action and command, he asked himself how the shops had been
getting along without him. He felt out of place, useless, idle; he
had at last become bored, he wandered about with a sort of restlessness until finally the day of departure arrived. For he was not
used to long periods of idleness and the air of the engines was his
nourishment.

Thus Antoine's life unfolded in the age of his maturity. He was
surrounded by a soothing peace. Among the metaphors men use
to describe existence, that of mountain topography is not inappropriate. There are plains, sharp, steep inclines, precipices, and pla-

teaus. People themselves say they are "at the bottom," "at the peak," of the range, that they are going down "the other side." They are well aware that they are travelers and that their course crosses invisible divides, great stretches without storms or accidents, where their eyes discern the next stage from afar.

Antoine had had his ups and downs. There had been times when his every effort seemed futile and when he had known weariness and despair. He had stumbled through deep hollows where the daylight did not penetrate, where the heights of the sides overwhelmed him with a hostile shadow. Then he had climbed back, he had cast off the weights that encumbered him without worrying over their possible value, and now suddenly he finds himself walking with his full stride. He breathes to the full capacity of his lungs. The country round about seems so endless and tranquil that he does not stop to ask himself whether he is whole or mutilated. He does not see where his journey will end. He has come to a plateau greater than any he has traveled over hitherto, and his fellow-travelers congratulate each other on the ease of their journey. Antoine has reached the age when man feels endowed with his surest strength. He thinks he is utilizing all his resources. He believes that he is firmly established on earth, that the landmarks of his position are visible from afar. He advances with an even tread. Antoine thinks his life has taken definite shape. He is a man who has made good; many people greet him and envy him. His wife is not sorry she married him. His parents in the fastness of their age and solitude tell each other that the sacrifices they made to raise him were not in vain. He is the man whom schoolteachers point to as a model for workers' children. When Anne asks him if he feels happy, he answers that he does. Barely does a recess of his being harbor a certain resistance, a tiny solitary force of protest and torment which is crushed beneath the structure of the social man but which is waiting to expand, which cannot die. It is this force within him that makes Antoine always hesitate an instant before replying that he is happy. For he must cast it off. When it is cast off he finally sees himself with the same eyes as other men do. He approves of himself the way others approve of him, and he stretches his arms to right and left in the space of his day, like a being at peace with the world. For him the sun is at its zenith. It is as though eternally suspended in a cloudless summer sky, whence it will never go down.

But it will go down.

Part III

That night passed; all nights—even the starless night before dissolution—must wear away.
—Charlotte Brontë
in *Villette*

17

July 1914 was a splendid month.

Day followed stormless day; the temperature slowly rose toward August. The huge trees on the Allées de Tourny, the Cours Bugeaud, and the Cours Montaigne, the lindens bordering the canal, began to lose their less resilient leaves and were coated with white dust. Puddles spread around garden hoses and dried up almost immediately. The dust shrouded the red and black paint of the shops. All the cabs and landaus had their tops up. The cafés, in the shelter of their red-striped awnings, exercised a power of attraction that passers-by could not resist. The waiters emptied the lukewarm water from the carafes on the sidewalk. In the coolness of back rooms the manille enthusiasts hung their coats on the rack and played in their shirt sleeves. The public parks were full of children whose mothers idly knitted mufflers that wouldn't be needed till autumn. The last classes ended at the Lycée and there remained within the hollow empty walls no one save the assistant headmaster, the assistant bursar, and the handymen.

In the factories the workers wore nothing but their overalls. The streets were empty and women lay half-naked on their beds behind closed shutters. The only passers-by wore black alpaca coats and straw hats. In the station square, the horses hung their heads under their canvas bonnets and the drivers idly chatted in the shade of the acacias.

In the evening, the city awoke to life. Workers' families

strolled along the canal embankment and down the alleys of the lower town. On the river, rowboats went as far as the Campniac ferry, as far as Maladrerie, and young girls cooled their moist hands by letting them trail in the water. Along the boulevards, men in white trousers, women in light dresses with white lace trim strolled about as on holiday evenings. Never were the fireworks more impressive than they were that year. In the big cafés, at the Comédie, the Café de Paris, orchestras played romances and waltzes. The violins gladdened all hearts with the graceful turns of "Dream Waltz" and the "Merry Widow." The screens of open-air cinemas two stories high billowed at the least breath of wind. The newspapers lay piled on the marble tables and the café management supplied the ladies with cardboard fans that bore the figures of graceful women clad in airy garments, with long wavy tresses, decorated with flowers and ribbons.

Around July 15, after school closed, bourgeois families began to leave. In the peaceful districts of the southwest you saw whole rows of closed shutters; landaus laden with trunks and suitcases headed for the station. Trains leaving for the mountains or the seaside were full. They had to double the expresses, and the passenger division was driven to distraction. The people who remained in the city awaited their turn to go on vacation. Men whose wives and children were already in the mountains or at the seaside met at the Café de la Comédie and killed the fine July evenings with the awkwardness of bachelors. Then they returned home to houses that smelt of moth balls, where the armchairs wore striped covers. Along the way they saw couples who kissed lingeringly, and the sight of love disquieted them. Some spent their evenings in the brothels of the lower town. Drops of perspiration coursed on the perfumed skin of the brothel girls, it was so hot that, stifled by the stuffiness of the windowless parlors, they sometimes got up and went to sit by the door, letting the night surge over them. Others slept with their servants. Others slept alone.

There were perhaps a hundred people in town who every morning unfolded the Paris papers impatiently, with a worried frown: a few pessimists, a few workers belonging to the unions, a few socialists. Those people were expecting not a vacation, but something very different. In these houses, on these streets, a few ears attuned to the subtler noises of the earth anxiously caught the first rumbles of the gathering storm and were aware of the danger signals in Europe. But all the rest of the town lived on in peace, with a bright confidence in the future. The Sarajevo assassination, the diplomatic notes, the conversations of Cambon, Grey, and Sazonov were all part of the season's news. Wise commentators remarked that in summer the least bit of news is exaggerated. Others said that the strength of armaments made war utterly impossible. The workers in the shops believed with all their might that socialism would prevent the war. The readers of *l'Humanité* passed around their paper on account of Jaurès' articles. But the Caillaux trial aroused the interest of more people than the threat of war. They discussed at length Caillaux's rude interjections, the fight of his two wives around the republican hero, this whole tangle of love and politics that gave a scandalous and romantic appearance to the intriguing struggle of the Right and Left. There was Poincaré's visit to the Tsar. The first pictures of the military parade at Tsarskoe Selo flashed on the billowing cinema screens. The town's inhabitants felt proud of the reception that ancient Russia had accorded the little man.

The last week of peace rolled by. The orders for general mobilization flashed over Europe like streaks of lightning. The last diplomatic telegrams winged through the sky. Even these shocks barely ruffled the town's serenity. The number of men who were worried slightly increased. Antoine Bloyé was finally among them. In the railroad world, there was already a certain bustle, a certain noise of preparation perceptible to a man as familiar as he was with his company's atmosphere. Instructions began to pour down from the main office. He discovered that war was completely assembled, like a mighty engine. To start it moving all that was needed was to press the button. On July 31, Antoine bought *l'Humanité* as though to find a ray of hope. He guessed that the only voice capable of truth was to be found there. He read:

Crowds may yield to such insane panics and we cannot be sure that governments will not do the same too. They spend their time (delightful occupation) frightening each other and reassuring each other. And this, if we are not mistaken, can go on for weeks. Today we must appeal to the people's intelligence, to their reason, if we want them to be able to retain self-mastery, subdue the panic, overcome nervousness, and dominate the course of men and events, that the human race may be spared the horrors of war. . . .

Antoine was a man without political ideas. He was merely a man who wanted to continue doing the work he knew how to do in peace, and he turned toward his workers as toward the sole force capable of protecting his own life, his own peace. There were millions of men in France like him—men who, like him, had no knowledge of why wars occurred. Antoine telegraphed his wife to return from Brittany immediately.

The evening of the thirty-first Jaurès was killed.

The white notices of the general mobilization were pasted up on the walls. Under the August sun, a tremendous patriotic exaltation suddenly filled the peaceful hearts of this town, too remote, too steeped in its ancient happiness to believe itself endangered by the ill outcome of battles. Processions swept through the streets and Jewish stores hastily drew down their blinds. On the Rue de Bordeaux, the Maggi branch was burned. The café habitués felt civic, warlike hearts surge within them. They embarked on adventure. They let their fighting instincts and their hatred, long wrapped up in the cotton wool of bourgeois life, take their course. The tales the newspapers started to print fanned their ardor. The stories and the songs they had learned in school, the reflex motion of saluting the flag, the legends of far-off Alsace, the words which were part of their vocabulary—right, civilization, science, liberty —were all brought to bear. In the squares, they discussed the first war news. Men would announce, "I am leaving in two days, in three days."

The reserve officers, already in uniform, lounged in the station doorways, their binoculars and map cases stacked together. At the theater the orchestra leader harangued his little group and shouted: "I am exempted, gentlemen, but I shall enlist. I ask that I be allowed to leave im-me-dia-tely! Have you seen Lavedan's admirable declaration? He shows us our duty."

He thereupon pulled a clipping out of his pocket and read:

At this moment, just as I was coming out on the Place de la Concorde, I saw Barrès a few steps away at the corner of the Rue Royale. I clasped the hand he tendered and I cried in a choking voice: "Ah! my friend! what can I say to you?" "There is nothing to be said," he answered. "What can any of us say? The hour has struck. That's all. I am full of hope." And with an accent of charming, youthful simplicity and a well-bred motion of his upraised chin, as though speaking of some whim that one should forgive him, he declared: "I am enlisting," and with these words the president of the League of Patriots left me to lose himself in the crowd that had made way for him, friendly and respectful as though it understood and realized that he should not be delayed.

"There, gentlemen! There's an example for you!"

The infantry regiment and the artillery regiment left amid hurrahs and war bouquets. From the sidewalks, men and women shouted: "Hurrah for the war! Hurrah for France! Hurrah for the army!" The statue of the fighters of 1870 was smothered in wreaths and bouquets. The president of the Veterans of 'Seventy said in the cafés, "This was bound to happen. For forty-four years they've been insulting us!"

Train followed train out of the station. The waiting rooms

were full of distraught civilians who had missed the last train available before the transport of troops started. The Ladies of the Red Cross, already attired in the white linen uniforms they were to retain till the last day of the war, organized buffets under the station awnings, awaiting the first contingents of sick and wounded.

In the offices of the railway shops, the order for the departure of the eligible workers was posted. This work was done in the evening, when the machine tools slept and when only a tiny thread of smoke issued from the central chimney. The workers waited, shuffling about in the silence; when the engineer arrived they entered the office in small groups. The engineer craned over the workers' backs and smirked at his own thoughts. The second evening he said suddenly, "They should be kept amused, these children."

And he began juggling with two chairs. They fell and he tried again. Antoine pulled him by the sleeve, saying to him in a whisper, "Control yourself!"

The doomed workers remarked between their teeth, with the hatred that was in them, "He's still drunk, the swine!"

The first war bulletins appeared on the boards of the Havas Agency. The patriotic papers started coming out and all the children began to read *Les Trois Couleurs* and to stick little flags into maps of the front. In the company shops, the turret lathes forgot their peacetime output and began to bite steel shells and copper caps. Under the sheds rose piles of "75" shells, rapidly absorbed by the war. The factory men were in the war. Antoine was in the war. He accepted it at length with the same credulous meekness as the rest of France, and when the troops filed past he doffed his hat like everyone else. He kept saying, "It's a matter of six months, or a year."

The town had rapidly taken on wartime habits. At the end of the summer months, when autumn tinged the hilltops, when the victory of the Marne had spread an intoxication of triumph through all the departments of France, it settled down to a new life. Towns are as pliant as the softest women. It does not take many strong men to mold them. As in other years, the smell of truffles, *foie gras,* of apples and walnuts rose from the market place. The town did not forget its peacetime pleasures. The Institut Saint-Joseph, the convent of Sainte-Marthe, received the first batches of wounded with their cargo of mutilation, gangrene, pus, and suffering. The lady nurses fluttered around the bedsteads of the wounded. Some of them, who had been regarded as rather fast in peacetime, seduced the convalescents. At Saint-Joseph, Mme Astier never passed the cot of a sergeant whose testicles had been torn off without saying with a sigh, "What a pity! My handsomest patient!"

The ladies who had not given up civilian life brought the wounded baskets of peaches and grapes. In the autumn of 1914 grapes cost three sous a pound. In winter, they knitted caps, scarves, and sweaters. From their old linen they made strips and bandages, which the doctors did not dare refuse. They patterned their lives after stories their mothers had told them of the war of 'seventy-one. Bourgeois houses opened their doors to the convalescents, but the mistresses of these houses were relieved when these "heroes," who took up so much room at their dinner tables, left for the front. Soon they learned the names of the town's first dead. Old Monsieur de Leyment received news that his two sons had been killed on the Marne and the town saw him go about like a phantom of the war. He walked along with drooping head, then suddenly would lift his face and wail like a dog excited by the moon. At the Lycée the chaplain wore red frock and blue cape when he said Mass. He had a big white face like the chorus man of a traveling show and he walked like a woman in disguise.

Batches of refugees reached town, fleeing southward, from Pas-de-Calais and Belgium. As winter asserted itself the war stole in slowly like a subtle poison. The blooming enthusiasm of the first months began to wilt. You heard people say, people who were former enthusiasts, "You'd better start thinking of yourself. Everyone should look out for his own safety."

The orchestra leader was working in an office.

The town's inhabitants sank back into their little lives, solitary and mistrustful. The outward signs of the war gradually grew fainter in the town. There were no more uniforms on the streets, men walked about with canes and crutches, stylish women wore hats that imitated policemen's helmets. The children at the Lycée, poorly watched by old schoolmasters who had been summoned from retirement, ran off to go sliding on the ice on the swimming area and the canal. There was a certain imperceptible disorder. The cathedral began holding services in memory of the dead.

At the shops, Antoine's thoughts were taken up with the shells, the upkeep of the machines, which were suffering from the wear and tear of war. Military inspectors prowled about the plant and Antoine no longer felt at home. Again he experienced the tension of former times when he feared catastrophes, again the weariness, again the fear of committing irreparable mistakes. These fuses, these shells were unfamiliar objects. The engineer told him, "Don't you worry, Bloyé. I'm on the job, I'll protect you. I'm an old artillery officer myself. Everything'll be all right. I'm on excellent terms with the inspectors."

How could he rely on this man who was perpetually drunk, unhinged by the war and who, when he was tipsy, praised the strength of the Germans, the organization of the Germans, and prophesied the defeat of the Allied armies? The catastrophe came with a threatening and obscure telegram that was confirmed two days later by a letter couched in military terms:

18th District Artillery
Inspection of metal plants of Toulouse

Depot of Bordeaux

No. 457   Confirmation of telegram
The battalion commander and detachment commander to Monsieur the engineer of the shops:

I have the honor of confirming my telegram of today to the following effect:

You have committed errors in verifying imbalance of "75" shells. External plate should have cavity that could be moved off center to correct imbalance. Cease further verification. Explanations follow letter.

Antoine read these explanations. He could not grasp the meaning of these words; his brain was not yet accustomed to them.

When a shell has been retouched for balance, the surface of the body is no longer cylindrical. It must therefore be ground on the high spot and on the groove between the band and the base.

The engineer said, "We're mixed up in a messy business. They're determined to accuse us of deliberate sabotage. What are those inspectors up to?"

Bloyé answered, "We can't see to everything, we can't verify every delivery ourselves. That's what the artillerymen are here for."

M. Huet smirked. "We're the ones who'll pay for it, my dear Bloyé, and not they. We'll be held responsible, and there are plenty of people who would be only too glad to have your job and mine. It's obvious you don't know these dear artillery fellows as well as I do. We'll be bounced, I'm telling you!"

An investigation started. Antoine discovered he would be blamed for a production accident capable of harming national defense, which had become the sole deity in these years of upheaval. He presented his case and defended himself. But old peacetime virtues, "a past of work and honor," were scant protection against the rigorous requirements of the war and the manufacture of arms. His whole career, his growing importance, were unavailing against an error of a few tenths of a millimeter in the thickness of the base of a shell, a shadow of inaccuracy in the diameter of the groove. Painstaking inspectors examined the shells in the rejected shipment. These officers took on the airs of judicial investigators. The investigation dragged on, they no longer questioned either

M. Huet or Antoine, but the inspectors, the head workmen. The town started talking of the incident at the shops. It was a time when their patriotism filled all Frenchmen with a sort of fever of suspicion, a faculty for making mountains out of molehills. People talked of the defective shells on the avenues and in the cafés. They said, "An error? Don't tell me that! Negligence in supervision? Maybe, but such negligence is a crime. There are circumstances when negligence in supervision or an error borders on a deliberate felony."

Antoine kept saying, "All the same, you can't be at every machine at once."

People would answer him coldly, "Undoubtedly, undoubtedly, but it's very mortifying for you all the same."

In the lower town, the women doing their marketing would say, "The shells were made so badly that they would have turned back on the French and killed them. There's something crooked in it."

In their gardens, Antoine's neighbors pretended not to know him. These potterers felt the cares of public safety weighing down upon them. When Antoine neared a group of strollers, he often perceived that the conversation had just changed subject. The inspector told his friends, "Bloyé is cooked. There's a job for someone."

These things were passed on to Antoine. He was given to understand that a widespread campaign was being conducted against him from which he could not defend himself. He fell from the heights of his importance. He was no longer anybody. He was, in fact, removed. M. Huet was "bounced" as he had predicted. They were given to understand that they were lucky to get off so easily in a period that swarmed with "traitors" and spies. Antoine finally left. The local paper did not mention his departure. But on the eve of the day he took the train, his workers presented him with a bronze statuette on a green velvet pedestal. It portrayed a woman with the haunches of a smith and the arms of a stonecutter standing behind an anvil; it was a mocking personification of Industry. In a shed of the shops, along a table laden with bottles and plates of biscuits, the managers and workers were lined up. When the time for the speeches came, M. Huet said with a smirk, "The adieu of Fontainbleau."

A foreman got up to read a speech. At this same moment, the workers who had not taken part in the toasting were remarking, "A blackleg is going to throw bouquets at the boss, if that means anything."

The speech began.

"Monsieur Bloyé,

"Today the personnel of the shops conveys to you its feelings of esteem and gratitude on the occasion of your departure.

"We know you as an intelligent, considerate chief, who long ago discarded the outworn forms, the theatrical and haughty mannerisms which were all very well for our former chiefs but which, in the socially minded times we live in, are obsolete. Motivated by justice and truth, despite the inflexible strictness of company rules, you have known how to obtain from your large personnel the maximum measure of effort and conscientiousness in work, while at the same time you treated them with the friendliness that has made you so popular among us. At the moment when a decision from above calls you to a distant post, we are especially sorry to part with you. Permit us to tell you publicly how great will be the memory you leave among us. The name of Bloyé, if it has not been engraved in the manner of the great in the marble of posterity, will yet remain deeply graven in our memories. To have been a great chief, to have undertaken the heaviest responsibilities in the times of greatest difficulty, to leave accompanied by the unanimous regret of his personnel, is not that the loftiest of rewards, the most sublime of moral satisfactions? May the bronze that is offered you today, into which each of us has placed a fragment of his heart, bring back your thoughts to us and cause you to relive the long years of good feeling and steadfast toil we spent together. In the name of everyone, Monsieur Bloyé, we thank you!"

It was like the day they handed out the prizes at the secondary school in Saint-Nazaire. Shades of Epinal! The good student, then the good boss. But where were the leaders of the plant, the secretary of the union? While the pompous phrases of the speech were slowly unrolling, Antoine thought of the men who were not present. Their absence betokened an enormous silent disapproval. It was their presence that he would have prized the most. Their presence would have justified him. But he knew that there were men in blue, with oil-smeared hands, who had not forgotten the strike of 1910 and the groups of soldiers in the courtyard.

This foreman with his bushy mustache like that of a police agent and his gross empty flatteries! I was polite to them, I didn't treat them like dogs, like soldiers, I got help for their wives in childbirth and after that I made them sweat just the same for the King of Prussia, for Baron Rothschild, and there was more than one who had an arm torn off, and Brevet whose skull was fractured and his brains oozed out, his companions placed his shoes to the right and left of his head like candles, when I talked to them they were polite and knew how to keep their distance. I flattered them to encourage them in their work, I appealed to their pride, obtain the maximum effort from your personnel, the locomotives come out from a complete overhauling in twenty days, that speeded them up and I'll no longer order them, I'll no longer be the boss and I like being the boss and more than one of them knows that I'm against them and my being against them got me nowhere and I am thanked like a pickpocket. They put their heart into this bronze, that's a lie, I wish it were true but it's a lie, an utter lie, years of good feeling because I was not rude in talking to them, hypocrite, old scoundrel who knew the worker for the company's benefit and who is it who's getting up there, it's Lafarge, the strikebreaker, another speech, no, a poem.

We offer you this bronze in everybody's name
It is the fruit of a unanimous desire
Our tribute to a chief who leaving us can claim
Our deep regret for one we always shall admire
Accept our bronze; to you with every coming year
It shall recall a brilliant past of radiant light
A noble page whereon the honor of a whole career
Inscribed in golden letters that are ever bright
This bronze our glowing tribute does personify
The tribute no adversity can modify
A block that was chiseled with worthiest views
Where each put his heart in by giving his sous!

Idiot, with his grammar school alexandrines, he doesn't mean a word of it.

Antoine replied, thanking these men who did not know the truth. He thanked them in the appropriate tone as though he were a priest. Somebody sang. It was quite a little party. The farewell became a get-together. The inspector, who had a bass voice, sang in his turn.

O ma locomotive
Quand ton âme captive
en vapeur fugitive
sort de tes flancs brûlants
tu pars, belle d'audace,
tu dévores l'espace
et ta colonne passe
comme un éclair dans l'air

He was the very one who was counting on getting his, Antoine Bloyé's, post. Louse, said Antoine between his teeth.

Then he left. For the last time Antoine crossed the threshold of the plant that had been the scene of his pride, of his advance, the period of his greatness. The little blue spruce stood utterly motionless. Men passed along the tracks. Everything went on perfectly well without him. There was no longer a single paper, a single personal object in his old drawer, on his old desk. Outside the weather was fine. Dusk was coming on. A slight breeze rustled over the housetops. The abandoned cemetery that he passed every day was choking with green plants, with grass and flowers, like a garden, and the iron cross where the paths converged was covered with bindweed and clematis. A brook flowing from the hills ran over a bed of pebbles where you could see the hollow imprint of fossil seashells; it was an unusually gay and lively brook. The women's faces began to be gilded by the sinking sun. Children cried on stairways. Cats started to head for the houses after a day of idleness. Along the boulevards, the passers-by stopped to read the bulletins. It was the forty-fourth week of war. The heights of Notre-Dame-de-Lorette had been attacked, the Germans were attacking the sugar refinery at Souchez, the French soldiers were attacking the labyrinth of Neuville-Saint-Vaast. The papers reprinted Lloyd George's speech at Manchester, where he said: "We need shells, guns, machine-guns. Each time you send our army all the munitions they ask you for, tell yourselves that you have saved so many human lives, so many brave soldiers. Shells, more shells." What irony! Antoine hung his head. The springtime was more oppressive than the frost or the August sun. He walked like a man disgraced, like a man let out of prison who wears his shame on his brow and on his clothes, which do not have the creases of a free man. When he reached the end of the Rue de Paris, he discovered he was hungry. He thought to himself, "It's curious to want to eat in spite of everything."

That was how things were.

He would go on eating; all his life, whatever happened, he would go on eating and sleeping. He no longer had any pride, he was like a soldier who has been demoted. He suddenly remembered the proverbs that his mother-in-law quoted: "An empty sack does not stand up. . . . While there's life there's hope." He entered the house. His wife began to cry when she saw him. Pierre looked at his parents worriedly, for he felt an atmosphere of dismay and defeat in the house. The servant served the dinner.

"Eat," said Anne, "you must keep up your strength."

Thus did shafts that issued from the cloud of the war strike from afar a man who thought himself happy.

18

Thus began the decline of Antoine Bloyé.

The men who govern the railway from their Paris offices high above the Austerlitz line had appointed him director of stores for the southern suburbs.

From commanding fifteen hundred workers, from a position of authority, Antoine was reduced to humiliating idleness, to the command of sixty men.

Between Vitry and Choisy, in the midst of the wide desolate plain that extends from the Seine to the hillocks of Thiais, stood a jumbled pile of buildings and sheds strung along the tracks. Here were stored provisions: grease, soap, bales of oakum, logwood, rows of oil tanks, and barrels of pitch. Behind the buildings, in the thick shade of chestnut trees, stood the wine cellars of the catering division. Tarpaulins were made here too, stretched out to dry in drying rooms. They looked like huge black sheets. The only machine was a planer that made the logwood fly into splinters, and Antoine would go and watch it work in its obscure corner, because it reminded him of his lost power over a multitude of flashing machines. He was shrunken, humiliated. He felt he had become "a wholesale grocer." For a man of his kind, it was an irreparable misfortune to be torn from production. He, a producer, had suddenly become sterile like a withered woman.

He pictured with considerable shame what his friends of yesterday were saying. "Oh, Bloyé, haven't you heard? Why, he got into a mess, he was kicked downstairs and sent I don't quite know where."

Kicked downstairs, those were the words they would use. It was almost a phrase of the profession. That was what it was, a fall. He was shoved to one side like an object no longer of any use. Round about the stores lay old locomotives, old chassis, rusty boilers, rows of wheels, all overgrown with blackberries and catnip. He was indeed like these scraps of metal that had once seen service. He had not been completely thrown overboard; they had taken a sort of pity on him, as on a retired soldier, or maimed workers who are found a quiet post, the job of guard or nightwatchman. A man who has based his entire life on his professional pride, and only on his professional pride, does not allow this pride to be destroyed without anguish.

Antoine did not have much work, his leisure weighed upon him. He had never learned to enjoy leisure, and he ran like a machine in low gear. He shuffled along the aisles of the silent stores. Once he had finished a few experiments with linseed oil in his little laboratory, oil that dried in streaks on a copper plate, once he had made the round of the stores and signed the mail, he was through for the day. He went to sit on some kegs at the corner of the plant. The electric trains from Paris to Juvisy shuttled back and forth along the tracks and long sparks shot out from their brake shoes. A low-lying murky sky overhung the plain. There were a few fields of lilies where nurserymen from Vitry worked, then a great expanse that stretched unbroken to where distant factories smoked on the horizon. From time to time, tugs towing a line of barges toward Bercy would moan in the fog; an express would thunder past. It was a poor region, where the air always smelled of tar and acid, where the grass was grimy and strewn with debris. In the direction of Vitry, stone houses had begun to break into this expanse, houses where workers lived in the center of vegetable patches. It was a bit of steppe, like the treeless dreary places where Asiatic nomads pitch camp. Antoine gazed at this plain as he would have gazed at the sea, with a sort of dizziness and a heart as empty as this bleak suburban world.

Beyond the railway tracks, a chemical products factory reared its white brick walls. The surrounding air was charged with the pungent smell of chemicals. They manufactured poison gases there, and on some days, when the wind was bad, Antoine and his workers wore gas masks on the job. The poison of war blighted the wild plants that had grown along the edges of the tracks. The men spat and wiped their eyes, fearful lest an explosion should let loose a torrent of gas and death from the factory across the way. Occasionally a container exploded and the air suddenly gagged in the workers' throats. There was a casualty in the plant across the way.

The Bloyé house stood five hundred meters from the stores at the end of a row of gardens. It was a long two-story house with a long wooden annex painted brown. Around the house grew a ring of tall beeches and Japanese lacquer trees. A great acacia towered over the lawn. Because of the trees and of the high embankment where the Alfortville road crossed the tracks, the house never emerged from a heavy green shade which was barely pierced by the morning sun's rays. There was also a very large garden enclosed by a hedge of hops higher than a man, full of hedgehogs.

Beyond the hedge was a stretch of land peopled by ragpickers, foreign workers. But the hops were too dense for them to be able to see what went on at the Bloyés'; while the latter merely knew that a few feet away there existed a terrible den of misery and sickness whence the smoke rose as from a savage village buried in mud and offal, where children and dogs ran about looking for scraps. What a comedown for Anne Bloyé to have such neighbors right after the glorious days of the Rue Combe des Dames! But the house, the factory, and the garden formed a fairly closed little world of their own. Sometimes, however, ragged children, small, pale-haired, thin-legged girls climbed up on the embankment and gazed from afar at the Bloyés' elaborate flower-filled garden. When the little girls saw Anne seated on the lawn knitting, and Pierre playing near her, they hurled insults at these quiet people, insults full of a fierce hatred that welled from their misery.

"Fat arses," they shouted.

On such occasions, Anne would get up and say to her son, "Let's go inside!"

And she would murmur, "The dirty little scum."

Antoine exercised his body in the large garden. He reaped his alfalfa, dug his potatoes. In season, he went to the flower market in the morning. He passed whole afternoons idling about the tannery shed and around the booths of the grain and poultry merchants. But this was not a pastime that could dispel his boredom and his shame. He was over fifty and he was out of the run, out of the events of the war, out of the attacks of fever that convulsed great enterprises. His past suddenly bore down on him. He began to feel terribly tired, the decline of life racked his huge idle body. He thought of his age, he told himself that age does not stage a comeback. He had not fallen to rise again. This realization exasperated him. Age had deposited its sediments and poison in every recess of his body and his memory. The years mounted up, one on top of another, and the cumulation had gone on in silence, unobserved. During all these years, men think they still possess the lightness of youth and their hopes unfold before them without diminishing, without melting away. They see their future, stacked up in a neat little pile in front of them, always intact. But the tide of years breaks of a sudden. It appears without warning. Antoine, who had spent his whole life waiting for a new nameless something—and every year he told himself it would happen next year, like the Jews who comforted themselves by repeating "next year in Jerusalem"—Antoine, who had not perceived his metamorphosis from youth to manhood, of a sudden underwent the transformation from manhood to old age. This transformation was more difficult than a change of skin.

First had come the poor cramped peace of childhood, the troubles of youth, then his profession and its breathless tempo, the engines, the tools, the workers, marriage, offices, fatherhood, little ambitions nurtured by the memory of youthful humiliations, then the petty successes of middle age, vanity, solitude. Antoine had never had time to take his bearings. He waited. He waited, hoping perhaps to discover he was happy. Nothing had ever made him take a special interest in himself save for brief feverish intervals. Nothing had ever apprised him of the occasions when he had been a man; never had he seriously asked himself the meaning of the phrase "to be a man." Barely had he known what it meant, in the words of his environment, to be "somebody." And, when all was said and done, between the ages of forty and fifty he had been "somebody" in the bourgeois sense, a man who knew locomotives better than anyone else and whose name was known to several thousand people. Once this was taken from him, he was brutally aware that it was nothing, that it was a success that did not count, a success that left him empty-handed. He felt himself stripped bare and poorer than he had ever been, in this ghastly physical and mental unemployment. His fate was swallowed in the shadows. He was over fifty. How could he reverse steam, change the course of his life? What more could he hope for on his desert island outside the ways of navigation? He had nothing more to look forward to. No human struggle, no pastimes, no resources. He found nothing in his past life to help him. He had laid up no treasures in those years consumed by the passing days and nights. Ah, those endless days at the depot of Tours and that sort of idiotic pride that possessed him then! Cities, children, friends, companions, Marcelle—all these things were born, all these things passed away—Sunday walks, short carefree vacations, for-

gotten like the making of a world without a history in an unknown sky.

In 1917, Jean-Pierre Bloyé died. All the people you love die
off, one by one. They take away, with the contemptuous greed of
the dead, all that was built upon their presence. Those structures
of friendship, occupations, habits, quarrels, pleasantries, conversations, and walks, whose foundations they were, collapse along
with the visible frame the moment the heart stops beating or the
mouth hangs agape on the last breath. Among his various roles,
Antoine Bloyé was a man who was the son of another man just as
he himself was the father of a son. He was not alone in the lineage
of men. He had ties upstream and downstream and one of these
ties had snapped. His daughter Marie was dead, M. and Mme
Guyader were dead, and now Jean-Pierre Bloyé died. His grand-
parents had died in his childhood, he had barely known them. He
retained only a dim recollection of his paternal grandmother—an
old white figure covered with a veil over which buzzed green flies
chased off by chattering women. How many lives are borne away
at the sleepwalking pace of funeral trains and their listless black
horses! Every death is accompanied by this destruction, this ruin,
this form of defeat. A whole section of your being is mortified.

Antoine left for Redon, Anne remained with Pierre. On the
train, Antoine tried to bridge the gulf that separated him from his
childhood.

Every year, returning from their vacation, the Bloyés stopped
at Redon. After their retirement, Jean-Pierre Bloyé and his wife
had lived in a hamlet called La Châtaigneraie on the road to
Rennes, in a little house that consisted only of one large room and
an attic. It was surrounded by large walnuts and hedges of holly.
Sunken roads led to the farms of the hamlet, and wheat covered
the upland that was called the upland of Galerne. On the trodden
earth floor of the one room stood two huge beds with red quilts

and feather mattresses as soft as sleep, a table, a wardrobe, and a pearwood chest of drawers. To the walls, which Jean-Pierre Bloyé whitewashed once a year, were nailed images of the Virgin and a crucifix surrounded by a heartshaped rosary. On the chest of drawers, a pendulum clock ticked away between an orange blossom under glass and a glass ball with a mountain landscape in it. If you shook the soapy water in the ball, snow fell and the landscape, which had become unglued, bobbed about like a fish. All the worldly possessions of the old Bloyés could have been loaded on a cart.

"It's plenty for old folks like us," they said.

As they grew older, the compass of their lives shrank further, lives that had always been so small, so unimportant, that had set off so few echoes, that had touched so few beings with their ripples. Jean-Pierre Bloyé retained his large straight figure and the glistening teeth that he had been so proud of ever since the girls made eyes at him in Allaire. Marie Bloyé had become an incredibly thin and bent old woman. A network of deep wrinkles lined her forehead and cheeks and encircled her lips. She had red cheeks and eyes sunk in hollow sockets that presaged death. Under her headdress done in the fashion of Redon, under her black shawl, you saw the white strands of her hair, which she often smoothed with her hand.

Every year, for three or four days, Antoine again saw the furniture, the ghosts of his childhood. He opened the closet and the chest of drawers, where the clothing and other objects were still in the same place. On the top shelf of the closet still lay the prizes he had formerly won at Pontivy and Saint-Nazaire. At meals, his parents told stories he alone could understand. His wife was outside this charmed circle. She did not know those people of Saint-Nazaire. She became slightly bored, she smiled a bit at the mistakes her parents-in-law made in their speech, and felt she came of better lineage than her husband.

"How untidy your mother is," she told Antoine.

Pierre scampered along the roads of La Châtaigneraie. Soon they departed.

"Till next year," they would say.

Antoine gave his parents money. He was worried by the fact that he saw so little of his loved ones—three or four days a year, what a mockery! He asked them to come and spend the winter at his house, but they refused. They said, "We would only be a bother to you."

For they had acquired the habit of living with an imaginary son who seemed too far above them. Once the topics of childhood memories, of the village news were exhausted, they had little to say to him. They lived in separate worlds. Antoine felt more keenly than they, perhaps, the solitude of their old age. On the train homeward bound, he experienced regret, a feeling of obscure uneasiness, which the activity of his daily life soon dissipated.

In the house at La Châtaigneraie, Antoine eyed his father's corpse, the thin wasted body that once had been so stalwart, that had cast a shadow on the ground when he walked. He thought of his daughter who had died long ago, of the old wound that still hurt. His mother told her beads. Another part of his life had ended with Jean-Pierre, son of Joseph, son of Aoustin.

There were the activities of life, meals together, arrivals, departures, letters, reunions, the palpable presence of a human being, a familiarity, a half-spoken understanding, the common game of memories and of the half-secret, half-uttered words of people who love each other, who have breathed the same air. And when death quenches life, there remains only the emptiness of shattered thoughts. Vainglorious men, with their lives made up of other lives, dying deaths other than their own deaths.

Antoine was no longer young. His father's death wounded him more deeply than he knew. Wounds on spent bodies do not heal quickly, the flesh no longer retains the reserves of its youth. Its tissues do not mend so easily. This death struck a man whose recuperative powers were already impaired. This death presaged his own death, it was like the first stage of his own death. Antoine experienced the gnawing grief of an old man without a future who does not hear within him the mysterious premonition that the young experience, the assurance that they will triumph over sorrow. His mother was a very old woman, she wept over her husband's death with that secret indifference of beings in whom the fountainheads of grief have been dried up by age. She did not grasp the emptiness that engulfed her life. Almost all her distant memories were already lost. Along the road that led away from the cemetery across the upland of Galerne, Antoine asked her, in an effort to recapture his childhood, to retrieve the warmth of his early years: "Do you remember the day, mother. . . ." But she answered, "It's so long ago, Antoine, I can't remember any more."

Thus Antoine lost his first existence. He could no longer compare his memories with other images. His father no longer answered him as he had during those three or four days a year at that time of his vacation when Antoine renewed his store of youth, re-established contact between the extreme limits of his years. He left. His mother remained alone in the house at La Châtaigneraie.

19

Antoine dreamed. He did not dream while awake, he did not seek to lose himself in a world conjured in broad daylight. He really dreamed, at night, and in his shattered life these dreams took on an importance that his dreams had never had before.

The expeditions and encounters men take part in in their sleep are endowed, after all, with a certain wisdom. A man's dreams are not always bad counselors. They do not always lie, and they are ill-acquainted with the precepts that daytime dwellers in houses and guardians of morality must know by heart. The man whom they haunt is unable honestly to free himself of their hidden sincerity. When questioned in the consciousness of waking, they answer with telling words despite their habit of being mysterious, of speaking in parables and riddles and of ridiculing the most worthy idols of good morals and geometry. But the sleeper little knows how to question them on waking, he does not know that he serves as a sounding board for so wise a voice. He does his best to be deaf and to forget. The awakened man loses what he has gained in the night. He leads a divided life. He is his waking self, later he is his sleeping self, and the sleeper and the waking man rarely merge. What man knows how to triumph over this division? He will not triumph over it alone, for the causes of his division are not in himself.

In the bosom of the solitary idleness of night there appear in veiled form all the things that day forbids, desires condemned by

the tribunals of good daytime citizens, by their customs and virtues. Shame, discipline, suppressed desires, lack of leisure crush
the obscure recesses of a man's character, where his truest needs
may perhaps be hidden. For as long as men are not complete and
free, sure on their feet and on the earth that supports them, they
will dream at night. They will satisfy all their hungers, their real
hungers—all men who do not eat or drink their fill in the world,
wretched men with their thirsts for vengeance—they will score
victories over their daytime oppressors, they will conquer willing
women. The nighttime man will impart his confidences to his
daytime shade who does not heed him. A few men have the key
to their dreams. They do not look for prophetic secrets, for vi-
sions of the future, they do not seek a false magic in these mysterious adventures where it is not gods, demons, and ghosts that appear, but the child formerly humiliated, the man crushed under
his duties, his burdens, his taboos, the man shorn of everything.

In this period of despair, when the threat of death gnawed Antoine without his being able to defend himself against it by the
proofs, the testimonies of a life and of a past, without his being
able to accept it like men whose potentialities have been realized,
whose desires have been satisfied—for he discovered in his real
past nothing but the emptiness and leaden skies of bourgeois life
—he dreamed. Bit by bit, he acquired the habit of accepting his
dreams in his waking hours, of conceding them a measure of cre-
dence simply because all real appearances crumbled, were swept
from him as a canvas tent in the wind and left him on the threshold of a vast desert like the plain that began at the edge of his
plant. These dreams of his were not all apart from him, were not
all formed in inaccessible recesses of his being. There were some
whose testimony and advice he could record. He blushed in the
beginning, but the ill-humor, the mortal wrath that encompassed
his life, made him at length forget the impropriety of some of his
nocturnal explorations. He retained a fear of them because they
voiced requirements he would doubtless never have the courage

to satisfy. Some of his dreams were too complicated for him to know how to interpret them. He would say in the morning, "Last night, I again had another of those absurd dreams. Where should one look for those things one dreams of but has never seen?"

Others were forgotten with the first flush of dawn that pierced the slanting shutter bars, and he sought to recapture them. He sensed somewhere a strange—or seductive and terrible—recollection, but it evaded him like one of those small animals of the undergrowth one hears rustling through the grass without knowing whether it is a rodent, a lizard, or a bird. All that remained of this dream was a vague elusive presence. Some of them did not erase themselves. They accompanied him through the day, scarcely less vivid than an evil or a pleasant memory. Only toward evening did they weaken and melt away.

What element of man is more humiliated than his manly needs? Pride may well allow itself to be crushed; it is not the deepest attribute. Thoughts on pride are not forbidden thoughts. This passion that the company of others instills in us does not survive at night, when we are alone. Pride is a passion of the waking hours of work, of the ant hills of the day. The sleeper sheds his pride. Antoine, like most of his fellows, left his pride when he went to sleep, the relations he had with others between eight in the morning and seven at night sufficed to nourish and to wound his pride, to give it exercise. But his sexual life was poorly satisfied.

Antoine was a married man, a man faithful to his wife for twenty-six years. There are many men who are faithful to their wives merely through laziness, through lack of spare time, through fear of domestic rows. Most cases of fidelity are not examples of heroic virtue, of sacrifices offered to a great love, but of weakness and laziness. It takes courage, it requires effort, to be unfaithful. You tell yourself by way of consolation: "This act is the same with every woman. . . ." You appease yourself with this lie.

Antoine had a lawful wife. Formerly, at thirty, he was convinced that he loved her. With time, with the endless years, stale
as an old newspaper, there remained nothing but the lazy habit.
And a woman, after all these years of proximity, scarcely gives
more pleasure than a thousand other habits, a thousand other nets
where one by one the days and years are enmeshed—than meals,
cigarettes, and desk drawers that must be put in order from time
to time. How many scruples, lessons, and virtues are marshaled to
protect this lawful habit! Love does not make so many demands,
nor liberty. No one ever speaks of codes of love, or scruples of liberty. Anne felt Antoine's eyes searching her, appraising her. She
had become a heavy, shapeless woman. Age had not only lined
her forehead, puckered her lips, and fretted her legs with varicose
veins; she had become fatter and heavier year by year. She began
walking about her house with the heavy rolling gait that had been
her mother's. The years had slowly deposited their thick coating
of domestic taboos and sacred habits. It was like an inorganic shell
encrusting the mentality of a sentimental young girl. Anne still
read little romantic novels in illustrated covers with the same sort
of feelings as she had had at sixteen. She was the epitome of years
in which nothing had happened. In the Bloyés' bedroom there
was a little stand on either side of the bed: the stand on Anne's
side and the stand on Antoine's side. On Anne's stand for the past
fifteen years, there had lain a book that shed pages every time it
was opened—*The Woman's Little Secrets*; it contained beauty and
household recipes. On Antoine's stand lay the faithful and unread
Life of George Stephenson. When Antoine had finished reading
his paper in bed, he would re-open his "favorite book"—it always
opened at the same page because of a break in the binding.

"Aren't you going to put the light out?" Anne would say.

He would set down the book, and reach for the switch. It was
darkness; it was the image of life. This life had no place for the
warmth and impetus of love.

While all the young girls of the world walked around Antoine, they were utterly beyond his reach. A mysterious glass separated them from him, and he could not simply stretch out his hand to reach them and pull them into his dreary world. Undoubtedly, when they passed him they thought him old, or perhaps they did not even think of him at all. He was just one of the various movable or immovable objects, he was just part of the sidewalk; they did not notice him as a woman notices a man, but as a pedestrian notices a paving stone, or a gas lamp. Formerly, it had never worried him that by choosing one woman so quickly he lost all the rest. This loss was irreparable; it was too late—no other woman would ever love him, never again would he touch the skin of youth. The springs of youth would never more well within him.

He was continually aware of the presence of all these women. He was forever on the lookout, just like adolescents. Women take a seat in a train or a streetcar and show their knees. Women dressed in linen smocks blown part way open by the wind wash the store windows in the morning. Women go by on bicycles, and gusts of wind clap their skirts to their bodies. All these bits of bodies seen in a flash go to form a sort of huge nameless body that makes its presence felt everywhere. Why spend your whole life in the company of one woman, of one body? Almost all men ask themselves this question; few of them know the answer. Antoine was no wiser than his fellows. The surest of all forces deterred him from making the last effort in the direction of one of these unknown women. Wherein lay the power of this force? He knew nothing about it. He was fettered; he would continue his fettered existence, always restricted, unable to give himself rein. Now that he was suddenly left without work, he came for the first time to have an inner life. A whole world was revealed in the shallow seas of night, when the ebb tide of sleep uncovered their reefs, their strange vegetation, their submarine personalities that caricatured the man. He dreamed dreams of power; he killed people in cold blood; he scored victories; he followed funerals where lines of men applauded him. Women played the main part in these shadowy kingdoms, these colorless dependencies. They peopled them with a female carefreeness. Among them he was a naked man, no longer a voter, the father of a family, and an engineer. Men lose all but their name in this world which destroys every law of the civil state. There, every man becomes an animal poised on its hind legs, that wakes within the prostrate bodies of sleepers in dark rooms, unhampered by houses, pitfalls, clothing, and ideas. No town, no sky confines these ignorant animals that know nothing save the most ancient secrets of humanity. These visitors cause the waking man to blush. Antoine blushed like anyone else. There was a whole period in his life when he dreamed thus, when he was dominated by these dreams just as he had formerly been dominated by work and by the image of activity. Many women figured there, many declarations were made to him, many bodies were possessed by him; the postures, the manners of these relationships would be judged obscene or ludicrous by the morning censor. The real women whom he encountered, whom he met in the daytime, whom he greeted, with whom he chatted of their husbands, of the war, were delivered to him by the night. These images filled the night; they trespassed on his waking hours. He no longer blushed at harboring these desires, at giving them all the light they required. The barrier that divided him from real madness grew lower every day. He sank into a world where his factory, his wife, and his child became more and more insignificant. He hated them like obstacles. And he was still alarmed by this descent, whose end he did not foresee. Certain voices still decried this metamorphosis, this flight, this invasion by a chronic temptation. A moral man does not allow himself to succumb without a struggle.

The Bloyés had a servant named Lucie. She was a girl from the south who wore pink dresses and silk stockings. She walked about the house singing. Pierre, who was thirteen, blushed when she looked him in the eyes and asked, "Do I frighten you?"

Antoine began following her with his eyes, spying on the movements of this young untalkative girl. When you watch a woman persistently, you discover many of her bodily secrets—the shape of a breast, an armpit, a knee, the skin of a haunch, the base of the throat, the curves of the loins. These are the glimpses that nurture desire. Lucie began casting furtive glances at Antoine, and Antoine would shift his eyes like his son. The days Anne went to Paris—she would fetch Pierre from the lycée and would not be back till six—Antoine would return home for things he had deliberately forgotten. He would enter the kitchen, where Lucie was cooking dinner or ironing or sewing, and ask, "Have you seen my lighter?"

Lucie would answer, "No, I haven't seen it. Monsieur may have put it in his pocket and forgotten about it."

Antoine would take several steps into the kitchen, he would drink a glass of water at the sink, then he would go out, mechanically feeling his pockets without saying anything. He had forgotten how to make up to a young woman, since the time . . . He was bald. He trembled lest she should make fun of him, lest she should go and tell Anne everything in the evening. Already Anne asked him, "Why are you always hanging about the kitchen? You keep the girl from doing her work."

She would say to Lucie, "It seems to me your dresses are extremely short, my girl."

Lying awake at night, he thought of this young girl with the misplaced ardor of youth. He remembered having seen her during the day sitting in a deck chair, and one could see her haunches as far as her underwear, and his son had followed his glance with jealous eyes. All he need do was get up noiselessly, cautiously climb the squeaky stairs to the floor above, push back a door without a latch, and touch Lucie's shoulder. But she might scream. It would be better to have a cautious word with her first. Offer her something. She had the insolence of youth. She laughed at him. Antoine took some drops of valerian to put him back to sleep.

One Sunday morning he saw Lucie talking to a young man, in an empty street, her back against a factory wall that was pasted over with bills, and the man was leaning over her and looking her intently in the eyes. Antoine hurried by with a sort of childish pang.

Then she left. Anne said, "Did anyone ever see the like! You may pack your bag, mademoiselle."

Outside the house, events rolled past without Antoine's taking notice. The streets were thronged with soldiers of all the services. There were convalescents who limped. Women wore dresses that were more martial than ever. These passers-by bespoke the presence of the war, an adventure in which Antoine played no part. Now and again he would help his son stick little flags into a big map of the front—with indifference, as though he were re-constructing a chess game played somewhere in the Southern Hemisphere. Air raids began to disturb the nights of people in the rear. Airships in flames floated in the black sky, pursued by the searchlights from the forts. The anti-aircraft guns roared. Bits of steel fell on the rooftops. When the alarm was over, Antoine would climb up the railway embankment with his son and point to the glow of the fires. "Look," he would say, "it's burning near the main shops."

These fires filled him with a kind of sneaking satisfaction.

In the shelter that the workers of the plant had dug, the people of the neighborhood would gather, shivering from the strain and from the cold. Dogs howled as during a storm, consumptive women coughed, children cried. The men whispered as though fearing that they would be heard by the German pilots passing some three or four thousand meters overhead.

"It's further away now. . . . Can you hear? They're sounding the 'all clear' in town."

The armistice came. Then peace. There were processions that children watched with empty eyes. In peaceful parks German cannons were pointed toward the clouds. The soldiers returned. Women surrendered themselves to the sex hunger of the returning men. People felt they could breathe again. The whole world forgot the cannon roar which you had been able to hear in Paris during the second battle of the Marne. Antoine withdrew before this invasion of men.

20

One day in June 1920, Antoine was walking along the Boulevard de la Gare. As he had a spare hour before his suburban train left from Orléans-Ceinture and the weather was fine, he casually turned toward his old neighborhood. Spring was in the air. Antoine was thinking of nothing; as he walked he could see the tips of his shoes appear and vanish beneath him. Presently he took his coat off. He walked on and on. There was a great vacancy within him, a vacancy that waited for the presence of ideas, for the coming of feelings. It was not the expansive emptiness of contentment, joy, or merely carefreeness.

And suddenly, on the sidewalk of the Rue de Tolbiac, where men and women passed with their accustomed stride, busy with their everyday affairs, Antoine discovered he was going to die. He was suddenly cut off from the passers-by, who continued calmly in their eternal life. He knew this thing by a single stroke of his cognition, with a special and unerring knowledge.

In the course of human thought, ideas come to light whose very appearance involves the formation of a certain conclusion. An idea has coursed along the channels of sorrow and memory. It has looked for tributaries and found them, it reaches the light of day like a new spring, a pool that man has never sounded. It is unexpected, it overwhelms the living man. Thus was Antoine overwhelmed by the presence of death. It pierced his boredom and emptiness with a blinding flash of light: the world was blotted out

218

by its concentrated clarity. Doubtless he had always known he
would die, but like all his fellow men, in so vague a manner that
this knowledge did not deeply concern him. Like others, he
would say, "We are all of us mortal. I shall die like everybody
else."

He would joke about his own funeral. He would say, "I'd like
very much to be burned, but it's a bit too expensive, cremation is
more than I can afford."

And day dawns, night falls; men go on eating and sleeping,
doing their tasks, loving their women. It is one of the realizations
people accept mechanically, like the motion of the planets, the
course of the solar system, the destruction of the Temple of Jerusalem. The earth revolves around the sun. All men are mortal.
Nothing is changed, nothing is disturbed by the prediction of
death. Nobody applies the consequences of this cardinal truth to
himself, for it seems to the individual to concern humanity in
general rather than his own flesh. But on that day Antoine knew
everything with the knowledge of certainty, and no longer
merely as a platitude that people quote. It was no longer that all
men are mortal, but *me,* I must die. It was no longer like the account of a crime, or a misfortune, the details of a bad business that
was no particular concern of his personally. It was no longer like
a lottery stake. It was a warning launched from the moist, seeth-
ing depths of his body, from the fibers of his muscles and arteries;
it was the knowing voice of the heart itself.

Antoine was a man of flesh and blood. He did not have a conscience so pure as to be disinterested in the body that nourished it
and which for so many years had furnished it at every second
with the remarkable proof of existence. Death is the cataclysm of
the body. Antoine's body ceased to live with its carefree animal
assurance; the bad news came from its most inner recesses. It pro-
ceeded from the very structure of its organs, of its elements and
functions. The body gasped. In the depths of his chest Antoine
felt an elemental pang, a pang in the roots of his being. It was a

suspension of motion, a pause that crushed the walls of his chest and his lungs. He raised his head and tried to catch his failing breath.

At the time he was on a small deserted square that seemed quite familiar to him, a semicircular square with low houses shaded by acacias, standing behind gardens and iron fences that converged toward the center of the square. Along the chord of the semicircle rose huge buildings with straight blind walls. The sweetish smell of the acacias filled Antoine with nausea. He opened his mouth, and a passer-by could have seen his gums with half their teeth missing, and the red shadow of his windpipe. He remembered the hunting dogs he once had killed with a revolver. From their black breasts issued a string of bloody bubbles that burst, and they opened their hideous throats, gasping just as he had today, and he saw their black and red palates streaked like a strange seashell. He sat on a bench with his derby hat on his knees and tried to remember when he had seen this sleepy square. In his dreams apparently, but dreams are not born of nothing. It was a square he had strolled through in other times, in the time of Marcelle and the engineers, a time that he had never dared recall save in his dreams.

Death was in him, it filled him with a disheartening anxiety, without images, without ideas. One has no ideas of death, one experiences nothing save a naked anguish. He remained a long time alone on his bench. He might have died, no one would have seen him die as he had seen the four dogs die. They would merely have found him the following morning, when the street cleaners and the patrolmen passed. He had a respite, he managed to breathe, he did so cautiously, in order not to awaken the icy spider that had seized his lungs and heart, that had pressed against his ribs and breastbone. All that remained of the mortal warning was an almost agreeable numbness that coursed the length of his left arm and centered around the crook of his elbow.

When it was dark, he took a train that left much later than the one he had intended to take. There was no one walking in the Rue Danton between the railway tracks and the long endless walls of a park, where Danton had once strolled. By the pottery factory wharf two old canoes were rotting under the chestnut trees. Further on, on the Rue des Epinettes, children from the neighborhood waded in a stream fed by the drainage water of a factory. Above the trees of his house, the chimney of a factory under construction began to rise between the scaffolding, like a tower still soft and needing to be propped up. At home, his son was doing a Latin translation, the acacia on the lawn was blooming like the acacias of the square. Anne came toward him.

"How late you are," she said. "I was beginning to get worried. Why didn't you take the usual train? You haven't been to the café again?"

"That's right, I went to have a glass," he answered with so much weariness that Anne was not annoyed, "with Huet, whom I met at the Forty-One."

A man has a perfect right to lie to hide his own death.

Antoine never ceased thinking of his death. He would ask himself what would happen the day the sentence would reach his body. How should he accept his loss? Should he rebel? How would things look after he was dead? One cannot conceive these things, one cannot be truly dead and see oneself dead, stretched out in death. There is only dizziness. His own death was not imaginable. Barely could he picture himself hovering above his body like a shadow, but this severance was not death. He was irked by the problem of trying to grasp the fact that his nothingness could not be represented. Men are so used to conjuring with ideas and images that they cannot adjust themselves to a sorrow that scorns all palpable forms.

All other men, the friends he met, the women he saw, were the accomplices of life; they inhabited another world, they played an entirely different game. They went about, they loved, they still had ambition, they formed plans, they bargained with time, certain of the future. These disgusting living beings, these living egoists who were not empty, who had hope before them—Antoine began hating them, he even hated his son who said, "When I am grown up . . . ," his son who was like the visible image of all the years that had escaped him. Which of these fools loved him enough to shield him from death, to provide him with reasons to continue living, to keep on. But they all regarded him as one of their equals in life.

Comrades whom he met would say to him, "Well, Bloyé, haven't you begun to think about retiring? I am making my plans. I have another two years to serve and then I'm through. I'll thumb my nose at this dirty shop. We've pulled the yoke plenty since the days when we were journeymen engineers."

But Antoine would answer vaguely, "I am taking stock of myself, I ask myself what I should do. What constructive work will you do when you're retired? I have plenty of time to think about it. Retirement is not a life that suits old railwaymen. We are like old horses that die when they no longer feel the traces. I don't make any plans. Plans never turn out. Are there such things as plans? In three years, in four years—but maybe we'll all be dead by then."

His comrades would tell him he saw things very black, he would see them all buried and would make speeches over their graves. Antoine thought with irritation of those people who ordered their lives as though the future were a piece of property, as though one could order a given year to have a given form and another year to have a different form. The future is not a house that you inherit, to which you may add a wing, a bay window or a chimney at will. The idiots thought themselves immortal, they acted as though some almighty person had promised them an eternity on earth, as though they were made of incorruptible materials, of diamonds, and not of blood, of fat, of albumen, of things that rot, that decompose, that do not endure. They saw the years issue from the clouds with clear and recognizable shapes. They were familiar ahead of time with the only possible outlines of their lives. Antoine felt that a plan is not an ordinary undertaking. The least decision contracts for an unmeasured fragment of time and perhaps all time. In the end he hesitated to give orders, make an appointment, or tell his secretary, "Mademoiselle, I am going out; if anyone phones tell them I shall return in two hours and will call back."

These were the sort of phrases that rolled off the tongue mechanically, phonographic habits, but he felt that the moment he uttered them, he was asking for a miracle, the miracle of the prolongation of his life. You have a stroke, or an attack of angina pectoris. You collapse in the street and people drag you to a pharmacy; a small crowd collects in front of the colored glass jars. You are grimy with mud and dirt like a run-over cat. How brash you are with your talk of being back in two hours. There, he was going to die like that, and he had not even lived. His wife would sometimes say—it was all a part of that dinner table philosophy, that philosophy of everybody—"Would you like to begin your life over again knowing all you know? I shouldn't, I have had my share of sorrow, I have had my joys. One only lives once. I shouldn't like to begin over again, it would surely be just the same."

But Antoine answered this question badly, it involved too much, it would involve telling Anne things she would never forgive, things that would spoil her last years. A real study of the question, so he felt, would have carried him far, would have made him blush, run away, cry. In everyone's philosophy there are traps. What a question! Begin again a life where there would not be the threat of death, not too soon at any rate. If only one were sure of a little time before death, if only one did not live precariously, if only mistakes did not count, and were never more than mistakes—bad roads that in the end led back to the main highways.

But everything forbids men turning their attention to their eventual deaths. They do not have this knowledge within them. Antoine himself did not have it before that June day in the little square. Nothing inclines them to this contemplation, they do not know they are wasting away their time, they do not even know that time can be wasted among the living things that people the world. Men and women go out and move about the streets. These cowards have their work, their children, their table- and bed-mates. They let themselves be dragged along by the irresistible movement of the chains of their lives. Beings of the opposite sex sleep in their beds, walk at their sides, give them the semblances of happiness, exercise the shades of unhappiness for them. They are surrounded by the barriers and the ramparts which the species builds with coral-like obstinacy and patience to screen from living eyes the chasms and tremendous suction power of death. Well-built walls of houses, children's games, pride, misery, the antics of stray dogs in springtime, the budding trees, the changing clouds, factories, barracks, prisons, theater façades, the white tables of cafés, printed words, flags, screens, families, duties, profits, states, gods—all reassure them constantly of the stability, the unshakable motives of life. But there is human poverty behind these screens which keep men from telling themselves that time presses and that they must really live.

Antoine had long lived within these fortifications reared around him, around the good husband, around the good worker, around all these good "characters" that he had been. He had been a party to the conspiracy in favor of life, of that life that was not life. And lo and behold, he put this certainty to doubt, he spurned the protecting hedges, the sham thoroughfares, the solemn farces. All that remained was a dizziness within him, a whirl of pitiless force, a maelstrom turning slowly in the depths of his chest, sucking into its blind current all appearances, all the assurances that came within range of its greedy attraction. All waters reach the sea, all wreckage reaches the depths. All this happened to him merely because one of the barriers that hid death and nothingness from him had collapsed—the social barrier of pride, the barrier of his trade—merely because one day he had received a warning from his heart.

In this vast surge of nothingness, Antoine abandoned his oldest pretexts, his wife, and his son who eyed him with the uneasy frightened-animal looks of children who infer the sufferings of adults, that absurd factory where he stagnated, his garden full of fruit, vegetables, dahlias and gladiolas, his forgotten friends—the whole structure he had called his life, that had risen over him like a mollusk shell. He wandered in a world of apparitions, of deathly personages and trappings. He did not clearly unravel his state of despair, the absence of hope. He could not have explained to anyone the nature of his ill. He was a man with a small vocabulary and he doubtless would have lacked words had he wanted to describe his bankruptcy and destitution. This anguish could not be translated, articulated. He examined himself, he worried, he aired his illness. In those days he walked a great deal, he could not sit still, he felt lost. The most ordinary objects at times seemed unrecognizable. He reached the point where he would touch the bark of a tree, rough as the skin of a large animal, and he would press his hand against it as though to reassure himself. He handled his most familiar tools, his spade, with shaft and handle polished as though oiled by his own hands, his test tubes and scales, and he suddenly forgot how to use them. Under his eyes, in his hands, they changed their shape and meaning; they seemed to belong to an incomprehensible world whose ways were strange to him, and he laid them down, he discarded them.

At night, his bed would carry him like a ghost ship to a land whence no one returned. The misshapen walls of his room were the docks whence one sets sail on a deathly voyage. He did not sleep. At first, he tried to keep perfectly still, not to waken what was inside of him; he held his arms at his sides as though he were dead, as though he had been laid out on his deathbed, or else he crossed his arms on his chest. He tried to picture what would happen after his death, but it was a useless effort. He did not see himself, it is impossible to be dead and see oneself dead. Later he became restless, the bed burned him up. He sought parts of the sheets that were still cold, but soon they too became scorching hot and he had to get up. He took care not to wake his wife who slept heavily beside him. He slung his clothes over his arm and dressed at the foot of the stairs with the precautions of a thief. He went out; in the black garden he felt like a successful strategist, as though his wife and son were enemies who wanted at any price to hold him within their little well-ordered world, their little world of barriers, of false barriers against death. He would smile maliciously and then set out. Using his hands, he climbed the embankment opposite his house and reached the road of the overpass. Beyond the railway bridge, the Alfortville road descended to the Seine and then followed the bank. This river road bordered on huge empty lots crossed by godforsaken railway junction lines. Here and there rose somber factory walls. Row on row of piers with cranes on them jutted out above the Seine. The air was charged with fumes of chemical products and a pungent smell of gas mingled with the river vapor. Antoine stumbled over piles of sod and cinders. He put his foot into puddles. Some nights it rained and he turned up his coat collar. He was chilled through by the cold and dampness. He gazed in the direction of Alfortville, at the twinkling misty line of lights. Near him flowed the river, lit up here and there by feeble lamps that seemed in league with death. On the leaden surface of the Seine covered with its film of oil, huge whirlpools drifted downstream without altering their slow and lackadaisical rotation, their speed and shape. These whirlpools regarded him like staring eyes and drew him toward the river's secrets.

Those nights, Antoine pondered what his wife and everyone called "his dark ideas," his ideas of the night. His life was too precarious to be worth saving. What should he do with his life? "My life was given me without my having bargained for it, it is added to the lives of others like one tile to a pile of tiles. I might as well admit it, my life neither helps nor hinders anyone. It is entirely in place for me to think of my own death. My life is empty, it deserves nothing but death." There are men who make a place for themselves, who cannot be ignored. Such is not the case with Antoine Bloyé. When such men die, their place is long visible, like the traces of a fire on the grass of a cliff. It's like a scar on the earth's surface. By dint of rolling over and over, like dogs fixing a place to lie in, they make themselves an almost perfect couch. "But how about me?" Antoine asked himself. "No foundation laid, no road opened. Nothing to show for myself. I could have built bridges. I'm an extra number, I'm superfluous, I'm useless. I've already ceased to exist. If I let myself fall into the water, no one would notice. There would be the usual messages of condolence. Anne would add a big crêpe bow to her black hat. I'm a failure, I'm through."

He felt as though he had been dismissed after an unsatisfactory test, like a bad worker. All lives that do not attain fullness are relegated to the shadows of attempts that failed. That was the key to the matter, that was the conclusion, and he could let himself die as there was no reason for his being granted a reprieve, since no force was capable of retaining him, since all human forces were out of his ken in these nocturnal sorties, in the hours when other men stir lazily near the bodies of their wives. Antoine no longer kept to earth. Where then were the people that might have lent him confidence? There was nothing left but anguish. The lack of earth beneath his faltering feet and this sickly feeling from his throat to the pit of his stomach, the heaviness in his shoulder and the numbness in his fingers. He moved like a blind man and he knew his illness was not imaginary, that it was an incurable illness that could only lead to death. After walking for two hours, he went home. As he had been walking through grass, his trouser legs were almost invariably soaked to the knee and he was shivering. He put his hand to his face and discovered his beard had grown in the night. Near the house, his wife and son, awake by now, were looking for him, calling him. He heard their shrill voices from afar, but he gave no answer. He let them worry till the last moment, as though to punish them. They feared that he might have killed himself, that he might have been lured by the attraction of the electric third rail or the whirlpools that drifted on the Seine. When he reached them, he would say with a choking irritation, "I no longer have a right to do as I please. I always have to be spied on."

He climbed to his room, ignoring them. He lay down in stony silence.

People who met him said, "Have you noticed how white and old Bloyé has grown, how sad he seems? He must be having troubles."

Others said, "Bloyé's completely neurasthenic."

He was neurasthenic. You couldn't give his ailment a reassuring medical label, a familiar name; he had headaches and stared for hours at an electric light bulb; he had digestive problems and couldn't eat; pains shot like lightning through his arms and legs. It was the perfect picture of a routine ailment, of an ailment that could be healed with medicine, treated like a cold; he possessed that familiar hatred, the sly maliciousness that invalids have, the absurd fits of anger. He exhibited an outer shell that was truly like an illness, and his wife and son sought hope in telling themselves he was sick, in saying to him, "Tell us if you feel ill, if you have a pain somewhere. Take care of yourself, you can't go on this way."

But beneath the shell was hidden a store of misery deeper than all the diseases provided with a name and responsive to remedies. The influx of nothingness. He was beyond all help. When nothingness appears, all else is destroyed. Worries, amusements, people, treatments, and pleasures afford men little protection from the pang of nonexistence. It takes a great deal of force and creation to escape from nothingness. Antoine had created nothing. He had let his forces go to waste. He had invented nothing. He had not dealt with men. At last he vaguely understood that he could only have been saved by things of his own making, by making use of his power. All the content of his life fell to dust. If only he could begin his life over again and fill it!

21

They kept telling Antoine he was sick. His wife, his colleagues called this visible transformation of his face, bearing, and voice, of his "character," an illness. The framework in which they had been in the habit of setting him no longer fitted his new appearance. Antoine clung to the idea of illness. If he were sick, then he was no longer to blame, he was no longer lost. At last he gave in. He went to see a famous neurologist, a famous professor who healed neurasthenia, phobias, fixations, who had a magical reputation.

Boulevard Haussmann, a large house with caryatids that gazed at the houses across the way over trees parched by the summer. It was one of those proud, well-shaded houses that the policemen on the beat eye with respect. They include a whole world of cellars, garages, servants' quarters; they are decorated with glass tulips, velvet benches, wrought-iron balustrades. They are comparable only to cages and aquariums inhabited by rare birds and fish. Antoine did not take the elevator, he preferred the stair that ascended between stone walls, bare as the vault of a crypt. His feet sank into red carpet. He sat down in a large salon where he was alone in the silence of those huge apartments whose inhabitants are separated by magnificent distances, by the opaque thickness of the walls. There was a grand piano covered with an embroidered silk shawl with hanging fringes, bronze statuettes of animals, watercolors of flowers, period furniture with shiny gilt. A curtain was drawn back. Antoine entered the professor's study.

The professor was a white-haired man who looked like Henri IV. He exuded the air of polite authority of a man who has always dominated others, who is feared and respected, an air bred by ascendancy over his patients and his pupils. He made you feel then and there that you were nobody, that he was the arbiter of death and recovery. He spoke: his voice, famous for its warmth and depth, like the voice of a minor prophet, imbued the sick with faith. He examined Antoine for a long time, he walked around him, he tapped Antoine's knees and fists with his reflex hammer as though he wished to evoke echoes whose meaning he alone could understand. He looked Antoine in the eyes for a long time and told him, "You must have taken plenty of antipyrine in your life?"

"True," said Antoine, as though he had confessed a sin.

The professor then said, "What sort of life did you live between the ages of thirty and forty?"

"I worked very hard," answered Antoine.

"One pays for work as one does for dissipation, monsieur."

Antoine answered questions about his body, his most distinct pains, those he could name and locate. But the essential pain he could not name. He felt that the wisest magicians of the body had no cures for it. He said simply, "And I think constantly of death. I have ideas of suicide."

He left this beautiful house with a diet for his heart, a diet for his liver, a diet for his kidneys, and some advice.

"You are at the dangerous age," the professor said. "All men overwork. You are neurasthenic. What does that mean? That means that you are decharged like a battery. A battery can be recharged. The battery must be recharged. With a little willpower you'll manage it. Do not tire yourself, but change your ideas. Go for long walks in a crowd, lose yourself in the crowd. Isolation isn't good for you, and allow me to give you a piece of advice that a doctor can give—a doctor is somewhat above morality you know. Try women . . . you understand what I mean. Keep yourself occupied, see people. And come back and see me in three months. I have given you Veronal for cases of extreme insomnia. But don't abuse it."

In the street, Antoine thought that the entire consultation had been beside the point. He would obey, however. It was an order. Besides, it was a means of escape from his life. He could say: I am neurasthenic. This doctor had at least given him a name to call his loneliness and death.

Antoine "treated" himself. He had medicine bottles standing on the table. Anne would say, "Have you remembered your drops?"

He had the illusion of doing something. Around him buzzed an atmosphere of activity and hope. His wife and son collaborated in the treatment. This illness with a name reassured everyone. An illness is a familiar, intelligible thing, against which people no longer feel powerless. Once he was sick, Antoine ceased to be strange, mysterious and cruel in the eyes of his relatives. Anne said to her son, "You mustn't irritate your father, you know, on account of 'his' illness."

Everything was simple, as though he had rheumatism, or some other of those long illnesses that take months or years. But Antoine was not his own dupe, he was not taken in by these efforts to believe in his illness, in a state that possessed such a clear ticket. "With a little willpower, you'll manage it . . . a battery can be recharged. . . ." What efforts he made to get out of the consciousness of nothingness, to break the shell of mortal loneliness, to restore the barriers that had so long concealed from him the advance of nothingness, to bury his head in the sand.

Adventurers and fools are not the only beings that have neither roots nor friends. In rows of bourgeois houses along city streets live sedentary inhabitants whom nothing attaches to the world, who no more mix with men than oil with water. Antoine sought to mix with men. All his life he had moved among men. He had imitated their ways, he had spoken their speech and adopted their sayings, but he had not mingled with them. He had not developed among them. Doubtless it was rather late for association, for human society to lend him the illusion of no longer being alone. Human atoms lost in the emptiness of bourgeois life come together in order to forget that they are nothing but dust. To share this great illusion it would have been necessary for Antoine to begin earlier. Some twenty or thirty years before he should have entered one of those constellations that the bourgeoisie of the provinces constitute. A lodge, with its secrets, its signs, its thin conspiracies, a political committee that got wrought up around election time, a musical society or a hunting and fishing club. Some group or other when he was young enough to believe in it. That time was past. All his life Antoine had vaguely realized that real union, union that defied loneliness, that was even now sweeping away the dust of bourgeois life, was the union of workers. He still thought of that season of his youth when he had experienced the warmth of revolt in Saint-Nazaire, and of the demonstration that headed for the doors of the railway shops as though a new world had already replaced the world of loneliness.

Antoine remembered that he had graduated from Arts and Trades. Like the graduates of all the big schools, the graduates of Arts kept in touch with each other. They published a big yearbook. When one of them died, the yearbook contained an obituary notice and the Association gave the deceased a bronze palm to embellish his last passage through the city. They held banquets. Antoine rarely attended the banquets of his class. Now, however, he began accepting all these invitations written in a style that seemed funny only to the initiated.

Dear comrade,

Twenty-five (or forty) summers have rolled by since you left the old school and certainly your absent or white hair, or your prominent bay window make it unnecessary for us to remind you of the fact, were it not the custom among the old boys of the Arts to celebrate in proper manner the twenty-fifth (or the fortieth) anniversary of your freedom.

We would gladly have summoned you during the warm weather. But humanitarian sentiments restrained us. For some of our boys have become asthmatic and it would have been unpleasant for them to expose their adipose tissue to the oven-like temperature of the trains. So we have chosen the cool weather of December mindful that this coincides with the automobile exhibition which is of interest to so many comrades.

So, on December 6, at noon, we will gather for a banquet at Marguery's, Boulevard Bonne-Nouvelle.

Above all let us have no abstention and come prepared to enjoy the feed.

In the stuffy Marguery salon, amid the plaster ornaments, the wrought-iron lamps, the rails, the glass, the potted palms, men who had aged stirred the memories of their schooldays with a sort of lofty melancholy. During the first half hour of the meal, perhaps, they were again a band of boys without a future and without a past, struggling with all their might against a joyless barrack-room life, a band of companions united by their common tasks. Then they called the roll of the missing. They did not weep for the dead any more than a group of young people would have done, well protected by common strength and living resources, able to heal its wounds and fill its gaps. But by the time the cheese came, these men, separated by social distances, by the families they had raised, by the variety of their professions, the different marks they had made in the world, with their inequality of manners and success, had little left to say to each other. When the reminiscences of classrooms, refectories, walks, dormitory incidents, the words of a slang they no longer used, had exhausted their charms, whose spell waned with every passing year, they again became middle-aged and elderly men weighed down by the sauce-covered meats and over-rich cooking. They conversed like people who know each other slightly, who have met for the first time. They knew each other slightly; the years had covered the young men they had been with their accretions and their sediment. They talked of business, of their professions, and sometimes they made deals. They proposed jobs, gave recommendations. The first gaiety of youth ended in the stuffy buzz of a business lunch. At the end, out of respect for tradition, those who had been the merrymakers of the class sang songs that mature men do not sing. The others forced themselves to laugh. And from this gathering welled the ironic sadness occasioned by the imaginary return of lost time, the conjuring of shadows. On the Boulevard Bonne-Nouvelle, which spread before the restaurant like a lake, the crowd surged around these provincials to whom their Parisian comrades explained things with a certain pride. The double stream of traffic passed, the omnibuses started up with a noise like broken glass. It was afternoon, idleness made them restless, and they began thinking of the trip they had to make, of their train schedules. They walked and they felt heavy on their legs. They talked about those comrades who had died in the course of the year, between banquets, and those departures which earlier, in the restaurant, they had regarded lightly weighed on their shoulders like a foreshadow of their own death. Antoine again saw Vignaud, Le Moullec, and Martin. Rabastens had died at thirty.

Antoine said to Martin, "You remember Hefty Marie?"

Martin answered, "And do you remember Marcelle?"

Vignaud left them—Vignaud who had become an important man. He said to them, "I have to go, my business is waiting for me."

When he had been swallowed by the crowd, Le Moullec, who had remained depot master, murmured, "Some people have all the damned luck."

And they separated until next year, until the next banquet.

Antoine tried living for a few months with the regional group of old boys. He was treated with the conventional respect due an "old-timer." He studied questions that occupied the group, he made reports. He spoke at meetings on the retirement home and the benefit fund. He made speeches on the loans, on enrollment, on apprenticeship, speeches which ended in pledges of allegiance to the Public Authorities. Antoine was not deceived, he was perfectly aware that this was only a cure he was trying. No profound human end united these men. They were motivated only by rather petty interests for which high-sounding words served as a window dressing. These technicians of industry and transportation, placed on the scale of work between the foreman and the directors, tried to give themselves importance. In their speeches, they said:

At a time when competition is becoming sharper among the engineers of all the schools, it is absolutely necessary for our comrades to meet frequently, bring their ideas from everywhere, exchange them, and take them back in their different formulations.

Since the new industrial schools increased competition, they had to make an effort to hold their own. They defended themselves, they defended their functions and privileges. The solidarity that they referred to as a virtue was, after all, nothing but a weapon aimed against the graduates of the Central School and the Polytechnic. In these rather sordid encounters Antoine bitterly experienced the artificiality of his new activity. He was acting merely for men situated between the owners whom they served and the workers whom they commanded. Their activities, poorly embellished by a certain sentimental exaltation, aimed at nothing more than to maintain them at their rank, with the hope, nourished by a few dazzling successes, of rising in the bourgeois firmament. Antoine realized that ésprit de corps has never provided anyone with a valid reason for living. His mortal detachment gave him a clearer vision than he ever had before. He drifted away.

The evenings after the reunion, he stayed at home in his house lost among the factories. On the other hand, the new arrivals from the younger classes, the ex-soldiers, brought with them new ways, appetites, and words that a man of Antoine's generation could not comprehend.

"Lose yourself in the crowd," the famous professor had said. Antoine wandered through Paris, he tired his body, but the inner unhappiness that he carried with him everywhere did not tire. Men and women passed. They were fenced off from him by a frozen impenetrable space. There were some who talked to themselves as they walked along; there were others who had nervous twitches. It was human dust that whirled in the wind of the boulevards, a conglomeration of bodies whose actions were less intelligible than those of a swarm of ants. The autos and the traffic divided them, cleaved them. They bore no relation to each other, they flowed in every direction. Young women wore colored dresses and coats, but all these people in the mass formed a black crowd. In France, almost all the men, almost all the women, are dressed in black. They had rubber-stamped faces; they all had the same face, and in this gray monotony one forgot the details of particulars of such and such a face—a prominent nose, protruding eyes, a goiter, a birthmark, the beautiful face of a woman from another world. People turned in at doorways, shops, and the métro entrances. They got on street cars and buses. They looked as though they knew where they were going or rushing to. Some of them left the avenues, the main thoroughfares, and lost themselves in the little sidestreets that ran between sheer cliffs. Antoine sometimes followed them mechanically. He saw them enter dark shops or cafés from which waves of sound issued. And sometimes they cast furtive glances over their shoulders. It was an alien crowd. Arms and shoulders jostled him as though he were invisible, or as though the passers-by were blind. He encountered not a single glance. No expression crossed any of these foreheads, as

alien as the horned foreheads of insects. He had never had the
luck that young men have of meeting the lingering smiling look
of a young woman in the crowd. Only at night, when the lamps
were lit, prostitutes who were the only leisurely attentive beings
in the world came up to him and offered him their enticing faces.
Some were beautiful and seductive like corrupted young girls.
Others were women already aging, with fat naked arms and big
folds of fat below their breasts. Others had gold teeth that shone
as in the mouths of the dead. And he spurned all of them and they
retired to the shadows. He gazed at shop windows full of articles
that the window display made to appear unusual—stacks of
knives, guns, suitcases, dishes, colored boxes, chains, pictures,
portraits. Some windows contained stockings, chemises, corsets
stretched over bodies of headless women or on complete bodies
covered with icy smiles. Almost all the men let their eyes rest on
the silken haunches, the shiny breasts, the lace fringes. Others
hunted contraceptives amid pyramids of sponges, medicine, red
rubber tubes. Women inspected themselves in mirrors.

Antoine walked on. Some boulevards crossed the railway.
Under the arches of the métro, men and women abused each
other in shrill tones. Sometimes Antoine was attracted to a local
festival. There were knots of people. The crowd became at last
intelligible. Young men in caps fired at eggs in the shooting gal-
leries, shouts and laughter came from the flight of the swings,
from the waves of the roller coasters. Tall merry-go-rounds,
adorned with armored warriors blowing trumpets, turned to the
creaking metallic music of hand organs. Girls were borne aloft on
fishes, cows, and pigs. And a ring of heads craned to watch legs
laid bare by the wind of the ride. The lottery wheels turned and
clicked. The Japanese billiard balls bumped each other. That doctor was an idiot. Antoine fled, and returned harried to the fastness
of his suburb. He arrived like a cork that has bobbed about for
hours and has reached a still backwater along with bits of straw,
paper, and flotsam.

One day he entered a brothel. He had not been in such an establishment in twenty-five years. He scarcely had any feeling of guilt, however. It was a modest brothel on a boulevard where the métro passed. It was like a little country hotel. The corridor was bright with porcelain tiles. At the far end, a woman was doing the bookkeeping behind a counter. Antoine entered the parlor. At one table, two petty officers were talking in low tones to two of the girls, who wore green combinations. Other girls entered. One of them came over to sit by Antoine and tried to start a conversation. Antoine, leaning his head against the back of the bench, gazed at the wall, the mirrors, the paintings of mildly erotic pastoral scenes.

"Is there anything wrong, old boy?" asked the girl. "You aren't very chatty."

She placed her hand on Antoine's leg and rubbed it with her palm.

"I don't excite you?" she asked.

"Not very much," said Antoine.

She continued. One of the petty officers set the mechanical piano going; it started up joltingly, like an old truck. The two of them and their girls danced. One had the look of a big little girl with dimpled cheeks and a reddish knot of hair. The other was short and plump. At every turn of the waltz, her combination rose, revealing the lower part of her white powdered behind. Antoine's companion asked, "Aren't you coming up, then? I'll be very nice to you."

"No," answered Antoine. "I just came in for a drink. . . . I'm going out."

The girl drained her glass and got up. Antoine rose heavily from the bench. In the hallway, the woman at the cash counter spoke to him, "Monsieur can't make up his mind today? Perhaps some other day?"

It was raining on the boulevard. Heavy gusts of wind pursued the pedestrians. Each of them was as lonely in the city as though

walking at the edge of a cliff during a storm. All men were engulfed by the oncoming night, which rapidly extinguished the
whitish light of the tempest. Antoine hunched his shoulders and
dabbed with his hands at the drops of water that rolled down his
cheek.

All his life reduced itself to this thin trickle of water flowing
down to death. Nothing was left to defend Antoine any longer.
No screen hid his end from him. The very hopes he had formerly
placed in his son, he had himself neglected and destroyed. He
sometimes eyed this taciturn adolescent already embarked on the
adventures of youth, who abandoned childhood with a kind of
avid exaltation. During vacation time he would ask him to go for
walks with him. But they spoke only of strange things, of events,
of studies, of Pierre's future. It was too late to recapture from
other times the exchange of manly, telling words. That secret was
also lost. No help was forthcoming from this young man, lonely
as himself, who had nothing in common with the child that once
had walked beside him along the poplars on the Bordeaux road.

22

Nantes is a town where the sea trade, the banks, the factories, the white faces of devout women, death, and restlessness are the mysterious elements of a life that no other French city imposes on its inhabitants. The people of Nantes, accustomed since childhood to the ways of their city, take no notice of the air one breathes on the banks of the Loire. Of all towns this was perhaps the place where Antoine was least likely to find the rest he sought, the absence of uneasiness which should provide the moral atmosphere of old age for a man at the end of his task.

He settled there by chance, and because Anne was strongly influenced by the fact that her daughter and parents were buried there, that she could "visit her dead" as often as she cared to. This funeral motive sufficed perhaps to locate Antoine's last years in this provincial capital under the signs of mourning and death. For him, Nantes could only be the town one settles in awaiting death, the town whence one never will move. What he really needed for his old age was one of those cities in the south that seem to defy death. He had long dreamed of going, after he retired, to Palavas-les-Flots, where he had formerly been on Sundays. But the call of the dead, the vague idea of returning to the region of his birth, to the scene of his youth, this idea so powerful over many men, whom a perverse fidelity attaches to stones and countrysides, the presence in Nantes of numerous comrades of his youth whom he had "lost sight of" and with whom he promised himself he would resume the course of his life as though his mature years had not existed, as though old age succeeded youth without any interruption—all these motives in the end made him give up the genial south to settle in a town which he had never liked, where he had always felt a certain oppressiveness, the dim feeling that he could never be happy there.

When he was once more settled among the furniture, the knickknacks that had followed him about for so long, in one of those detached houses that the natives of Nantes call *hôtels* and the Parisians *pavillons,* once he had found his bearings in the new rooms and had learned to adjust his gestures to the angles and the passages of this unknown tent, once he had gotten to know the place from where he could call his wife and hear her answers without having to move, the idleness of his retirement began to weigh upon him heavily.

For a man such as he, "retirement" was charged with all the severe meaning it could contain. He had withdrawn from the crowd of men who worked, displayed their ability and knowledge, met each other, and talked to each other. He had withdrawn from all the things that had been essential to his life. His son was already a man launched on his own track, who inspired him with a sort of timidity. Pierre wrote letters as concise as reports, letters that made no appeal to his father's experience. No human being had any need of Antoine.

He had finally reached that fearful time of life when the earth lies utterly bare beneath the feet of a man on the slope going down to death. It was a period full of dread. The light grew dim. From the depths of air came huge nameless figures shrouded in veils. Cold allegories like dead men on a holiday. Antoine summoned to his aid all his justifications, but none of them gave him a valid answer. He acted like all men who want to die satisfied with having lived. At a certain stage of life men feel a need for justification. This is the time when many men adopt God and seek to believe they will appear before him just and pure in conformity to his will. Others ignore the gods and are their own judges and their own witnesses. They act in obedience to the fearful precept: "Man, prove thyself." Thus the king of Scripture trembled before the words deciphered by the prophet: "You have been weighed in the balance and found wanting." How many men will be found wanting? How shall they resign themselves to seeing so many identical days, of efforts, sorrows, and brief joys quickly consummated, fall away into a vast forgetfulness? Death, whom they have fought through seasons more evanescent than a grass fire, lifts a strong cold voice that they must silence with the proofs of their deeds.

But Antoine's past was cloaked in a shadow so black and was shrouded in a silence more fearful than the apparitions which he seemed to see. It was an undefined mass like the countryside one travels through at night in the foggy season. Antoine lacked imagination, but when he searched his past he always likened it to a familiar countryside. Once, on his summer vacation, he had climbed Mont-Saint-Michel de Braspartz, on a windy day in mid-August, and he saw the vast submarine landscape of dark marshes and naked shoals, the long, broad undefined and silent expanse, sullen and formless, with winding paths between the hedges and sometimes, on the farthest edge of the horizon, the strange glitter of the sea. His past was like this shadow country where no voice breaks the uneasy silence. Where were the friends who could have justified his past, told him of his virtue and his worth, shown him what he himself was unable to see? Scattered over the face of France, and under the face of France, living, dead. One of them was mayor of a town in the Pyrenees—and he might have written him to ask for hotel addresses before leaving on a trip, but not for favorable testimony on his life. Another was still absorbed in the thoughts and routine of his profession. Others, like him, felt idle and uncomfortable in the irksome leisure of retirement. They were already bored with the boredom of the dead. Another was a paralytic, blubbering the syllables of the words he had formerly uttered, smirking, worth a million. And as many others were really dead, the inhabitants of cemeteries, scattered among the graves of unknown people. How could he question them? Such friends had utterly vanished. They had bequeathed no footprints, no advice. Some men leave behind them deep impressions on the earth; one can long discover secrets and advice in their books, in their actions, in a certain serenity or a certain strength they were endowed with.

But the dead whom Antoine had known, when like himself they were alive, laughing, talking, in their offices, before time-tables, on street corners, in factory courtyards, had bequeathed him nothing. In vain did he seek refuge among his last living friends in the town. What did they know? Were they also seeking impossible proofs, proofs that did not exist? What did they say at night when they lay down beside their old wives or on their widower or bachelor beds? What did they say in the morning when they washed, reviewing the ill-recorded thoughts of sleep? Were they calm, restless, indifferent, wise, terrified, or like machines? Antoine did not formulate these questions very clearly. He did not couch them in well-ordered words. Yet he fully felt that they existed, that they were threatening, that they counted above everything. But he did not actually question his friends. Men who are stranded on their little lonely islands call this silence shame.

Antoine went for walks with his friends and he awkwardly turned these things over in his mind. They talked of things that came within their range, wherever their steps happened to lead them, of the news in the papers, or of people of whom they had received news, of marriages, births, and deaths. A new ship flying a foreign flag was moored in front of the Exchange, near the suspension bridge, across from the Steps of Sainte-Anne, just like the ocean liners from Santander in the harbor of Saint-Nazaire long ago. These stationary men knew all the flags of the world. The Loire flowed along between the green piles that marked the channel, it flowed to its estuary, it flowed on with its former swiftness toward its great delta, between Saint-Nazaire and Mindin. The Brittany express with its long metal coaches rushed over the tracks. Groups of sailors strolled along the street, they were heading for the little cafés painted in water-green whose windows were spattered with mud from the carts, toward shops selling souvenirs, penholders, colored inkwells, pictures of the suspension bridge and of the chateau of the Duchess Anne, painted on slabs of wood. Ropes were coiled like gray serpents among the lanterns and rockets in the windows of the ship chandleries. Along the side streets you could see the large lanterns of the bawdy houses. Sometimes you noticed a woman standing in the shadow and you saw her silk-covered knees below the fringe of her combination. Sometimes she even beckoned to the old men, who passed by on the river front, with a gesture they pretended not to notice, for they thought with a sense of humiliation, as terrible as the fear of death, of their impotent member that was nothing more than a hunk of meat, a urinal tract, and not a source of strength and joy, an affirmation of manhood.

On other days, Antoine and his companions would go and sit in the botanical garden where swans swam about under the branches of magnolias and exotic trees whose names they did not know. At the end of the afternoon they would go and sit on café terraces and drink muscatel and Anjou. Some of them drank beer because they had acquired the habit in the towns of the east and north. A long crowd climbed and descended along the Rue Crébillon hemmed in on both sides by the houses. Coming out of the shops and offices, stenographers and salesgirls stopped before the display windows. Well-combed young men as vain as peacocks threw them a few passing words. Big girls with make-up eyes and lips, shiny cheeks and sleek hair, walked along with the lazy motions of ships, looking the men in the eyes. Their dresses outlined their thighs and breasts and passers-by would turn round stealthily to watch the motion of their haunches.

In autumn came foggy days charged with smoke and with a
smell of damp earth. The old men avoided winter and rain.

"The barometer went down again last night," they would say.
Or when they rolled cigarettes: "The tobacco's damp. The
cigarettes aren't fit to smoke."

Endless silences sometimes punctuated their walks, silences
that did not always have for pretext the noises of the traffic, the
horns of the river steamships or the thunder of trucks loaded with
steel bars. In the towns the old men stroll empty and hopeless;
they don't know how to spend their days, how to cope with old
age, and when they are silent it is perhaps because they are ob-
serving it as if they were only forty.

The old men sometimes landed unawares in streets and squares
that were utterly quiet and deserted, along whose walls they were
the only passers-by. At such times their silence was the silence of
their loneliness. It was like a disease that stealthily overtook them.
The muffled sound of the tread of the two or three sixty-year-old
men was not enough to break the silence. It was not the din of the
world that caused them to be quiet on these long white streets
with their gardens, their convents, barracks, and garden walls.

They also talked. But their words were no longer connected
by verbs of the present tense or by those wonderful future verbs
that young and mature men employ. They spoke in the past.
They would sometimes stop and face each other, their hands behind their backs, as though for an important conversation that the
motion of walking would interfere with. Was any dignity contained in these sentences in the past tense? Since these men had
all been engineers, calculators, machine-builders, timetable keep-
ers, since their lives had been full of professional events and since
they had known many men, they still had memories whose dates
and figures they knew. They still retained the exact patterns of
these memories, which differed as much from the true possession
of time as blueprints covered with figures and white lines differ
from an engine in the fullness of its strength. Their memories

were fragments detached from their lives. They tried hard to derive pride from them. They told each other of their exploits: the engines they had salvaged, the industrial records they had broken with their heads and the arms of their workers. They repeated old anecdotes about workers they had employed, about their superiors, about famous chief engineers who had since died.

But they realized well that these deeds did not belong to them. They were isolated acts imposed on them by an external and inhuman force as cold as that which directs the workers, acts that were not part of a genuine human life, that had no real consequences. Acts that were merely registered in bound and dusty ledgers, that had merely helped ensure the profits of factories and companies and the submissiveness of the workers who worked in them. They recalled no real achievements or genuine human relationships, their workers and their superiors were to them strangers or enemies. They were solitary actors, actors devoid of any dignity. They pretended to be proud of their memories, but in their secret hearts they did not cherish them.

What Antoine needed in those days was to find one man capable of proving to him that his past was worthy of being admired, that it contained elements worthy of gratitude and friendship. It was rather late to find secrets that had been lost so long ago. It was without hope of finding them that he sought them now. That was why he did not always sleep peacefully. He ate, he talked with Anne of the familiar shell of his days. At night the avenues of his habits led him toward sleep like an animal herded to its pen. Shut all the doors for the night, inspect the windows, make fast the bolts against robbers, against the dangers of the night, bank the furnace fire, say good night to the maid, put out all the lights, undress while walking through the rooms on the second floor, feel eyes heavy with the weight of sleep. He would stretch out heavily on his half of the bed.

"Antoine, don't toss about so much. I want to sleep."

Sleep. In the still silence of the night, sleep? He dared not light the lamp. A body lay at his side just as it had for thirty-odd years, a body that no longer had the light breathing of youth, a fifty-year-old body that did not like you to disturb its first sleep, less easily recaptured than formerly. Antoine had acquired the habit of lying with his eyes open in the darkness, against his will, in order not to disturb his wife.

"You are impossible with your lamp," she would say. "You know perfectly well that it wakes me up and I can't get back to sleep. Put it out or go sleep in the guest room."

She would heave over with a single motion, as though in quest of sleep on her side of the bed, on the side that belonged to her, toward the wall which was her wall. She would question him: "Is anything wrong with you? Are you worried about something, are you ill?"

"Not at all," Antoine would answer. "I simply don't want to sleep. Go to sleep, go to sleep."

He remained alone in his prison of the night, a prey to thoughts that crowded in on him without his having the strength to dispel them. He could not concentrate on what he wanted to think of. He could not go to sleep at will, as he had read that great statesmen, Napoleon and Hannibal, could. Restlessness made him toss about on the chafing bedclothes. It was in his body like a child inside a woman, and it stirred within him, it lived within him like his lungs, like his heart. "Maybe it's that aorta? See the doctor—go on a diet—what is my blood pressure?" But this deep anguish that had haunted him for years probably bore no relation to bodily symptoms. It was fear. In a region deeper even than the blood system of the body where the warnings of diseases come from, he harbored an ill more radical than arteriosclerosis. It was no longer bodily death that he feared but the shapeless image of his whole life, that defeated image of himself, that headless being that walked in the ashes of time with hurrying steps, aimlessly and chaotically. He was decapitated; no one had ever noticed that the whole time he had been living without his head. How polite people are! No one had ever called to his attention the fact that he had no head. It was too late. The whole time he had been living his own death. But a man cannot long endure these torturing thoughts, and Antoine ended by clinging to the most exact, the clearest of his uneasinesses. He told himself it was merely his heart that was not working properly, that he decidedly must consult a doctor. It was so long since he had had himself examined. "At sixty, one's arteries are as brittle as clay pipes. I shall make an appointment with the doctor, I shall have my blood examined." He pictured himself at the telephone, at the doctor's buying boxes of pills, drops, measuring his tobacco, his meat. These thoughts would at last put him to sleep, like a story.

One day among other days, Antoine came home, took off his coat, and put on an old robe to which his shoulders and arms were long accustomed. He kissed his wife and went into his study, he opened his paper, he rolled a cigarette. He was not feeling very fit. He felt a kind of nausea. His cigarette tasted badly and he threw it into the fireplace. What was bothering him? The clock ticked loudly, its pendulum made a reverberating noise. The walls around him seemed to fall away. Above the sofa, his portrait gazed down at him with a terrible insistence. From the kitchen came the familiar crash of a broken dish. He rose, as from depths of the sea. Antoine felt the heaviness in his left arm that he had often experienced. What was the meaning of that heaviness? It coursed along his arm toward his shoulder socket. He stretched his fingers and bent them. He would have liked to talk to a living being, to be reassured by a peaceful human presence. He turned toward the door, the porcelain switch was glaringly white like a painted bone. All other light grew dim. He took another step, a single step, a step that followed on the millions of steps he had taken since he learned to walk, in streets, rooms, factories, countrysides, a step made with great effort, like an act of heroism. He wanted to call Anne, Anne who had loved him. But he uttered no sound; his tongue and his lips were motionless as ice, he could no longer utter a sound. Around him life had ebbed away suddenly like the sea. There was a crash, a noise like the pop of a big electric bulb. Antoine fell on the carpet from his full height and moved no more.

Later, Anne came in and let out a shriek so loud that a passer-by heard it from the street and rang the doorbell. But Antoine, cut off from human forms, could no longer hear Anne's familiar voice, nor any message from the world. He lay on the blue carpet, dead. All the blood had already drained from his face, which was calm as a lake. A big black vein began to swell between the two bumps on his forehead.

Anne called him, she placed a mirror to his lips. She pierced the lobe of his ear with her scissors: no blood flowed.

Modern Reader Paperbacks